WILD LAND, WILD LOVE

"For a moment, I'd imagined strangling you, but this is far more agreeable. I had no notion you could be so accommodating." Lids lowering, Iain glanced down the length of her body to her feet before his eyes returned to her face.

Iain was so close that Leeanne could count the laugh lines around his eyes. So close she could feel his warm breath fanning her mouth. She moistened her lips. "I can't afford to be," she said in an oddly breathless voice.

Iain was primal—like the land in which he lived, Leeanne thought. Primitive, sensual, and as impressive as the craggy bracken-and-heather-covered slopes that surrounded Glencoe, creating a natural fortress. As wild and powerful as the mist-capped mountains rising in the distance. In his eyes she saw reflected the noble blue of the Scottish sky, and the potential for things she'd considered impossible.

LOVE'S TIMELESS DANCE

VIVIAN KNIGHT-JENKINS

LOVE SPELL ◆ **NEW YORK CITY**

LOVE SPELL®

March 1997

Published by

Dorchester Publishing Co., Inc.
276 Fifth Avenue
New York, NY 10001

The name "Love Spell and its logo are trademarks of Dorchester Publishing Co., Inc.

Printed in the United States of America.

To Nancy K. and Nancy B. They know
the rhymes and reasons why.

To Karen Martin—a brave, bonnie lass
in her own right.

In loving memory of my mother, Vivian
Clotilda Helms Knight, and my aunt, Ruby
Knight Love.

To my mother-in-law, Grace.

To my sisters Trina and Teddy.
And to Betty and Elaine.

True heroines one and all...

O My luve is like a red, red rose,
  That's newly sprung in June;
O My luve is like the melodie,
  That's sweetly play'd in tune.

As fair art thou, my bonnie lass,
  So deep in luve am I;
And I will luve thee still, my dear,
  Till a' the seas gang dry.

Till a' the seas gang dry, my dear,
  And the rocks melt wi' the sun:
O I will luve thee still, my dear,
  While the sands o' life shall run.

And fare thee weel, my only luve,
  And fare thee weel a while!
And I will come again, my luve,
  Tho' it were ten thousand mile.

"A Red, Red Rose"
—Robert Burns

Prologue

North Carolina, U.S.A.
Saturday, February 29th
Leap Year, 1992

"This is ridiculous! It *has* to work," Leeanne Sullivan muttered to herself, gazing through the picture window and out across the dance studio's asphalt parking lot.

At any other time, the stark white snowflakes powdering the hood of her station wagon might have alarmed her. Due to the winter storm warnings, she'd allowed her dancers to cut out on rehearsal early. But she couldn't bring herself to lock up shop and follow suit. Not just yet. Not with the season's first performance bearing down on her like a fire-breathing dragon in search of human sacrifice.

Leeanne collected a forgotten soda can from the window's ledge, rolling the cool cylinder between her warm palms. If only the more difficult movements of the Scottish dance sequence she had choreographed were as malleable as the empty aluminum can, she thought, crushing and shooting it into the wastepaper basket.

"The reputation of my company is riding on a deadline. I've got contributors breathing down my neck. And to top it all off, the mortgage payment on this building is due in two weeks," she moaned to herself.

Perhaps she'd been crazy to accept a commission that more experienced choreographers had turned down flat, Leeanne mused. The trouble was that she'd always been rather willful . . . rallied to the call of adventure . . . the thrill of a dare. But in this instance, the risk of breaking new ground had cost her more than she'd imagined. She couldn't remember when she'd last eaten a home-cooked meal. Her boyfriend had stopped calling because she had no time for him. And though her muscles screamed with fatigue by day's end, she couldn't sleep for the stress created by her obsession.

The company's failure is your failure. Prove to your backers and to yourself that you can make this production a roaring success. The personal challenge drummed like a litany in Leeanne's head.

"All right," she responded aloud. "For whatever it's worth, I'll give it my best shot."

Retrieving a Highland-green and burnt orange plaid from the seat of a director's chair, Leeanne defiantly turned her back on the inclement weather, enfolding her shoulders and upper body in the generous rectangle of tartan cloth. Crossing the studio to stare at the sheet music cluttering the scarred upright piano, she trailed a negligent finger over the ebony keys. Like a flock of chattering birds, piano notes reverberated in the quiet studio.

"The musical scores are the perfect setting for the dance sequences. But the dance sequences just aren't doing the music justice," she said, reaching for a granola bar from the bagged lunch spread on the piano seat, rejecting it to nibble instead on a half-eaten veggie sandwich.

A frown marring her classical features, she set the sandwich aside, pivoting to face her images echoed in the mirrors lining the walls. What she saw was a professional immersed in the trappings of her trade. Sable curls brushed back from a widow's peak and twisted into a bun, she wore pearls in her pierced ears, a neon pink save-the-whales T-shirt, and black woolen jumper with a full skirt over her leotard, tights, leggings, and leather ballet shoes.

"Lady, I sure hope you haven't bitten off more than even you can chew," Leeanne said,

13

ignoring the dull ache between her shoulder blades.

Shadows semicircling her eyes, the slender woman stared defiantly back at her. Leeanne leaned toward the mirror to peer at her new, soft color contacts—royal blue lenses that only served to enhance the strain-reddened whites of her eyes.

"Incidentally, just in case no one has informed you lately, you look like you've been hit by a truck."

No matter. Looks are insignificant compared to the well-being of the show.

"So . . . why in the heck isn't the piece working?" Leeanne asked her reflection. "I *know* my dancers can do it. They have the rhythm, the movement. It's the spirit and sense of tradition that's missing. But how do I transmit that to them, when I'm not even sure what it is myself?"

Ultimately, the bottom line had to be her unshakable belief in the theatrical production, she decided. Her gut feeling told her it was the finest script she'd ever composed. Perfecting it made her happy, intrigued her because the dance technique was difficult; something out of the ordinary.

With visions of Broadway prancing through her head, Leeanne selected two items from the stage chest next to the piano. Her first choice was a replica of a Scottish sword—shiny and new, yet strangely lifeless. Rummaging through the props, she extracted another sword. A wealthy patron had presented the claymore to her company as a joke, insisting that she was spending time on a production that would, in the final analysis, be an unmitigated flop.

Cradling the claymore, Leeanne silently disagreed. The double-handed broadsword, with its rusting shell guard upturned toward the hilt, spoke to her. Even with the blade pitted, the point broken, and the settings studding the pommel bereft of gems, the sword possessed an arrogant grace, an energy, a sense of passion and raw power that Leeanne found mysteriously irresistible.

Gingerly, she placed the claymore on the maple dance floor, hilt to her left, crossing it perpendicularly with the replica sword. With a touch of the rewind button, Leeanne sent the studio cassette player zipping to the introduction of the musical score. Standing before the swords, she listened intently to a medley of songs before "Gillie Chalium" finally commenced.

Taking a deep breath, she cleared her mind, allowing the stirring pipe tune to lead her forward. Nimbly she avoided displacing the weapons as she danced counterclockwise inside and outside the squares formed by the blades.

"Discipline, persistence, practice, persistence," she recited as she concentrated on the tempo of the music, on her own strict sense of timing. She observed her body movements in the mirrors, her trained eye scanning for form, for the truth and eloquence of the strenuous number.

When the music skirled to a finish, she admitted to herself that although her performance had gone well, like the replica sword, something was missing in her modern version of the dance. Wiping the perspiration from her brow with the edge of the plaid, she rewound the tape, punched the button, and started over. Once more, when the music ended she had come up short of her own expectations.

"Damn!" she said, using a felt-tipped pen to scratch corrections for future rehearsals on a yellow legal pad. Cheeks flushed and breathing labored, driven by self-discipline, she began a third attempt.

"I've always heard three is the charmer," she whispered, pushing herself above and beyond the call of duty.

The telephone rang. Once. Twice.

Counting on her answering machine to pick up the call, Leeanne ignored it. Turning up the cassette player's volume, she blocked out the phone as she glided into position, aspiring for oneness with the music. Swaying, she allowed herself to be carried away by the melody, by the soul of the past. The worn floors flexed like a springboard as she danced, the music crashed against her athletic figure, lifting her, dominating her, giving her life meaning.

Leeanne had almost achieved the perfection

she sought when her toe hit the hilt of the replica sword, propelling it like a spinning top into a corner of the studio. With a resonant *pop,* a sheet of silver shattered on the far side of the dance floor.

Uninjured by the broken mirror, Leeanne nevertheless sensed her face flush red as her heart lurched, beating in double-quick time to the music's climax. Exceeding the beat. Pumping in her ears; in her throat; in her chest.

Although it seemed she'd physically slowed to a standstill, Leeanne watched in amazement as her image in the mirrors continued to whirl around the ancient sword, her expression like that of a terrified child trapped on a speeding merry-go-round, she thought. Then to her horror, like blood separating in a laboratory centrifuge, she felt her body ripped from the axis of her world.

Clutching her left arm as severe pain shot through her upper back, Leeanne gasped, "This can't be happening. I'm only twenty-eight . . . too young for . . . a . . . a heart attack!"

Chapter One

Glencoe, Scotland
January, 1692

The music pealed so loudly in her ears that Leeanne decided she must have somehow fallen into an orchestra pit composed entirely of bagpipes. She felt woozy, the veggie sandwich weighing heavy on her stomach as she attempted to focus on her unfamiliar surroundings, on the wild applause that erupted as soon as the pipe tune skirled to a halt.

Her stamina deserting her, Leeanne exhaled loudly, sagging like a leaky party balloon.

"You're a brave, bonnie lass to stand up to a dare like that, but I fear you've tested the quality of the claret once too often," a deep, husky voice whispered in her ear. "Otherwise I'm certain you'd never have danced the Blades of War, a man's dance, with such abandon." Bending to retrieve the claymore at her feet, the stranger looming like a giant by her side returned the sleek, double-handed broadsword to the leather sheath slung across his shoulders. "You're as white as sea foam," he stated. "Here now, let me help you find a bench to rest those weary gillies," he continued with quiet authority.

Awestruck, Leeanne babbled, "This can't be heaven—angels don't wear kilts." As incredible as it sounded, she recognized her claymore, with its shell guard upturned toward the hilt. But the blade was no longer broken or pitted. And instead of vacant sockets that gaped at her like sightless eyes, the flat-topped pommel was studded with twinkling yellow sapphires.

As for the man—she'd never before seen anyone like him.

Thonged deerskin shoes—hairy side out—protected his feet, and knitted hose hugged his muscular calves all the way up to his gartered knees. A belted plaid with a purselike leather sporran attached at the waist covered his masculinity, while a black velvet jacket ornamented with silver buttons emphasized the broadness of his powerful chest. A round bonnet sporting an eagle feather and heather badge topped a head of dark blond hair that hung well below his collar, reminding Leeanne of the pictures of

Norse warlords she'd glimpsed in history books while researching for her production.

Assessment complete, her shocked gaze traveled to his face—a face so ruggedly handsome that her knees almost betrayed her. His expression was serious, but his striking azure eyes, so full of humor, bedeviled her as he said, "Who's to say angels don't wear kilts, lass? I'd think a true Highlander would no' give up his *plaidie*, even if it meant standing on the steps of heaven for an eternity."

"Highlander?" Leeanne asked, troubled that her voice cracked, feeling that her vivacious imagination had gone berserk. That she'd finally outdanced reality.

"Aye. Highlander, and proud of it," he said. He tossed her a charismatic wink.

The earth ceased its erratic spinning, and Leeanne tried to view her new environment with the detached impartiality of a superior court judge. She failed miserably. Her audience pressed in upon her—fellow clansmen she supposed—costumed in seventeenth-century dress tartans, though few were as fine as the self-proclaimed Highlander's. Somehow, she'd exchanged her studio for a tapestry-draped building that reminded her of nothing so much as a stone barn with a roaring hearth at each end. Instead of the delicate fragrance of lemon-scented disinfectant, the smell of smoking peat fires, pitch torches, and roasting mutton encumbered the air.

Leeanne almost gagged. Sheer willpower prevented her from disgracing herself as she whimpered, "Pardon me, but I feel faint. My head is swimming. Please, I need some air."

"I fear the claret will have its way almost every time," he responded sagely, a high measure of sympathy evident in his voice.

Only when the Highlander took her elbow to urge her through the crowd did the sensual energy of his touch confirm to Leeanne that she had neither succumbed to heart failure nor was she imagining things. Mind racing, she acknowledged that there was no logical explanation for the precarious position she found herself in. There was, however, a bizarre, utterly fantastic alternative to logic: time-travel. With speculation dawned comprehension, uncertainty, and finally a fear of the unknown that Leeanne had never before experienced. How in the world had this happened to her? More importantly, what was she supposed to do now?

"Whose guest are you, lass?" the Highlander asked, breaking into her chaotic thoughts.

"What?" Leeanne stuttered, doing her best to keep pace with his ground-eating stride without stumbling over her own aching feet as they passed table after trestle table laden with food and drink.

When he realized the difficulty she was having, he slowed, gallantly offering her his arm to steady herself.

Leeanne hesitated. Because she was single, she'd learned to be wary of strange men offering assistance.

Her expression must have given her thoughts away, for he said, "It's no' as if I've asked to bed you, lass. I'm harmless enough unless provoked."

Eyes widening, Leeanne stopped dead in her tracks. "Are you always so blunt?"

"The way I see it, frankness and honesty run hand in hand. Come now, accept my arm before one of those brassy young stags staring after us decides you've grown weary of my attention."

Leeanne hastily scanned the room. The men *were* staring at her, young and old alike ... much to the undisguised dismay of their female counterparts. She shifted uneasily.

"It's your hair—it's a glorious wild mane you have draped about your shoulders." The Highlander lifted an errant curl, testing the texture between his thumb and forefinger.

Dumbfounded by his boldness, yet oddly flattered, Leeanne found herself tolerating his easy familiarity.

"Soft as Cheviot lambs' wool. Shiny as new coin," he said, letting the curl drop. "I'm thinking that like the light, no doubt your hair catches many a discerning eye. It did mine," he confessed.

It's the papaya and aloe extra body shampoo, Leeanne thought irrelevantly, raising a trembling hand to her hair, bewildered to discover that somewhere along the line she'd lost her barrette and hairpins. Without their restrictive influence, her natural curls would be encouraged to misbehave more outrageously than ever. She didn't even have a brush to smooth them into place, Leeanne thought.

Her face undoubtedly registered her anxiety, for he said rather quickly, "Here now, do no' fret." Loosening her plaid, he adjusted it like a hood over her head, securing it with an ivory pin from his bonnet. "There. That's better, but be careful of the *dealg* pin's point. We would no' want to draw blood," he said, patting her hand with his callused palm before hooking it securely under, then over his arm.

And I thought I was going to faint before! Leeanne reflected, her mind reeling in spontaneous reaction to his touch. Subconsciously, she assessed his hands. Strong hands. Capable. Competent. Sexy. His hands most definitely got a gold star.

When she realized what she was doing, Leeanne redirected her gaze to his face. She quickly acknowledged there was little refuge to be found in his square jawline or the intensity of his handsome blue eyes. She liked what she saw far too well.

It was incomprehensible. No man of her acquaintance had ever affected her senses as this one did. From his appealing physical appearance and his rough gallantry down to his quaint Scottish burr, the Highlander stirred something deep within her soul that had been napping.

Why this particular man? Why here? Why now?, Leeanne asked herself. She could assemble no ready answer. She supposed it was just one of those things, something that happened once in a blue moon.

"You're no' from the Highlands, are you?" he asked conversationally, jolting her out of her reverie.

Had the Highlander glimpsed her T-shirt when he adjusted the plaid? Leeanne wondered, teetering once again on the cutting edge of panic. Nervously she settled the material more closely about her shoulders, seriously doubting he had ever run across a piece of clothing as glaring as her aniline-dyed, screen-printed T-shirt.

Or as incriminating.

Striving for complete calm in the face of disaster, Leeanne reminded herself that a true professional winged it. It was a philosophical maxim that had been drilled into her subconscious since the age of three when her professional dancing career began. A maxim that was now ingrained in her character. Relieved to be alive, Leeanne stifled her weaknesses, drew on her strengths, and proceeded to carry on with the show, determined to give the impromptu performance of her life.

"What makes you think I'm not from around here?" she asked quietly, consciously controlling the tremor in her voice.

He chuckled. "A *sassenach* isn't difficult to spy, even when she dances as if Scotch blood flows through her veins."

"*Sassenach?*" Leeanne mimicked, thinking, *Scotch!*

He nodded. "Aye. *Sassenach* is the Gaelic word for outsiders."

"Am I to understand that you don't care for . . . outsiders?"

"I can take them or leave them, especially if they're of the English persuasion."

But I'm not British; I'm an American citizen, Leeanne almost blurted, catching herself in the nick of time. He wouldn't have the vaguest notion what she was talking about, and the last thing she needed was to complicate matters. She asked instead, "Then why did you rescue me back there, if you knew I was a . . . a . . . *sassenach?*"

"My mother was English." He rolled the statement off his tongue as if the words tasted sour, making the admission sound more like an accusation.

"Oh." That accounted for his soft accent, for the reason she understood him so readily, Leeanne mused.

He continued. "Too, I regretted being so caught up in the festivities that I allowed the perpetrators of the dare to make use of my sword."

"Your sword?"

"Aye."

"Of course it was your sword I used in my dance. That makes even more sense," Leeanne muttered to herself, trying to comprehend the chain of events that had fueled the backlash which had sent her reeling into the past.

"Afterwards, you looked so lost. I thought perhaps you'd gotten separated from your escort. Did you?" he asked pointedly.

I wish it were as simple as all that!

Suddenly discomfited by his piercing perusal, Leeanne cast her gaze toward the slate-gray floor of what she could only assume was a kind of primitive community center. "I, uh . . . didn't come with an escort. I was invited to the, uh . . ." She paused, nervously glancing around. *To the what?* As if she'd asked the question aloud, he supplied the answer she needed.

"To the wedding at Glencoe."

Leeanne didn't want to lie, but cornered as she was she felt she had no alternative. Besides, nothing ventured, nothing gained, she silently encouraged herself. "That's right. I was invited to the wedding . . . by the . . . um . . . the bride. She's the one that insisted I attend."

Leeanne sighed in relief, smiling as if she'd just said the most clever thing in the world. Smiling because she finally knew where she was: Glencoe, *Scotland!* How she'd made it overseas without an airline ticket and her passport was something else altogether. Something the Highlander couldn't possibly answer;

probably wouldn't believe. She could just barely credit it herself.

With the tip of his finger he tilted her chin up to look her squarely in the eyes, a thoughtful expression crossing his clean-shaven countenance as the curve of his smile relaxed. "The bride, you say."

Lids partially closed to shield her eyes and hopefully conceal her ulterior motives, Leeanne nodded.

His arm tensed as he pressed her hand more firmly to his side. "And I thought I'd met all Sesi's female acquaintances before today. It seems you're one that's escaped attention. Until now."

Leeanne searched for a legitimate response. "You wouldn't know me. I'm a teacher." Though off-the-wall, that at least was the unvarnished truth.

"One of the teachers from that finishing school in England that Sesi attended?" he persisted.

The lie reared its ugly head and leered at her. "Yes," Leeanne answered, less smoothly than she intended.

"Let's go and see if we can find Sesi. I'm sure she'll be overjoyed to learn you've arrived."

"Have I ever!" Leeanne exclaimed, thinking, *Why me? What did I do to deserve such a mind-boggling misadventure? I'm a dancer, not an astronaut! I'm not trained for this kind of stuff . . . put my foot in it for sure.*

"What's that, now?" he asked, bending to catch her words above the din of the merrymakers.

Leeanne's chin rose a degree higher without benefit of his aid. "I said, lead on. I can't wait to congratulate Sesi on her good fortune. She must be pleased, to be marrying someone like you," she offered tentatively.

She watched him stiffen. Eyes narrowing, he said, "I did no' realize you were *that* tipsy. Perhaps we should bide a wee before making the customary presentations."

"What do you mean?" Leeanne asked in startled amazement. His attitude had changed immediately and completely—from that of knight rescuing damsel in distress to suspicious Highlander casing archenemy numero uno.

"Take a hardy peek at my plaid, lass. Tell me what you see in the sett."

Glancing down at the hem of the kilt swinging about his knees, she contemplated the woolen tartan. Puzzled, she asked, "What am I supposed to see in the pattern?"

"Black-and-white bars and stripes."

Leeanne blinked. "What have stars and stripes got to do with anything?"

"*Bars* and stripes," he corrected impatiently. A fierce sense of protectiveness ringing in his voice, he clarified, "Only a *sassenach* up to no good would talk such blether when my status is as plain as the pert little nose on her lovely face. I'm no' Sesi's groom and well you must know it. I'm Iain MacBride, her elder brother and rightful guardian. And if you've come to cause my sister grief on her wedding day, think again, my bonnie lass."

"I believe there's been some kind of mistake," Leeanne protested. A big one! she thought fearfully. She had no immediate family to speak of since her parents' death in a sailplane accident, but she'd watched enough "Wild Kingdom" in her day to recognize a sharp-toothed lion in defense of the pride when she smacked headlong into one.

"You're right about a mistake. And I'm the man who made it," Iain ground out. "You seemed so harmless for a wee while there. Who set you up to this?"

"No one, I—"

Iain cut Leeanne short. "I realize that reiver, Parlan Macdonald of Glencoe, has stolen more than a few maidenheads in his day, but he's a changed man since Sesi. It took some dire convincing on his part to open my eyes, but I see now that it's true. I'll no' allow you to threaten Sesi's future happiness, even if it takes locking you up until the ceremony is performed and the commitment sealed. She deserves that much from me since I'm the one that introduced her to Parlan in the first place."

"Great! Out of the frying pan and into the fire," Leeanne muttered under her breath as Iain MacBride tugged her along beside him. She fought the numbing sensation of helplessness seeping into her bones, realizing that beneath Iain's seemingly placid exterior lurked a formidable opponent; one she'd prefer not to rub too far the wrong way if at all possible.

"Will you please *listen* to me for a minute! I've been tried and convicted on circumstantial evidence," Leeanne said, thinking that perhaps she should scream for help, then promptly rejecting the idea. Depending on who came running, she determined she might just find herself trading bad for worse. At least Iain hadn't harmed her. Yet.

"There's nothing you can say to change my mind," Iain assured her, slipping his arm around Leeanne's waist to force her intimately against his muscular thigh while manipulating her like a puppeteer along the perimeter of the crowd. Veering away from what appeared to be a receiving line and heading toward a plank door which Leeanne supposed constituted the rear entrance of the community center, he cautioned, "You'll only dig yourself in deeper if you try to explain this away, lass."

He was absolutely correct; she'd never talk herself out of this one, Leeanne reasoned as he kicked open the door onto the bleakness of a snowswept glen. A blast of frigid air struck her full in the face, causing a reaction of near panic.

Perhaps it's time to yell after all, Leeanne advised herself. *You've never before played the passive role, and if you want to survive I have a feeling this isn't the best place to start. So go for it, girl.*

"Fire! Help! Fire!"

Although her tone of voice sounded more like a squeaky-toy that had been stepped on than a scream, curious faces swiveled in their direction.

Iain grimaced. "Ach, lass, now see what you've done. You've disrupted Sesi's receiving line."

"I don't care who I upstage. There's no way I'm going out in that weather!"

A spark of anger flared in the Highlander's clear blue eyes. "We'll just have to see about that now, won't we?" he said, obviously unaccustomed to opposition.

"I'm serious."

"Serious or no', you'll get little assistance from the people of Glencoe against me. The clan Macdonald might follow us with their eyes, but they'll no' interfere in my personal affairs. It's no' their way, to take blood-brotherhood lightly."

"Who said anything about blood-brotherhood? We're talking Popsicles, buddy!" Leeanne said, fighting down hysteria.

"Popsicles?"

"Icicles, then!" she supplied, sadly lacking the patience that Iain had incorporated when explaining the word *sassenach* to her.

"*English*," Iain grumbled beneath his breath, continuing more forcefully, "I think it's only fair to warn you now that I've committed myself to the Macdonalds through Parlan and my sister, Sesi."

"That's all well and good. As long as you don't drag me into it." *Literally.* "I didn't travel this far to freeze to death in the snow. I could have done that at home without half the hassle!" Leeanne shoved against his rigid chest, struggling in the earnest now.

Iain spouted a universal curse that Leeanne decided must have come down to modern man through the ages intact because she understood it perfectly. "Do no' create such a stir. You'll give me cause to regret being so tolerant of you."

Leeanne opened and closed her dry mouth several times in rapid succession, drawing a shuddering breath. "Tolerant! Why I . . . You . . . This is insane!"

"Your coming here certainly was," Iain agreed.

With a wide, don't-trouble-yourself-about-this-because-it's-all-taken-care-of smile, he managed to doff his cap to a petite, exceedingly pregnant young woman robed in a white gown and tartan shawl who stood at the head of the receiving line, mouth agape, staring after them. Then with grim determination, he flattened Leeanne's arms to her sides and presented her a swift, well-placed kiss on the lips. The liquid heat of his searching mouth sufficiently stunned her into silence; the bold laving of his tongue across the sensitive inner lining of her mouth zapped everything except the unexpectedly pleasant taste of him from her mind.

Then, before she knew what he was about, he withdrew from her, lifting her pliant body in his strong arms and tossing her over his rock-hard shoulder, caveman fashion. Dazed, head bobbing in a downward slant that sent her blood rushing to her cheeks, Leeanne clung to Iain's torso for dear life.

"For God's sake! What do you think you're doing?" she demanded.

"Keeping my word to my sister," he said.

"By manhandling me?" Leeanne asked, her glowing thoughts of escape disintegrating to ashes as she completely lost control of the situation. Of her own destiny.

"I do what I must when pushed, lass," he said.

"But you don't even know my name," she sputtered, her words muffled against the softness of his velvet jacket, his sword sandwiched between them, pressing into her breast.

"It makes no difference. You're here and that's all that counts," he stated solemnly.

Iain MacBride was right again, Leeanne admitted with a shiver, wondering frantically how she'd managed to traverse the time barrier . . . how she was going to return home . . . and how "a true Highlander" disposed of party crashers.

Chapter Two

It was incredible, the way Iain MacBride doggedly plowed through the driving snow, bearing her weight as if she were no more than a sparrow perched on his shoulder, Leeanne thought. But she wasn't a sparrow. She was a woman. An angry, apprehensive, confused woman whose veggie sandwich was now riding like a lead ball in her stomach.

How much valuable time had passed since she'd been dancing in her studio, her only concern the completion of the theatrical production she was working on? she wondered. She calculated it to be mere hours, though it seemed at the moment like light-years.

An eerie wailing in the distance disrupted Leeanne's introspection. Unconsciously she clutched Iain's waist more tightly, squeezing her eyes shut as she asked, "What's that?"

"You're accustomed to the city."

"You can bet your bottom . . . coin I am," Leeanne said, recalling his reference to her hair in comparison with the local currency. "Now what *is* that?" she demanded. "It sounds like banshees on the prowl."

Iain stopped for a breather, adjusting her more securely on his shoulder, and Leeanne marveled once again at his incredible patience with the weather. Her face was snuggled against his velvet-clad back, protected from the icy sting of the snowflakes by his body. He faced directly into the weather's diagonal onslaught, undaunted by Mother Nature's winter fury.

"It's no' banshees, lass. It's wolves you hear. And hungry ones at that," he added.

Eyes flying open, she shivered. As a rule, she wasn't easily intimidated. But these weren't normal times, Leeanne reminded herself. Under certain circumstances, wimping out was only human. Prudent even. "I wish it was daylight."

"It will be soon enough," Iain said.

"I wish you'd put me down." *And hold me in your arms instead.*

"I'll no' put you doon until you're safe inside my cottage," he countered.

"Is that where we're going?"

"We aren't going; we're there," Iain said, swinging around to shoulder open the door of a windowless, one-room, turf-roofed stone cottage.

Mouth grim, Iain unceremoniously tossed Leeanne onto the bed—a boxlike four-poster carved with mythical beasts that only served to encourage her fanciful mind.

At a loss for words, Leeanne huddled in the center of the massive bed and watched apprehensively as Iain divested himself of his bonnet, sword, and jacket, hanging them on a peg by the door. His long-sleeved linen shirt, open against the strong column of his throat, emphasized the breadth of his chest. Her gaze dropped lower to his trim waist where the shirt disappeared neatly beneath his belted kilt. There was no doubt about it—Iain MacBride was a fine specimen of a man, she decided. That, however, did little to allay Leeanne's doubts about being cooped up with a stranger during a snow storm, even if she felt oddly comforted by his presence.

"Do no' look so dour," Iain advised abruptly, turning his back on Leeanne to retrieve a brick-shaped clod of peat from the stack in the chimney corner and toss it onto the smoldering embers banked in the fireplace. Flames licked greedily at the fresh fodder, instantly bathing the room in a warm, orange glow that sent shadows cavorting across the unadorned walls.

Marveling at the clean, pleasant aroma of the burning peat, Leeanne rose to her knees, moving almost involuntarily closer to the foot of the bed and the heat of the fire. She hadn't realized how cold the walk had been until they were sheltered from the harsh elements—the wolves, the severity of the weather, and the possibility, though remote, of bumping into the Glencoe banshee patrol.

Feeling cut off from civilization, wishing she had a tape of classical guitar music and a battery-operated cassette player handy to sooth her rattled nerves, Leeanne asked, "Do you live here? Alone?"

Iain's clear eyes darkened to midnight blue, and Leeanne could have sworn she saw a flicker of pain skitter across them though he quickly suppressed it.

"Aye. When I'm in Glencoe, I bide here. Alone."

Feeling nervous and isolated, Leeanne experienced a burning desire to keep him talking, so she wouldn't have to listen to the discordant rumble of her own thoughts. "I take it you have another home elsewhere?"

"I'm no' a wealthy man, if that's what you're at."

"I'm not *at* anything. There's no crime in being curious. Or is there? I'm not sure anymore."

"No crime," he said, busying himself with the fire.

"So, where's the other cottage?" she prompted.

"Actually, it's a small manor house. Closer to Loch Lomond."

"I know that place. There's a song . . . something about a high road and a low road," Leeanne said to herself.

"What's that, lass?"

"Nothing important."

Hands on his hips, Iain turned to face her. "You mumble too much, do you know that? It's a distracting trait."

And maybe what you need is a topnotch hearing aid. "From now on, I'll try to speak more clearly when I'm addressing you."

Her sarcasm went over his head.

"I'd appreciate that, since we're forced to entertain each other's company," he said.

"Tell me, how is it that you got involved with the Macdonalds, besides being blood-brothers with Parlan Macdonald through your sister, Sesi?"

"The Macdonalds and the MacBrides are each a different sept of the same clan."

"I'm not sure I understand," Leeanne said.

"Distant relations, branches of the same family, lass. As determined as William of Orange is to run us over, you'd think he'd teach his subjects something about us."

"William of Orange?" Leeanne asked, pushing the makeshift tartan hood off her hair and onto her shoulders.

"I'm speaking of the King of England! You act as if you've never heard of the man, though more than one Highlander wishes he could claim as much. We were quite happy with our own James the Seventh until he came along."

"Well, yes, of course I've heard of William, and James, too." *In books.*

"Och, lass. Will you never recover from the effects of the claret? I thought that icy trek through the snow would cure you for sure. And here you are, still spouting blether."

"I suppose a walk in the snow is your version of a cold shower," Leeanne quipped dryly.

"More blether."

Leeanne shook her head as if to clear it. "It's not blether, it's just that I'm . . . terribly thirsty."

"Drouthy, are you? Well, they'll be no more claret for you this night," Iain declared in an emphatic tone.

"Fine!" Leeanne sighed, rolling her eyes toward the turf ceiling. She was sick of hearing about claret. It was useless to explain to Iain she'd never tasted the stuff before in her life. "But a cup of decaf—hot tea—to settle my stomach would be nice."

"I should have guessed. The English do enjoy their tea parties."

He advanced toward the bed, squatting to drag an iron-banded, trunklike strongbox from beneath it. "It seems to me that Sesi usually keeps a sack of tea leaves hidden in one favorite spot or another."

"A leftover from her finishing school days in England?" Leanne asked, peering over the footboard of Iain's head. His hair was nice; not too long, not too short. Attractive in a careless sort of way. Clean.

Iain glanced up; Leeanne drew back.

"She did no' learn of tea at finishing school. Our mother bequeathed Sesi the habit. She's been coveting the taste since she was a wee bairn. I think perhaps it came through in her milk."

"And not yours?"

Iain flipped open the lid of the strongbox. "My father demanded his firstborn have a wet nurse," he responded dryly.

"And what did your mother have to say about that?" Leeanne encouraged, determined to keep him talking, to keep fear and panic at bay.

"Lord luve me, lass! I would no' know. We never spoke of those kinds of things. Suffice to say I do no' care for the flavor of English tea."

"Nor anything else English," Leeanne said, but he was no longer listening.

"Och. Here we are," he said, extracting a small, lacquered tea caddy carved with Oriental designs from the strongbox. Moving to the fireplace, he poured some water from a pewter pitcher on the hearth into a matching mug, crumbled in the leaves, and set the concoction on the hearth to steep.

"There now. You'll soon have your tea, lass."

Leeanne frowned, thinking how primitive the seventeenth century really was. No tea bags. No glazed ceramic teapot. No lemon or half-and-half. Probably no pure cane sugar either. Definitely no sugar substitute or chlorinated water. It was downright scary, the things she took for granted.

Visions of smiling, comic-strip-style germs swimming happily in the untreated water temporarily superseded her other concerns. "I like my tea hot," she said.

"As you wish," he said, nudging the cup nearer to the flame.

"Just a little closer. I mean, I really like it best when it's boiling."

Iain nodded slowly, doing as she requested.

"Thanks," she responded, thinking it wasn't often that a man went through such a hassle simply because she asked it of him.

When the tea was finally done to her satisfaction, it took another ten minutes for the mug to cool. Each lost in their own thoughts, an uneasy silence grew between them.

When Iain finally handed the mug to Leeanne, he said, "Mind how you hold it. The bottom's still fair warm."

As if he'd plotted it, his hand closed around hers, capturing her fingers as he held the cup between them. Their eyes met, hers distant, his compelling.

"You must know, I do no' care for having to closet you in like this, lass."

"Are you apologizing?" Leeanne asked.

"Just stating hard fact."

"I'm sorry my presence in Glencoe seems to threaten you," she said, the nerves in her fingertips tingling as she attempted to withdraw her hand. But he held her fast.

Suddenly Leeanne had the disturbing notion that Iain might make a move to kiss her again. He watched her lips as though tempted, doing nothing to hide the physical desire reflected in his azure eyes. And yet he refrained.

"A wee slip like you a threat to me? What an unlikely proposition," he said instead, his thumb caressing the side of hers.

Struggling with mixed emotions, determined to put distance between them, to curtail her irrational sense of disappointment, Leeanne asked in a brittle voice, "Then why am I being detained here against my will?"

His natural courtesy faded. "It's the certain notion that you'll disrupt my sister's wedding that causes me to hold you captive here." He abruptly released her fingers, along with the cup. The dark brown liquid sloshed over the rim, splashing the back of her hand.

Leeanne's first impulse was to dash the tea in Iain's face and run like hell, but escape was impossible. Even though no lock secured the door, Iain stood between her and freedom. A freedom which consisted of darkness, snow drifts, and hungry wolves.

And even if she escaped Iain, what then? She'd still be caught in some kind of weird time warp, Leeanne reasoned. No, escape at this point would prove futile and dangerous. Best to sit tight for the time being, she advised herself. At least she was warm, with a roof over her head, and hot tea in her stomach—and on her hand.

A frown of concentration marring her face, Leeanne glanced around the room.

"What now?" Iain questioned curtly. "You look as if you've lost something of considerable value."

Only my own world. Perhaps my mind. "Uh . . . no . . . nothing," Leeanne said, readily admitting to herself that she had in fact been instinctively searching for a paper towel rack. A napkin holder. A dish towel. Something familiar. Quickly rejecting the use of her plaid, she licked the warm tea from her skin like a cat.

Through the wavering firelight, Leeanne watched Iain while he watched her. To counteract his intense perusal, Leeanne busied herself with sipping her tea, straining the leaves through her teeth. Obviously, his English mother had failed to explain to Iain the finer points of brewing tea—such as straining the leaves before you drank it. But in her present state, the tea was better than nothing. Already it was beginning to loosen the knot in her stomach.

Finally, to Leeanne's relief, Iain moved to add more fuel to the fire, saying over his shoulder, "On the morrow, I'll escort you to Loch Leven and the old road to Invercoe. From there, you can travel to your own country and forget you ever visited Glencoe."

Travel to my own country! I wish. Leaning over the side of the bed, Leeanne set the half-empty mug on the floor.

"You're going to let me go in the morning?" she asked tentatively, wondering if she dared go anywhere, even during daylight hours. In the snow. Without a car. Without a road map. With only colonial America awaiting her, should she attempt to travel home by ordinary methods?

The magnitude of her plight stabbed through her brain. Her sense of uneasiness grew by leaps and bounds, and suddenly Iain MacBride seemed the lesser of the evils bedeviling her. Doing an abrupt about-face, Leeanne acknowledged she was more frightened to be without Iain than to be alone with him in what amounted to his bedroom.

"By dawn, this episode will be finished. Until then, try to get some rest. You have a long day ahead of you."

Iain tossed Leeanne a hairy coverlet, which she caught in midair.

"Och. Good catch, lass," he commented. And with that, he moved aside the armchair and fireside stool to fashion a pallet on the floor near the hearth, effectively dismissing her.

Leeanne sniffed the animal skin, wrinkling her nose in distaste. Of all things, *Bambi*, she thought, glancing around for alternative bedding. There was none.

Chilled to the marrow, Leeanne snuggled deeper into the feather mattress, drawing the deerskin coverlet up to her nose, missing the womblike buoyancy of her own heated waterbed. Missing crisp percale sheets. And polyster-filled comforters. And the sureness of purpose she'd known in her own world.

Leeanne tried to relax, but her body felt like a live wire. She couldn't rest, much less sleep. It was beginning to register that Iain MacBride really had only a superficial hold over her. Time was her true warden, she its prisoner, she realized. Time made a graceful exit from Glencoe impossible because her world hadn't prepared her to survive on her own, exposed as she would be to the Highland elements with only her contemporary knowledge to guide her.

Dry-eyed and dry-mouthed, Leeanne listened to Iain's steady breathing, wondering how she was going to talk herself out of this predicament. It seemed she was damned if she didn't, and doubled-damned if she did.

Dreading the moment when Iain MacBride released her to her own devices, Leeanne finally fell into an uneasy slumber.

Like drumbeats pounding in her head, fists thudded against the cottage door, rousing Leeanne from a dreamless sleep. Bleary-eyed, she sat up and threw her legs over the side of the four-poster bed. But Iain was miles ahead of her.

Lifting the latch, he swung open the door to the diffused light of a lilac dawn. Behind the trio of unexpected visitors, Leeanne could see that the snow had stopped falling, but only after it had blanketed the glen in winter-wonderland white.

"Sesi, what are you doing coming here at this hour? You should still be abed with Parlan," Iain admonished cheerfully.

The pregnant young bride from the night before stumbled past Iain and into the cottage. Dressed in a lace cap and an empire-waisted, woolen maternity gown over which she'd draped her tartan shawl, Sesi reminded Leeanne of an ivory-skinned, golden-blond china doll.

Positioning her swollen body between Iain and the bed, his sister glanced over her shoulder, one quick unguarded look that spoke volumes. In that second, Leeanne took Sesi's full measure. Her love for her brother was evident in her delicate blue eyes. Still, her posture suggested hidden personal motives, prompting Leanne to back the underdog.

"Never you mind about Parlan and me," she said in flawless English. "What in the name of all that's holy has gotten into *you*, Iain MacBride?" she asked, her lips set in a thin line of disapproval.

For a moment, Iain's face went perfectly blank. Then he glanced past his sister to Leeanne. "I was doing exactly as I promised, preventing Parlan's English paramour from ruining your wedding."

Raising her hand to her lips, it was Sesi's turn to display astonishment. "Why, Iain, this isn't the woman I spoke to you about. She must have thought better of her threats and stayed away from Glencoe," she explained, in her agitation accidentally tipping over Leeanne's forgotten tea mug with the toe of her mule. A brown stain spread across the floor as the mug rolled from view beneath the bed.

Leeanne alone seemed to notice.

"Then who . . . ?" Iain began.

Distracted by the hollow thump of the mug as it came to a stop against the wall, Leeanne belatedly realized she'd become the center of attention. Rope supports creaking, she glided gracefully from the bed, smoothing down her woolen jumper and straightening her plaid. Feeling at a distinct disadvantage, she quickly realized that all the preening in the world wouldn't remedy the creases in her clothing.

She couldn't remember the last time she'd slept in her outerwear, never dreamed she'd consider her steam iron a dear old friend. But there was no time to dwell on it now. It was the moment of truth, as far as she dared tell it.

Color high, Leeanne cleared her throat, running her tongue over her teeth, wondering if she had tea leaves stuck between them and wishing for a container of dental floss and a mirror.

"My name is Leeanne Sullivan," she stated with a sense of confidence she was far from feeling.

A regal gentleman who reminded Leeanne of a stout, raw-boned Santa Claus, dressed in a kilt and army-blanket-like cloak instead of the traditional red suit, introduced himself in return. "I'm Alasdair Macdonald of Glencoe, laird of the glen and chief to the clan, and this shy lady peeping from behind me is my wife," he said in an educated tone, drawing a thin, salt-and-pepper-haired woman inside the cottage and closing the door against the cold.

At this point, Leeanne felt that her actions were crucial. She couldn't afford to antagonize the patriarch of the Glencoe Macdonalds, in a Highland community where a wrong word or incorrect move could prove her last. Stomach muscles tightening, she mentally crossed her fingers. Then, bending at the knees with her arms extended out to the side, Leeanne executed a simple ballet *reverence* in acknowledgment.

Alasdair Macdonald nodded agreeably, accepting her curtsey as if well accustomed to such physical gestures of respect.

"We're wondering from whence ye hail," he prompted.

Though cultured, his burr was thicker than Iain's. And because of it, Leeanne found herself leaning closer to better catch his sentences, holding her breath so she wouldn't miss something of consequence. His pronunciation was easy enough to follow if she listened intently, she decided. It was the meaning of some of the words that escaped her. But that was only natural—she was a dancer, not a semanticist.

Direct and to the point, the main Macdonald didn't leave Leeanne long to speculate on either his education, his burr, or his vocabulary.

"Did ye understand me? From whence do ye hail?" he repeated.

Leeanne faltered, plucking at her green-and-rust-colored plaid. How could she be honest—tell him that she was born and raised in the U.S.A, in a time and place so far removed from his own that he couldn't conceive of it if he tried? Because, as open-minded as she was, she was having a difficult time with the schematics of the truth herself.

Leeanne stared so intently at the plaid, seeking an appropriate answer, that the colors blurred before her eyes, merging until all she

49

could distinguish in the checkered cloth was Highland green.

Green. Perhaps that was the ticket.

With a quick glance in Iain's direction, Leeanne said, "Green Gables . . . I'm Leeanne of Green Gables."

"What an unusual name—Leeanne. I do no' think I've heard the like before," he said.

As often happened, Leeanne felt compelled to explain her first name. "I'm an only child, named after both my father and mother—Lee and Anne Sullivan."

The laird masked his expression of surprise beneath bushy white eyebrows. "English—I can see that now," he said thoughtfully, as if her foreign nationality answered any questions he might have asked of her. Returning his attention to Iain, he asked, "Well, what do ye have to say for yerself?"

"That I did no' realize you'd returned from Fort William," Iain said.

Alasdair Macdonald snorted derisively. "Fort William! Ye do no' ken the half of it. That damned oath of submission has had me in the saddle more than a man past his sixtieth winter cares to tolerate."

"But the fort is no more than a good day's ride," Iain said.

"I discovered the garrison commander, a Colonel Hill, to be a scrap leftover from the Cromwellian days. He lacked the civil authority under William's new regime to administer my oath of allegiance. That just goes to show ye how disorganized the English crown really is. It can no' seem to tend to its own business, much less see to the political welfare of Scotland. I vow, 'twas a sorry day when the Stuarts forfeited the reins of power."

"You know King William thinks of the clan Macdonald as nothing more than a band of cattle thieves."

"Aye. I'm no' so addled by age that I'd encourage an English King's displeasure while he has me under his thumb. Especially when he is sour on the clan to begin with. Colonel Hill furnished me a letter addressed to Sir Colin Campbell of Ardkinlas."

"The deputy sheriff of Argyle," Iain remarked.

"One in the same. My men and I rode to Inveraray to deliver the letter most personally."

"But that's over sixty miles, and in black hard weather!"

"To be sure . . . snow swirling so, ye could no' see before ye. But Inveraray is where I swore allegiance. Though it went against the grain, I gave my word to the sheriff that I'd carry the news to the people of Glencoe and that the poor souls who wouldn't swear for William would be imprisoned and sent off to Flanders."

"There was nothing else for you to do. You and Alexander MacDonell of Glengarry were the only chiefs who remained in defiance following the royal summons to London. Eventually, William would have crushed you both.

51

He has the power of the English crown behind him."

"Though I delayed, I set things straight for Glencoe. I'm of a mind ye must do the same, stand up and make amends for yer rough wooing of Leeanne of Green Gables while I was off gallivanting around a hostile countryside at William's behest."

Leeanne resisted the urge to laugh as Alasdair Macdonald continued, relieved that he hadn't given the Green Gables part of her name so much as a second thought.

"I blame myself as much as ye for this unfortunate incident, Iain. 'Twas my responsibility to be here in Glencoe, overseeing the wedding festivities. I was the only man with the power to check you last night."

"I swear I've done nothing to hurt the lass," Iain stated solemnly. "My bedding is on the floor. Witness for yourself."

"'Tis of little consequence at this point. 'Tis no' what ye did, but what ye could have done. Ye could have got her with child."

Iain's faced turned visibly ashen. "No' likely. Everyone present should know that."

Although she listened attentively, Leeanne felt lost. It was as if she'd walked into the darkened interior of a theater during the middle of a performance. Without benefit of a playbill. And no usher to assist her in locating her seat.

However, there was one thing of which she *was* sure. She sure was glad Alasdair

Macdonald's mounting displeasure was directed at Iain and not her. Iain seemed capable of handling it; for her, it might have been the straw that broke the camel's back, she decided as the elder man proceeded with his lecture.

"Regardless of what ye say, Iain MacBride, ye have compromised the woman's reputation in the eyes of the clan. Of that ye can no' deny."

"Only because I made a mistake," Iain replied smoothly. "If she'd been the woman Sesi was expecting—."

"She would have been considered brazen and deserving of her just rewards. But she was no'. We have numerous guests in the glen and none were carried from the wedding against their will without the laird in residence to administer a pause for thought," Alasdair Macdonald argued.

Feeling caught in the middle, Leeanne trained her eyes on Iain's face. The accusations swirling around him perplexed her. Still, she realized that contrary to Iain's adamant denial, the old laird would remain steadfast in his conviction that she'd somehow been wronged. Iain had made her quite angry, tried her patience, but in the end, he'd actually been quite the gentleman—all things considered.

Leeanne made a move to speak in Iain's defense. "I'm fine. Really. Iain built a fire, made me tea. We talked. That was it."

"That does no' change the fact ye spent the night together without a chaperon!" Alasdair Macdonald insisted.

"Sweet reason! I thought she was someone else," Iain interrupted impatiently.

"Do no' get black angry with me, Iain MacBride!" he boomed. "I've been acquainted with ye since ye were a cub. Ye spent your fosterage with me, here at Glencoe."

"And I respect you for the care you gave me in those growing years. But this is ludicrous," Iain announced, visibly controlling his anger.

Alasdair Macdonald extended his arm, palm facing out, reminding Leeanne of a highway patrolman directing traffic around an automobile accident. "Enough. Ye ken what I'm asking from ye—a contract of handfasting. That's no' too dire a consequence for the rashness of yer behavior."

Sesi interjected, "You know the old proverb, Iain. Better a good retreat than a bad stand."

"Sesi is correct," Adasdair Macdonald sanctioned.

Obviously agitated, the laird's wife added something in Gaelic. Though her words sounded like gibberish to Leeanne, the laird smiled, patting her beringed fingers. "Rest assured, the lad kens his duty, auld woman," he told her. "He just needs a breath or three to think it over."

For several moments, the group talked around her, over her head, behind her back, in every direction except to her face, Leeanne thought.

"'Tis up to ye to make an honest woman of her, Iain, and well ye ken it. I realize ye imagine marriage a bag of eels with only one tasty flounder in the lot, but I'll have this embarrassment settled swiftly," the laird said in a ruthless tone.

"Without a tribunal? A chance to defend myself?" Iain asked.

"There's no need for a forum of judgment. Public opinion leans in my favor. Besides, 'tis the right and proper thing to do. There's no arguing that bright point."

"Has anyone ever told you you're an obstinate auld chief?" Iain exclaimed.

"Thrawn I might be, but 'tis my sacred duty to the clan of Glencoe to administer justice as I see fit."

"Surely Sesi must have expressed my position on this?" Iain questioned.

"Och, to be certain. Like most women, she has her own thoughts on the matter of misconduct. But 'tis up to her to explain her reasoning to ye."

Iain looked sharply at Sesi. "Misconduct? I've been accused of misconduct?" The room fell deathly silent as Iain demanded, "Where's Parlan?"

"He's doing the morning milking, up at our croft," Sesi answered sheepishly, suddenly preoccupied with the toes of her mules.

"'Twas no' my nephew, Parlan, that brought this to my attention," the laird said. "'Tis Sesi who had reservations, and since she is yer own red-blooded kin, I deduced them well founded."

Iain's eyes narrowed. "I see the way of it now," he said thoughtfully. "You imagine you've done me a great favor, Sesi." He scowled. "A home-cooked luncheon of tatties-an-neeps is a favor. Darning my stockings when you feel up to it is a favor. This, my darling wee sister, is meddling where ye do no' belong," Iain said darkly.

Sesi glanced up, a pleading note in her voice. "Please, Iain, I didn't see it that way. What I did is for your own good."

"I'm thirty summers old, Sesi. Wise enough to know what's good for me," Iain ground through clenched teeth.

"I've entertained serious doubts about that recently," Sesi persisted.

"And what about the woman you misrepresented? Did you give no thought to how she might react to your high-handed brand of interference?" Iain shot back.

"Please, don't be irritated with me, Iain."

"Irritated? I'm furious, Sesi!"

Biting her lower lip, Sesi hung her head dejectedly. "I've been impulsive again, haven't I?"

Leeanne experienced the sneaking suspicion that she'd missed something vital in the interchange between Sesi and Iain. But she didn't dare interrupt. Especially with Alasdair

Macdonald looking like a thundercloud and Iain acting as if he'd like nothing better than to wring his sister's dainty neck.

Iain finally sighed, and to Leeanne's relief the tension in the room relaxed somewhat.

"Aye, Sesi. You've been impulsive . . . again. And dragged another into this kettle of worms with your maneuvering. Will you never learn to *think* before you act?" Iain asked.

"It's a difficult thing for me to do, Iain," Sesi said.

"I'll attest to that quick enough. But then, you've that much of our mother in you."

Iain pivoted to face the Macdonald chieftain, clenching and unclenching his fists. "I take it you'll no' reconsider?"

"I would have come to the same conclusion with or without Sesi's intervention. My decision's firm, Iain. Considering your strength and obvious ability to overpower her, the woman's innocence is without question," he said, arms folded across his barrel chest.

"Aye, on that there can be no disagreement," Iain conceded, hands relaxing against his thighs.

"She was vulnerable last night. Ye took advantage of that vulnerability, even if 'twas, as ye confess, in error," the laird said. "Her disgrace or salvation rides with ye, and ye alone."

"There's nothing for it, then," Iain said solemnly, the expression on his countenance illegible as his clear blue gaze impelled Leeanne.

She suddenly felt hot under his intense regard, as if he somehow knew what she looked like beneath her clothing.

Iain recited something in Gaelic that sounded extremely profound, deliberate, laced with an undercurrent of hostility that made her uneasy. "There. It's done," he ended in clipped English.

Alasdair Macdonald nodded, a smile of satisfaction curving his moustached lips.

"Aye, that's what I like to see about me—loyal and true God-fearing men. Like as no', ye will eventually come to see the rightness in this."

"I doubt it," Iain stated flatly.

Now she *knew* she'd missed something vital! Her patience shaved as thin as tissue paper, Leeanne blurted, "All right already. I've enjoyed enough of the suspense. Now, does someone mind telling me what in the heck is going on here?"

Iain raised a brow in her direction. "You mean, you do no' know?"

"If I did, would I be asking?" Leeanne snapped, anxiety making her voice ring sharply in the compact cottage.

"You should have spoken up sooner, lass. Now, it's too late."

Almost afraid to ask, Leeanne responded, "Too late for what?"

Iain's features tensed and for a moment he was completely silent. Then, as if shouldering an astronomical burden, he said, "To show just cause against our union."

Flabbergasted, Leeanne's mouth dropped open. Iain was handsome. No doubt about that. And she readily admitted she was physically attracted to him—woman to man. But that didn't mean she wanted to be permanently attached to him! "You can't be saying what I think you're saying," she said, rubbing her palms on the skirt of her woolen jumper.

Shoulders erect, eyes a cold, bold, penetrating blue, Iain nodded. "I can and am. In lieu of graver consequences, as of a few moments ago you and I officially became man and wife, lass."

Undoubtedly the wind outside had picked up, for it shrieked through the poorly insulated cracks in the cottage walls, straight into Leeanne's head. Or was it her mind shrieking in protest? Leeanne wondered.

She swayed. Iain was immediately at her side, taking her arm, encouraging her.

"Steady now, lass. No woman I name wife is going to faint before the laird of Glencoe."

Your wife! Good Lord above. Someone help me, Leeanne thought.

Acutely aware of Iain, Leeanne finally managed in a hoarse whisper, "We can't be married. You must be joking!"

"Am I smiling, lass?"

No, Iain certainly wasn't smiling, not the tiniest little bit. "But how? There was no ceremony."

"It's the way of the Highlands; common practice. In a pinch, all a man must do to wed is proclaim the woman of his choice as his bride in front of three reliable witnesses—those being Alasdair Macdonald, his wife, and my sister, Sesi."

"Doesn't the bride-to-be have to say something, to *agree?* To . . . to . . . sign something? I mean, don't I have any rights here?"

Iain frowned as if perplexed by her question. "It's your rights the auld chief is thinking of, lass."

"But he didn't ask me what I wanted. I mean, what if I don't want to be your wife. As a matter of fact, that's exactly what I don't want to be—your wife."

She looked to Alasdair Macdonald. "I don't want to do this," she stated bluntly.

The laird frowned, shaking his head slightly, but not unkindly. "Ye aren't already married, are ye?"

"Absolutely not," Leeanne answered quickly.

"Then, as I've said, 'tis the right way of things, Leeanne Sullivan of Green Gables. 'Tis done and can't be undone. Ye may honeymoon here at Glencoe. The harmony of the clan will help to establish the pattern for yer future relationship with Iain MacBride."

"Thanks for the offer, but if you don't mind, I think I'll pass on this one."

Leeanne turned toward Iain once again, bracing herself in an effort to deal with this new and unexpected complication.

"I don't believe this is happening. I do not even know you, and yet you've stripped me of my inalienable rights . . . the right to life, liberty, and the pursuit of happiness," Leeanne said, praying she wouldn't begin to hyperventilate.

"Hear me out, lass. I don't care for this any more than you," Iain said tightly, releasing her arm to slip a hand around her waist.

Leanne's heart started at Iain's easy intimacy.

"And that's supposed to make me feel better?" she asked, lowering her eyelashes to hide her growing alarm and regain a small measure of her normal composure. "I mean, I *like* being single. I have my work. My teaching career. My own apartment. My business. Control of my life—at least I did until I came here. Now, I just don't know anymore."

"You're no' making sense."

"Does that surprise you? It doesn't me," she said, a catch in her voice.

"Leave well enough alone, Leeanne," Iain suggested softly, his warm breath fanning her ear. It was the first time he had used her given name. She liked the sound of it on his lips. And for that she wanted to smack herself.

Leeanne moistened her lips with the tip of her tongue. "But this is a clear-cut case of entrapment," she said, trying valiantly to put things into their proper perspective. She had to think. But it was difficult with Iain's firm body pressed against hers.

"You heard the laird—we're only hand-fasted."

"What's that? I'm *English*, remember? If I didn't know I was getting married, I'm certainly not going to know what that term means, now am I?" she asked, determined to regain her own space.

This time Leeanne's sarcasm hit home. Iain abruptly released her.

"Handfasted means that if there is no issue from the marriage within one year and a day, we might choose to dissolve the contract and go our separate ways," he clarified grimly.

"A year!" Leeanne gasped, stunned.

"Aye. A year and a day," Iain repeated.

A year in this place and she'd be certifiable, Leeanne thought. Besides, she had previous commitments, things to do, places to go, people to see.

A performance to choreograph.

In the good old United States of America.

Back—or was it forward?—in the year 1992.

Leeanne considered her options. It came as a blow to realize that at the moment, regardless of how little she liked it, she obviously had none. Unless, of course, she could somehow get her hands on Iain MacBride's broadsword.

Chapter Three

Fine-honed and perfectly balanced to the size and strength of his hand, the sapphire-encrusted broadsword had been a coming-of-age gift from his father. He'd carried it since growing man enough to shoulder its weight. Not only was it a necessity in the Highlands, but a considerable comfort.

He slept, ate, and rode with it. In younger and less conservative days, he'd even made love while wearing it, Iain mused, buckling its leather sheath across his shoulder blades.

In more serious times, he'd severed the heads of the renegade soldiers who had ransacked his manor house and killed his parents. True-aimed, it had carried him through the battle of Killiecrankie when he'd fought beside the Jacobite Macdonald chief and Bonnie Dundee against William of Orange and his insidious Williamites. And more recently, it had saved Parlan Macdonald from a band of Glenlyon Campbells, intent on stretching the renowned cattle rustler's foolhardy neck.

But it had been at its rare best as a dancing partner for Leeanne Sullivan, lately of Green Gables, Iain decided. A woman who tested his temper and yet tempted him like no other. A woman whose striking blue eyes startled him with their intensity each time she glanced his way. A woman who was right now across the way, pacing in furious strides the length of the pony barn's sheltered walkway.

A woman whose feet, swathed in delicate leather slipper, must be sorely chilled by now, he thought.

Sheathing his broadsword, Iain opened the cottage door. Lounging against the door jamb, he studied his new wife—her proud posture, her willowy figure, the wild tangle of sable curls that intrigued him so.

Without a doubt, Leeanne stirred him. The slow burn in the pit of his stomach, a burn that insisted on spreading lower, was proof of that. But he was a man of control, Iain reminded himself, and control the burn he would, for intimate involvement was out of the question. His previous marriage had seen to that.

"If we're done with the tantrum, lass, I'd like

to get on with the day," he called out finally.

Leeanne glanced up sharply, glaring at Iain MacBride. "We? Have you got a mouse in your back pocket?"

"You talk in riddles. Besides, what manner of man would want a mouse in his pocket? And even if he did, it would no' matter. You know as well as I, a kilt has no pockets. That's why Scots carry these." He wagged the leather purse hanging from his belt at Leeanne. "The English, now they wear pockets in their clothes, and they do have some peculiar customs, but as for carrying a mouse around. That I would no' know . . . nor want to, if the truth be known."

"I wasn't serious. The phrase mouse in your pocket is a comeback."

"A comeback?"

"A comeback. A witty—" No. Not so witty. Not really. "Oh, never mind! I'm not in the mood to explain right now. Besides, you're just baiting me. You know it and I know it."

"Aye, lass. I am that. To my way of thinking, it's best all 'round if we make light of the current situation."

"Light of the situation! Now who's talking blether?" Leeanne muttered to herself.

"What's that?"

"Nothing important."

Iain leaned away from the jamb, his broad form filling the doorway as he placed his hands on his hips. "In case you're interested, the word's been passed through the great hall that we're wed."

Leeanne stopped pacing. "I imagine that caused quite a stir, me being English and all," she said dryly.

"According to Sesi, Alasdair quieted it soon enough."

"I don't doubt that a bit. He has a way about him." That of a souped-up steamroller.

"Sesi assumed you traveled here from Londontown with the Fitzgilberts—English cousins on our mother's side."

If she'd made up the story herself, it couldn't have been more plausible, Leeanne decided. So it seemed only reasonable to let Iain continue.

"Go on," she prompted.

"They left before dawn. I hate to be the bearer of black tidings, but Sesi says they seem to have absconded with your traveling baggage."

"And?"

"And so Sesi sent you a pair of her own wooden mules to protect your slippers from the snow."

Momentarily softening, Leeanne scanned the tracks her slippers had impressed in the virginal snow between the cottage and the pony barn.

"That was kind of her. I should thank her."

"Aye. You'll have plenty of time for that. We've been invited to break the morning fast with Sesi and Parlan. She's promised leg o' lamb basted with rosemary, thyme, and garlic glaze. My sister's a braw cook. And it's the least she can do for all the trouble she's caused us."

The snow from the night before had ceased falling and the Highland air felt marvelous against her skin—invigorating . . . pollution free. Leeanne sucked in a refreshing gulp, exhaling it in a great gust of smoke. "Ummm . . . sounds scrumptious. But what if I'm not hungry?"

Her sarcasm seemed to escape Iain.

"That's simple enough. You're a MacBride now. Do what your duty and station decrees— pretend to be," he said, a strange, tender smile curving his lips.

Tears of frustration welling in her eyes, Leeanne threw up her hands and presented her back to Iain.

"To my way of thinking, you're being petulant and a wee bit more than stubborn." His words sounded like a warning. Still, Leeanne ignored him.

"Surely you wouldn't want to distress a pregnant woman over such a small thing as breaking the fast," he went on. "You are no' that hard, are you?"

No, she wasn't hard. She was frightened, Leeanne mused. She'd been going over and over the events of the previous night in her mind in an attempt to sort things out. Devising and rejecting plan after plan to get her hands on a jeweled broadsword that seemed an extension of the Highlander who owned it.

But Iain MacBride wore his weapon like twentieth-century men wore their wristwatches —and it seemed that nothing short of a miracle would part him from the sword long enough for her to make use of it. And if she couldn't get her hands on the sword, she'd never get back to her own world.

And never was a long time!

Recently she'd been thinking of adopting a cat from the animal shelter. Good thing now she hadn't, Leeanne thought. Of course, her African violets would suffer . . . the mail would pile up . . . not to mention the answering-machine messages. She could hear the angry bill collectors now.

"Leeanne MacBride?" a deep voice prodded, distracting her from her introspection.

Leeanne whirled to face Iain. "My name is not MacBride! It's Sull—"

A snowball caught her in the mouth, chopping off her words.

Sputtering, Leeanne gently brushed the soft snowflakes from her eyes, careful of her contact lenses.

"You're really pushing it, MacBride!"

"You should no' have turned around, lass. I was aiming at your back," Iain said, a devilish grin replacing the tender smile.

Her body suddenly tingling with life, Leeanne rallied to the moment. Thoughtless of her slippers, she danced out into the snow. Bending at the waist, she scooped up a handful of the powdery precipitation and shaped it into a compact missile.

"You would no' dare," Iain said in a clipped tone.

Eyes narrowing, Leeanne said, "Oh, wouldn't I just?" She drew back like a baseball player on a pitching mound, pivoted from the waist to enforce the speed of impact, and let the snowball fly. It glanced off Iain's ear, knocking his knitted wool bonnet to the ground.

He blinked, his expression clouding. "Here now. You're getting snow in the cottage!"

Iain bent to retrieve his bonnet. Adjusting the eagle feather and heather badge, he repositioned the bonnet rakishly on his fair head.

"So what? A little water never hurt anything," Leeanne said, bending to scoop up another handful of pristine white.

A second snowball, larger and more deadly than the first, hit Iain in the chest, spattering his fleece jacket.

"Lass, I'm warning you—"

A third snowball sailed into his naked knee cap, filling the top of his cowhide boot.

"*To my way of thinking*, you can dish it out, but you can't take it, Mister MacBride."

Jaw tightening, Iain's body stiffened. "Put the snowball doon, Leeanne."

As a scholar of body language, Leeanne realized she was provoking Iain. But for some reason, she couldn't help herself. At the moment, she felt as though he was to blame for all her troubles.

A fourth snowball missed him altogether.

"Now be reasonable, lass."

"I am being reasonable," Leeanne replied.

The fifth found a mark that no man, not even a cowardly one, would tolerate. And Iain MacBride was no coward.

With movements sharp and sudden, Iain advanced toward Leeanne. "You should have told me sooner, lass. I'd no idea you wanted to get so personal," he said through gritted teeth.

Too late, Leeanne realized she'd gotten in over her head.

"I didn't mean it," she said, retreating toward the pony barn. "Seriously, I was aiming at your . . . That is, I wasn't aiming at your . . . What I'm trying to say is that I didn't intend to hurt you," Leeanne stammered, as surprised by the turn of events as Iain appeared to be.

Leeanne backed up as far as she could, until smooth planking stopped her cold. A shaggy pinto pony stuck its head over the stall door to nuzzle her elbow, and she literally leapt into Iain's outstretched arms.

"For a moment, I'd imagined strangling you, but this is far more agreeable. I had no notion you could be so accommodating." Lids lowering, he glanced down the length of her body to her feet before his eyes returned to her face.

Iain was so close that Leeanne could count

the laugh lines around his eyes. So close she could feel his warm breath fanning her mouth. She moistened her lips. "I can't afford to be," she said in an oddly breathless voice.

Iain was primal—like the land in which he lived, Leeanne thought. Primitive, sensual, and as impressive as the craggy bracken-and-heather-covered slopes that surrounded Glencoe, creating a natural fortress. As wild and powerful as the mist-capped mountains rising in the distance. In his eyes she saw reflected the noble blue of the Scottish sky, and the potential for things she'd considered impossible.

If only she dared to make a grab at the golden ring, Leeanne thought as he released her body, planting his arms on either side of her shoulders instead. Palms flat against the side walls of the pony stall, Iain imprisoned her.

"You smell of fresh-cut flowers, lass." He dipped his head toward her throat, inhaling appreciatively. "No' heather," he said, straightening to his full height once again. "Something else, something quite bonnie." A puzzled frown crossed his face. "How is it that, in the dead of winter and against the peat fire that warms the cottage, you smell so beguiling?"

Leeanne's legs suddenly felt boneless. Moistening her lips, she instinctively looped her arms up and over Iain's for support.

"The fragrance is Parisian." Chanel No.

5. Expensive, top-quality stuff. Very potent. Extremely long-lasting when paired with dusting powder and sachet.

The laugh lines around Iain's eyes contracted. "I've been to Paris, lass. It never smelled like this. Worse than our own Edinburgh in high summer, if I remember correctly."

Thoughts of open gutters and raw sewage spilling into the streets skittered through Leeanne's mind, breaking the amorous spell she'd momentarily fallen under. She whirled, dodging under Iain's arm.

"Personally, I wouldn't know," she stated flippantly as she stalked away from him. "I've never been to Edinburgh. Or anywhere else in Scotland, for that matter, until now."

His voice hardened. "You obviously didn't want to come this time. So why did you?"

"I honestly don't know! Call it fate, or destiny." Chalk it up to Einstein's theory of relativity. The possibility of a fourth dimension. "I'm not sure. Ask me again in a week, a month, a year and a day." *God, I hope not a year and a day!* "Maybe I'll be able to explain it by then."

"No need to get yourself into a frenzy again, lass. Sesi's invitation is explanation enough for me. I didn't mean to press you."

Leeanne wondered what Iain would say if she told him there had been no wedding invitation. That she was letting him believe what he wanted because it was less complicated than the truth.

Integrity warred with good old down-home horse sense, but the battle was short-lived.

Before Leeanne knew what he was about, Iain was behind her, scooping her into his arms. Cradling her.

"Iain MacBride! Put me down."

Expression serene, he angled toward the cottage. "This is the only effective way I've found of controlling you, lass. To keep those dancing feet of yours off the ground is to maintain a wee measure of the upper hand."

Leeanne began to struggle, throwing Iain off balance. He slipped, going down on one knee in the snow.

"Cease and desist, lass, before you maim me for life."

"Are you crazy?"

"I must be. You're more difficult to hold than an armload of squirming saltwater eels," Iain commented.

"Then it makes sense to let me go, Iain."

"No," he replied in a gruff voice. She felt his body tense as he gathered strength to rise to his feet.

It was so absurd, being carried around like a sack of potatoes by a man in a swinging kilt, that Leeanne almost laughed.

"You'll never make it. I'm too heavy," she said finally, clinging to his neck as he swayed beneath her.

Iain scoffed. "My sword weighs more than you do, lass."

At the mention of his broadsword, an idea popped into Leeanne's head. A self-serving idea of which she wasn't particularly proud. But she was desperate.

"I bet you couldn't make it to your feet with me in your arms if you started with *both* knees on the ground."

Leeanne felt Iain relax.

"Now why should I want to do that?"

"Because you're a man, and men always seem to be out to prove something."

With a slight jiggle, he balanced Leeanne's weight more evenly across his arms. "You've an odd sense of humor, lass."

"I'm not trying to be funny. I bet you a . . . a pleasant breakfast with Sesi and Parlan, with me dutifully at your side, acting the docile bride, that you can't do it."

A spark of interest flickered in Iain's blue eyes.

"So you're a gambler now, are you?"

"I've played gin rummy for change a time or two in my life."

"You English have a way with words. I only wish I knew what you meant above half the time."

Belatedly, Leeanne realized that gin rummy probably hadn't yet been invented.

"Rummy is a card game."

"Aye, I've played cards now and again. Are you sure you know what you're doing?"

Not really. But I want to get home, and your

sword is the only ticket I've got. Leeanne nodded.

"Will you serve me my plate before the fire at Sesi's?"

"Like a true domestic goddess."

Eyebrows cocked in surprise, he asked, "And speak only when spoken to?"

"Uh . . . yes. Though I might have to bite my tongue to keep that part of the bargain."

Iain chuckled. "And behave as befits a lady of your station without partaking of the claret, even if it's offered to you?"

Leeanne grimaced. "You'll never get over that, will you?"

"In time. Now do you agree to my stipulations?"

"If you insist." *If it's the only way I can get you to bite.*

Iain hesitated.

"And what, may I ask, is it that you'll be asking in return? That is, if you win the wager," Iain asked.

"Simple. Ten minutes alone with your sword."

Iain laughed aloud. It was a robust sound that started in his chest, quickly mirroring in his eyes.

"Are you daft, woman?"

Leeanne frowned. "No more than you. Is it a deal or not?"

In answer, Iain went down on both knees in the snow.

"I don't ordinarily gamble, but this time I'm thinking I'll take my chances against your promise of social good behavior."

Face grave, Iain closed his eyes and inhaled a deep breath through his mouth, letting it out slowly through his nose. Watching his face, Leeanne knew a moment of real consternation. She realized that, just as she sought inner tranquility through meditation before a performance, so must he before launching into a stressful task.

"Iain, maybe this wasn't such a good idea after all."

His eyes fluttered open. "Too late for second thoughts now, lass. Your fate is sealed."

Once again, she sensed him gathering strength. She saw his teeth clench and his lips press into a firm line of concentration, felt his shoulder and neck muscles contract beneath her hands. Then, like the professional he-men she'd seen lifting weights at the gym, with a single concentrated effort he was on his feet.

Bold and direct, Iain's eyes met Leeanne's as he tucked her more snugly against his warm body.

Flabbergasted, she exclaimed, "Well, I never!"

"Neither have I, lass. You've kept Sesi waiting more than long enough." With a triumphant smile, he crossed to the cottage, shouldered open the door, and set Leeanne on her feet.

"It's high time you made yourself presentable." Fumbling through the sporran at his waist, he extracted a comb with teeth on both sides. "To my way of thinking, you look as if you've spent the night making love. And we know that's not the case."

He pressed the comb into her hand and twirled to face the entrance. "The chamber pot is over in the far corner if you have need of it."

Chamber pot. Well, that should be a novel experience, Leeanne thought to herself.

"I'm going to saddle the ponies. My best advice to you is to be ready to go when I return," Iain said over his shoulder.

"The ponies? We're riding ponies to your sister's house?" The idea of riding ponies surprised Leeanne almost as much as the notion of using a chamber pot.

Leeanne's question momentarily stayed Iain.

"We have no regular carriages, if that's what you're at. The terrain is too difficult. But the ponies are sure-footed and hearty. And now that the weather's calmed to clearing, they'll do well enough." He stepped to the threshold.

"How far does Sesi live?"

"Glencoe runs seven and a half miles from the hills of Black Mount on Rannoch Moor to the shores of Loch Leven at Bullachullish. The clan Macdonald is scattered from one end of the glen to the other. Parlan's croft is only a stone's throw to the north along the River Coe, yet still too far to walk in the snow."

"Oh," Leeanne said to herself as the door closed behind Iain. She'd been thinking more along the lines of a cozy little urban development rather than a sprawling country community.

It was fortunate her parents had given her riding lessons when she was a child, Leeanne thought, staring down at the comb she held in her hand. And it was *unfortunate* that, like Iain's *dealg* pin which still held her plaid fastened together at the throat, the comb was ivory. She'd spent the last few years protesting the slaughter of endangered species, only to be forced by necessity to make use of the very item she'd boycotted so vehemently in her own time.

With a weary sigh, Leeanne reached up to run the fine-toothed comb through her hair, wondering what day it was. Or for that matter, what year. She supposed it didn't really matter, as long as she stayed close enough to the sword to make use of it at the first opportunity.

Iain returned to find Leeanne practically in tears, his comb ivory tangled in her long sable tresses.

"I can't do this," she said. "I need a brush. I need a pump bottle of conditioner. I need . . . something besides an old ivory comb that reminds me of a delousing tool." Her hands fluttered near her ears. "I've made a disaster out of it."

Her distress was so genuine that it struck straight at Iain's heart.

"You have at that."

"I'm a woman in desperate need of scissors, as you can plainly see for yourself!"

Aware of what she must be feeling, drawn to her despite his better judgment, Iain rested his hand on Leeanne's shoulder and maneuvered her to a sitting position on the side of his bed.

"Shears are for sheep, lass, not women."

Leeanne could have sworn she saw his lips twitch.

"It's not funny," she assured him.

"I did no' say it was. Here now, no need to get all thrang and taigled," he said. He lifted the matted comb. "Let me see what I can do before we resort to such rough means."

"But it's worse than—" She'd been about to say bubble gum, but quickly revised her sentence. "—anything I've ever seen."

"You're overreacting." His words were careful, calculated to be calming, Leeanne decided.

"Do you think so?"

"I'm that sure of it. Just rest easy. When Sesi was a bairn, I did this for her more times than I care to recount. And never did we resort to the scissor's blade."

"That's hard to imagine . . . a Highland warrior with a broadsword slung over his shoulders tending to a child . . . and a girl at that."

"We Highlanders are men of great patience, lass. We take our womenfolk seriously."

Leeanne arched a neatly plucked brow at Iain.

He grinned rather sheepishly. "Aye, I know what you're thinking—as the auld chief was quick to point out to me only this morning. Be that as it may, I would no' lie to you outright. Now, sit tight and let me see what I can do to help you out of this predicament."

Though it took him several minutes, Iain gently untangled Leeanne's matted curls from the comb's greedy teeth. Once the comb was free, he sat down on the bed behind her, turning her shoulders so that she faced the hearth.

"Be still now," he advised.

Holding her hair at the base of her scalp with the palm of his hand, beginning at the ends and working his way up, Iain combed the tangles from Leeanne's hair. The texture was just as soft as he'd imagined, the curls alive and springy to the touch. With each sweep of his hand across her hair, he felt his loins tighten.

Clenching his teeth, he ignored the sensation. For some reason Leeanne's defenses were down for the first time since he'd met her. She was vulnerable. A lesser man would have taken advantage of the situation. Honor and integrity, bolstered by an ingrained sense of guilt that he'd carried within himself for over two years, stayed him.

"I know how you must feel, lass," he began, talking to the back of her head while he combed, "married to a man you do no' know."

"It's not that. I'm a career woman. A teacher—"

"Who has been stripped of her right to life, liberty, and the pursuit of happiness," Iain interjected.

"Exactly. You see, I simply do not want to be married," Leeanne reiterated in a small voice.

"I can understand the sentiment. Neither do I. It's common enough knowledge that I don't care to be tied to a woman—English or otherwise. But I see no reason we can no' be friends these many months."

"Are you proposing a platonic relationship?"

"Aye."

Touched by his offer, yet unsure, she said, "I'll need some time to think about it. I've never made my decisions lightly."

"Is it that you find me undeserving because of what I've done to you personally? Or could it be that you've heard stories about me and mine before now?"

Hand at her throat, Leeanne clutched the edges of her plaid more closely together. She'd never felt so alone, so distanced from all the little things she'd taken for granted—like a sturdy, plastic, wide-toothed comb. "Neither. It's just that we're so different." From different centuries, with different life-styles, and different codes of moral conduct. "Worlds apart." Literally.

"I'll agree to that. Londontown isn't Glencoe. And the Highlands aren't England. But have you never heard that opposites attract, lass? We might even become fast friends before this is all said and done. The first step towards harmony is always the most difficult to take."

Leeanne twisted at the waist so she could see Iain's face. The face of a man who had offered her his friendship because, thrust as she was into an alien environment, she sensed that she desperately needed someone to lean on. "I've always been a firm believer that anything is possible."

"Aye. With a little assistance," Iain said, setting aside the comb to reach for the wooden mules that Sesi had sent to Leeanne. He slid from the bed and kneeled on the floor by her feet.

"Your feet are still chilled, lass. I can feel them through your slippers," he said, running his hands along the sole of her leather ballet shoe. Removing the shoe from her foot and bunching up her black woolen leggings to her knees, he massaged her toes through her color-coordinated tights.

"This isn't necessary—" Leeanne stuttered, attempting to draw her foot from his grasp, thinking that what she really wanted, if she was honest with herself, was for Iain MacBride to kiss her again. Like he had in the community center the night of Sesi's wedding. She wanted him to make her feel alive, and whole, and secure again within herself, as only a man desirous of a woman could.

His face a solemn mask hiding his emotions, Iain said, "I'm thinking it is between friends. We do no' want you to suffer from frostbite. The Highlands are hard enough on those that can walk, let alone cripples."

"A cripple! Heaven forbid," Leeanne exclaimed. Her life was based on her ability to perform, she thought.

Common sense, aided by Iain's strong, sure movements, prevailed, making it impossible for Leeanne the professional dancer to protest. Even if Leeanne the woman had wanted to do so.

Skillfully he worked his way along from her toes to the soles of her feet, then farther to dally over her ankles and the tops of her feet before gliding back down to her toes. His hands felt warm and enticing as they coaxed the blood to flow more effectively. Satisfied, Iain slipped back on her shoe, along with the mule, only to minister to her other foot in exactly the same manner.

Finally, as if the words were drawn from him against his will, he rearranged her leggings from her ankles to her knees. "If we delay much longer, I fear my sister's best intentions will become nothing more than a sorry excuse for noon's repast."

Iain lowered Leeanne's foot to the floor and with free-swinging strides launched himself at the door. "Come, there's a cloak in Sesi's box beneath the bed . . . too small in the girth for her, pregnant as she is. Bundle up and meet me outside. I'll be waiting with the ponies."

As Iain yanked open the door, a welcome breath of wintry air rushed into the cottage. It swirled around them like the erotic images eddying in her head, cooling whatever it was that had passed between them. At least temporarily, Leeanne thought, dragging the strong-box from beneath the bed as soon as the door closed.

She soon realized that it contained not only Sesi's things, but some of Iain's personal belongings as well. There were legal documents stacked within, documents Leeanne couldn't have deciphered if she'd tried, written as they were in a combination of old English and Gaelic.

Toward the center of the strongbox, she discovered a braided lock of chestnut hair tied in a silver ribbon, so long that it reminded her of the country singer Crystal Gayle. And an infant's handmade christening gown. A knife with a carved walrus-tusk handle. A dog-eared book of poetry bound in leather and stored in a green velvet drawstring pouch. Some lead tokens. Fresh bed linens. And near the bottom, a peat-colored woolen cloak embroidered with the MacBride family badge—an eagle feather surrounded by a sprig of heather.

Feeling as if she'd inadvertently invaded someone's diary, Leeanne hurriedly extracted the cloak, slamming the lid closed and shoving the strongbox firmly beneath the bed.

She scrambled to her knees just as Iain reentered the cottage.

"What's taking you so long, lass? Did you no' find the cloak?"

"I found it," she said, twirling on her tiptoes. The cloak swirled out around her, then settled against her figure like a dove folding its wings.

"Aye. It will do," Iain agreed, taking her arm and guiding her outside.

"Up you go," he said, grasping her waist and hefting her onto the goatskin saddle of a placid Highland pony. Iain handed Leeanne the braided-hair reins.

"The ponies may look as tough as winter, but they have tender mouths, so guide them lightly or you're in for a surprise. These ponies do no' take to heavy-handedness. They'd as soon dump you on your pretty rear as look at you."

"Thanks for the warning," Leeanne said dryly, wrapping the ends of the reins together around one hand. "Which way?"

Iain settled himself on the pony that had nudged Leeanne from its stall, his long, muscular legs practically dragging the ground as he reined it to her side. "That way," he said, pointing toward a stand of bare oak trees no taller than the average man. "We'll follow along the terraces of the River Coe. It's a more scenic route than—"

Iain stopped, cocking his head to one side as his pony shifted uneasily. Leeanne's snorted and rolled its eyes, trying to tongue the bit into its teeth.

"Lass, I suggest you hold your mount steady. Tighten up the reins a wee bit and dig in your knees."

"What is it?" she asked in alarm, doing exactly as she'd been instructed.

"Listen softly. It's a grand thing. You'll catch the gist of it in a minute."

And she did. The nasal cry of ducks. The thunderous pounding of their wings, so loud she couldn't hear herself think. Flying in tight formation like the B-52 bombers of World War II, Leeanne thought.

Astonished, she watched as the black shadow of their feathered bodies surged across the azure sky, hovering directly overhead, temporarily blocking out the winter sunshine. Then, as quickly as it began, the shadow passed out of sight.

"I've never seen such a huge flock of ducks. There must have been hundreds of them," Leeanne said in awe.

"Those weren't all ducks, lass. I spotted some herons and a few black-throated divers in the bunch. There were swans as well. Though they fly with the other water fowl, they have a special penchant for Loch Achtriochtan near Achnambeithach."

"What does that word mean—Achnambeithach?"

"Field of the birch trees."

"That's beautiful."

"Aye and aye. I'm thinking the swans are of the same mind. They're a splendid sight up close. Perhaps I'll take you to see them one day."

"I suppose there's all sorts of wildlife in the Highlands . . . besides wolves," Leeanne commented thoughtfully.

"We're no' nearly as domesticated as the English countryside you're accustomed to, but you'll find foxes aplenty if you travel high enough into the mountains. Wildcats range along the slopes. And then we've got our share of game—red grouse on the moors, deer in the cedar forests, herring from Loch Leven."

"And wild ducks."

"And more than enough wild ducks."

"For as long as it lasts," Leeanne muttered, thinking how modern man had abused the ecological system. How many animals had been hunted to extinction—the Atlantic gray whale, the sea mink, the California condor. She wondered, if she told Iain of DDT, of the wholesale slaughter of dolphins by the world's fishing industry, of the hole in the ozone layer, or the destruction of the rain forests, whether he would believe her. It was sad really, Leeanne thought, because she was quickly discovering the New World relatively pale in comparison to the Old.

Chapter Four

Iain and Leeanne entered the rustic stone cottage perched on the banks of the River Coe, if not hand and hand, at least on relatively amiable terms. Sesi greeted Leeanne enthusiastically, giving her a generous hug.

"Well, it's about time," she said, taking Leeanne's cloak and hanging it on a peg in the wall. That done, Sesi presented Iain with a brief peck on the cheek. "I feared the wolves had spirited off the both of you," she said to him.

Unlike Iain's cottage, Sesi's home was redolent of peat due to the hole in the roof which served as a chimney. Leeanne's eyes moved from the crude oaken picnic table squatting bullfrog like in the center of the room to the spinning wheel, loom . . . and live sheep penned on the far side of the room. Near the door, the bed proved no more than a frameless pallet upon whose foot reclined a collie.

The dog stood and shook itself, barking at the visitors. Shuffling and bleating as if at any moment it expected to be herded into a new corner of the cottage, the sheep instinctively reacted to the collie.

A red-haired man seated at the table rose to his feet, silencing the dog with a quick hand signal. Within seconds, the sheep calmed as well.

"A bit longer and Sesi would've beat me oot into the snow to hunt ye doon," the man said. "I explained 'twas foolish to worry so, but ye ken yer sister."

"Only too well," Iain responded as Sesi closed the door behind them.

Iain drew Leeanne more deeply into the dim cottage, and it suddenly hit her that, in her urbanized world, she'd never met his equal. She'd had boyfriends, and men friends, and male business associates, but none possessed his raw sense of power.

It wasn't so much his size as his sense of presence. Iain dominated the nondescript cubicle with an energy, a strength, an aura of self-confidence that the feeble man-made structure could barely contain. The cliché "larger than life" flashed through Leeanne's mind, its meaning as startlingly clear as filtered water.

"Leeanne, I'd like you to meet Parlan

Macdonald, Sesi's husband," Iain said, momentarily redirecting her thoughts.

Parlan was nothing like the boy Leeanne had imagined him. She would have bet her favorite ballet shoes that Sesi was no more than eighteen. Silver-gray peppering his temples, Parlan Macdonald was closer to Iain's age—mid-thirties if he was a day.

Hand settling at the small of her back, Iain nudged Leeanne expectantly. The contact was feather-light, yet firm and reassuring. She'd never been so aware of a man's touch, Leeanne mused. Her senses acutely heightened, she could actually feel the warmth of his splayed, blunt-tipped fingers through the material of her outer clothing.

Iain's hand deserted her back, and Leeanne almost cried out, the parting affected her so deeply. Then both his hands descended on her shoulders, easing her back against his hard body. He leaned over her shoulder, his clean-shaven chin rasping like fine sandpaper against her cheek, sending a delicious shiver down her spine. His warm breath tickled her ear as he whispered, "He only looks disreputable, lass."

Iain's hands slid across her shoulders and down her arms to her elbows, where he reached beneath them to contour her rib cage. With a gentle push, he advanced her toward Parlan.

With a start of surprise, Leeanne realized that Iain's masculine company was something she could oh-so-easily grow to enjoy.

"It's nice to meet you, Parlan," Leeanne said finally, automatically extending her hand.

The instant she did it, she knew she'd made a mistake.

A blank expression skittering across his ruddy face, Parlan glanced at Iain. Iain shrugged as if to say, "You're on your own, auld friend."

As the seconds ticked past, Leeanne felt her cheeks grow warm and her hand heavy. In her world, a handshake was a common form of introduction. But in Iain's, perhaps handshakes hadn't been invented. Or worse still, perhaps Parlan thought she expected him to kiss her hand—as she'd seen men do in movies portraying the courtly life of Mary, Queen of Scots.

Confirming that she'd guessed correctly, Parlan leaned awkwardly from the waist, grazing her knuckles with a brief, generic kiss.

Feeling self-conscious and more than a little foolish, Leeanne dropped her hand to her side, hiding it in the folds of her jumper skirt.

Obviously relieved to be done with formalities, Parlan redirected his attention to more familiar territory.

"Iain, I'd hoped to see ye dressed in something other than the black and white today," he said, a mischievous gleam in his hazel eyes. He clapped Iain on the shoulder. "Something more favorable to gaze upon, like yer new bride's own Jacobite *plaidie*."

Though Parlan's English wasn't as easy to

follow as either Iain's or the Macdonald chief's, Leeanne soon realized he was speaking of her costume. She glanced down at her Highland green and burnt orange plaid. So *that's* why she'd been so readily accepted into the Macdonald clan—politics. They believed her to be a Stuart sympathizer, Leeanne thought. Why hadn't she realized it before? It made perfect sense, even though the plaid had been chosen, not for the meaning of its sett, but for the bold coloring of the pattern. For the costume's visibility beneath bright-hot stage lights.

Iain frowned at Parlan. "I find the black and white sett favorable enough, thank you very much."

"Ach, he's a bit touchy this morning. I'll warrant he's na had much sleep. Best watch oot for yerself," Parlan said, winking at Sesi.

Sesi matched Parlan's playful smile with an indulgent one, and Leeanne knew a moment of envy. It was obvious, regardless of their differences in age, that Parlan and Sesi were deeply in love.

"Iain has been touchy for the better part of the past two years, but now that he has some feminine companionship to liven up his life, perhaps we'll see some marked improvement in his sour disposition," Sesi quipped. "Why . . . just look at what it's done for you, Parlan Macdonald."

Parlan reached out and affectionately patted Sesi's well-rounded rump.

"Ye, dearest lady, are too full o' yerself by half. And if I remember correctly, ye've na been forgiven for what ye did earlier this morning. The auld chief was worked up enough over the oath of allegiance and his trip to Inveraray without ye stirring the flames. And now ye have yer brother's eyes stabbing daggers at ye as well."

"Keep your fresh hands to yourself. We have guests," Sesi reminded with a becoming blush, physically removing Parlan's hand from the swell of her hip, but not before she'd given it a gentle squeeze. "Besides, I've already apologized to Iain."

"From what I understand, na in so many words," Parlan teased.

"Who told you that? Alasdair?" Sesi asked.

"He did."

"Then he also told you that I'm not above admitting how pleased I am that things worked out as they did. It's high time Iain put past griefs aside and got on with his life. He's a virile man. He can yet sire healthy children to carry on the MacBride name."

Sesi spoke to Parlan, while looking directly at Iain.

Leeanne thought she saw a flash of guilt on Iain's face. Just as quickly, it was absorbed into the shadowed pools of his azure eyes.

"I must have been mistaken," Iain said darkly. "I was under the impression we came here to break the fast."

Glancing between the siblings, Parlan agreed, "Aye, ye did at that, Iain." His gaze traveled to his wife's face. "Sesi, I must ask ye na to speak o' such private matters again. Iain has warned ye repeatedly that he does na care for yer prying ways."

"But he's my brother, Parlan. I'm only concerned for his well—"

"Enough, Sesi. The man is na only your brother, he's a guest in our cottage. Now, we've two weddings to celebrate. Break oot the claret and we'll drink a toast to each and make peace in the family."

"I suppose you're right," Sesi said with a sigh. "Sit, everyone, sit at the table and I'll begin serving."

Both men complied. Leeanne remained on her feet, mulling over the fact that Parlan considered them a family, wanting to ask the mysterious meaning of Iain's black and white plaid, but not quite daring to since it would have been obvious to a fence post that he didn't intend to discuss it.

Instead, she said, "Please, let me help you with breakfast, Sesi."

Leeanne watched as Sesi's angelic, china-doll face hardened with indignation.

"Heaven forbid! I'll not have it said that Sesi MacBride Macdonald had another woman wait upon her table. Right now, I admit my home isn't much more than a brigand's bachelor quarters, but it's my home all the same."

Unwilling to put her foot in her mouth again, uncertain of what she'd said to offend his sister, Leeanne glanced at Iain for enlightenment.

"I'm sure Leeanne didn't mean to insult your hospitality. You must keep in mind, she's new here, Sesi."

That's the understatement of the year, Leeanne told herself.

Iain gestured to a seat on the bench beside him. "Come, sit beside me, Lass. Sesi will serve the meal as is her right as hostess. And when they come to your home, then it will be your turn to do likewise."

Leeanne obliged Iain, thinking that she really must find a way to return home . . . to her *real* home in North Carolina. And soon! That she fit into Iain's world like a computerized engine in a Model-T. That it must be nearing nine a.m. and that her dance company, which met promptly at eight, *had* to be wondering what had happened to her. That surely they would contact the police and file a missing-persons report. Send out an all-points bulletin—which in her case would be about as effective as spitting into the wind.

"You look wan all of a sudden. Are you all right?" Iain asked, breaking into Leeanne's reverie.

Leeanne nodded, her mind backtracking through the centuries to the present. "I'm fine, really." *As fine as anyone in my position could be.* "Just a little hungry, that's all."

"I've got something that will fix you right up," Sesi said, placing three deep saucers with side-handles on the the table. From a flat-lidded flagon, she filled Parlan's saucer with a measure of dark purplish red liquid, moving next to Iain's.

Leeanne raised an eyebrow at Iain as the flagon progressed her way, not about to chance insulting Sesi further.

Startling sapphire eyes met and held solemn azure ones.

After a moment's hesitation, Iain shifted on the bench. Reaching past Leeanne, he placed his hand firmly over the mouth of her clay saucer.

"No need to fill Leeanne's *cuach*. My wife will no' be drinking wine today," Iain said.

The word *wife* sent a strange shiver rippling through Leeanne's body. Pleasure, or denial, or a combination of both? She really wasn't sure. She was sure, however, that even in profile Iain was drop-dead gorgeous. That he filled her senses without even trying. That his clean, natural scent moved her more than any over-the-counter men's fragrance. That he was utterly masculine and physically pleasing. And that his blatant sex appeal played havoc with her libido.

Righting the flagon, Sesi asked in surprise, "Well, why ever not?"

"Leeanne and I had a wager. Suffice to say, she lost."

Sesi's mouth narrowed into a pencil-thin line of disapproval. "And did it also include forgoing the meal I've spent the morning preparing especially for her?"

"No' that I recall," Iain said, a wry smile lifting the corners of his lips.

"Then I suggest you fill your trenchers . . . all three of you. I'll go and make tea since Leeanne can't partake of the claret, thanks to you and some silly wager you've made, Iain MacBride."

"No' made. Won," Iain called after her. "And she likes her tea boiling hot."

"Do you always speak for your bride, Iain Macbride?"

"No' always, Mistress Macdonald."

"Then might I ask my guest directly if she'd like milk with her tea?"

A teasing twinkle in his eye, Iain said, "You might if the notion strikes you, sister mine."

Eyeing the sheep's pen, Sesi asked sweetly, "Shall I collect some milk for your tea, Leeanne?"

It took a moment before Leeanne realized what Sesi was implying. Speculating on homogenized versus fresher-than-fresh, Leeanne decided that natural food sounded fantastic until one was faced with a saggy-uddered, hoof-stomping, cud-chewing refrigerator.

"None, thank you," Leeanne managed.

"You see, she has a mouth," Iain said, the

twinkle expanding into a bold gleam.

"And manners too, which is more than I can say for some Highlanders I know," Sesi muttered over her shoulder. Using the hem of her skirt as a pot holder, she adjusted the teapot whose spout was at right angles to the handle over the fire.

From behind his hand, Parlan said to no one in particular, "Pay no never mind to Sesi. She's well into her eighth month and as irritable as a bee trying to fill its hive before the first snowfall. But 'tis the first child to bear my name, so I've allowed her the moodiness."

"The first child to bear your . . . ?" Leeanne began, only to be stopped by Iain.

"From now on, it's only children bearing your name the MacBrides will be tolerating."

Leeanne thought Parlan blushed, but it was hard to tell with his ruddy complexion.

"Ye've my word on it, Iain. Sesi is all I ever want and well you ken it, or else ye would na have let me have her."

"Aye," Iain said simply.

He proceeded to carve the roast resting like a crusty lump on the round pewter dish that Sesi had placed in the center of the table. Leeanne watched in silent distress as he piled her platter high with thick, juicy slices of blood-rare leg o' lamb.

Though she felt hungry after their brisk morning trot, her stomach recoiled into a tight knot. Leeanne forced herself to reach for the only eating utensil in sight, turning the knife over and over to examine the finely carved bone handle. With the pointed tip of the blade, she toyed with the meat on her trencher, nervously rearranging the slices. Finally she cut a bite-sized piece, speared it, and raised it to her lips, finding to her dismay that she simply couldn't put the bloody morsel into her mouth. With a grimace, Leeanne set the knife aside without tasting the lamb.

"Once again, I see you look as if you've lost something, lass. What is it this time?" Iain asked.

She wanted to say, "What you *see* is a desperate woman. What she's lost is a handle on time itself." Glancing first toward Sesi, who was far too caught up in her tea-making to be entirely attentive to the table conversation, Leeanne whispered instead, "Iain, I'm so sorry, but I can't eat this."

Parlan almost choked on the slice of lamb he was stuffing into his mouth with his fingers.

Iain, on the other hand, simply stared at her.

After a moment of awkward silence, he asked in a low, controlled voice, "I thought I'd won myself a 'domestic goddess.' What happened to her?"

Before she could stop herself, Leeanne said, "The same thing that happened to serving your plate by the fire."

Leeanne couldn't help but notice that the lines creasing Iain's forehead hinted at anger.

Anger created by her sharp retort.

"It seems my sister prefers the more civilized social graces of a table," he said tightly.

Earlier, he'd been gentle with her. But Leeanne knew from experience that Iain could be harsh when crossed, especially when his sister's feelings were involved. And although Leeanne was at times fearless, she wasn't stupid.

Eyes lowering to her hands folded primly in her lap, Leeanne decided that her personal convictions overrode any displeasure she might cause Iain.

"I swear, I'm not trying to be difficult, Iain. It's just that I live by a strict code of ethics," she said.

With a careless grace that belied his muscular body, Iain scooted down the length of the bench. Uncomfortably aware of his intense regard, of his muscled thigh pressed intimately to hers, Leeanne glanced up, her body reacting even as her mind rebelled against the forbidden sensation.

"Would you care to explain yourself, lass?" he asked, his piercing gaze impelling her.

Leeanne's heart battered at the wall of her breast. Her breath tripped over her lips as she attempted to form a coherent reply, thinking all the while that she could learn to regret the pact of friendship they'd agreed upon.

"I'm a low-level vegetarian," she finally managed to stutter through the whirl of sensual thoughts hammering at her brain. "My diet doesn't include red meat."

Iain looked away, and Leeanne could only assume that he was attempting to make sense of her admission.

Chewing thoughtfully, Parlan said, "I've never heard of such an outlandish thing. Have ye, Iain?"

"No' that I recall."

"Most peculiar," Parlan mumbled.

Iain said nothing for a long while, and when he did speak his words were curt.

"What *can* you eat?" he asked, rubbing the back of his neck.

So, I am a pain in the neck, Leeanne thought. That was gratifying to know when all she could think about was his body pressed intimately to hers.

"Uh, grains, pasta, cheese, vegetables, and um . . . freshwater fish once in a while . . . for the protein." Unfolding her hands, Leeanne counted the items off on her fingers.

"I see." Iain said, though it was obvious he didn't.

"Really, it's not all that weird where I come from."

She wanted to tell him that lots of Americans had cut down on meat consumption in an attempt to lower their cholesterol. That eating animals wasn't as popular as it once had been. Of course, explaining that to Iain would only serve to confuse him more, and probably make it harder on herself in the process.

"I don't doubt that one wee bit, lass. You English and your peculiar sassenach airs do test a man's positive good humor. Especially a man who . . ." Shaking his head, Iain left his sentence incomplete.

Glancing up from the fire, Sesi asked, "What are the three of you whispering about?"

"Uh, nothing, luve. Nothing at all," Parlan said quickly.

He leaned toward Iain.

"Yer bride's preference is na a problem, Iain. There's more in the cottage than meat," he stated quietly. Then more loudly he told Sesi, "It seems Leeanne's stomach is feeling delicate this morning, as well any newly married lady might understand. Though the lamb is cooked to a perfect turn, ye might want to go ahead and serve something else with her tea."

"Something light?" Sesi asked, collecting the teapot and moving to the table to serve Leeanne a steaming saucer. Leeanne sipped at the bitter black brew, deciding it tasted nothing like the English Breakfast Tea she normally enjoyed each morning following a glass of freshly squeezed orange juice.

"Aye. Something on the lighter side would be more agreeable," Parlan said. "Porridge and smoked salt herring. Or mayhap she'd enjoy a slice o' the black bun ye've left from Hogmanay."

A bagel. A bagel. My kingdom for a whole wheat

bagel . . . and softened strawberry cream cheese,
Leeanne thought, asking, "What's Hogmanay?"

"It's Scotch for what you English call New
Year's Eve," Iain explained.

"And black bun?"

Sesi filled in where Iain left off. "Holiday
bread. You fill a paste jacket with almonds,
currants, raisins, sugar, cinnamon, ginger, all-
spice, and a touch of brandy, then bake."

Aha! An ancient recipe for modern-day sweet
rolls. Not too healthy, but blessedly familiar,
Leeanne thought.

"Would you care for a slice?" Sesi asked.

"That'll work," Leeanne said with a grateful smile, realizing she'd not only discovered
something meatless to eat, but the time of year
as well.

Leeanne breathed a silent sigh of relief when
Iain relaxed, giving a satisfied nod of approv-
al.

The tense atmosphere threatening to spoil
breakfast rapidly dissipated after that, and
Leeanne had to admit that the meal passed
rather pleasurably. The conversation went over
her head at times, but her tea, as Iain had
stipulated, was hot, the black bun delicious,
and the company congenial. Sesi, with her
quick wit and generous spirit, made Leeanne
feel welcome. And although Parlan was rough
around the edges, he had the earmarks of a
gentleman.

After breakfast, Leeanne was careful to leave

the clean-up to Sesi, moving to stand by the fire and warm herself while the men enjoyed a second cup of claret. To keep herself from dwelling on her own problems, to take her mind off Iain's broadsword and the probability of being able to travel back to her own time once she got it off his shoulders and into her hot little hands, and in hopes of learning more about the century she'd landed in, she listened to their conversation.

"Alasdair sent his piper 'round before daybreak with a challenge," Parlan said.

"Aye, he would, the auld fox. With Sesi out of the game, he's assured of winning," Iain said.

"The trophy today is a prize bull."

"The one John Macdonald drove in from the Glen Lyon two weeks ago?" Iain asked.

"The same. It's a braw specimen. Golden brown and sporting horns as long as I am tall. With a bull like that, Sesi and I could have a grand herd started by this time next spring."

Leeanne couldn't help but notice the gleam in Parlan's eye as Iain asked, "And what are they asking that you put up in return?"

"Three mature black-faced yews."

"That's stiff."

"The bull's worth thrice that many sheep to me."

His gaze drifting from the table, Iain said, "You know as well as I we have as much chance as a loch herring swimming on land, one person short as we are. That's the reason Alasdair's son is willing to put up the bull. It's a sure thing—a morning of *camanachd* with no price to pay."

Leeanne stood warming her rear by the fire, lifting her skirts slightly to allow the warm air to circulate beneath them.

"Wait one moment now. I'm thinking there may be a way to acquire that bull that I've overlooked until now," Iain said, his fair brows lifting speculatively.

"What are ye saying?" Parlan asked.

Belatedly, Leeanne realized she'd become the center of both men's attention.

Stroking his chin thoughtfully, Iain said, "Give us a look at your legs, Leeanne."

"What?" Leeanne asked, deciding that the mischievous gleam she'd glimpsed in Parlan's eyes must be the contagious kind because it was now playing in Iain's eyes as well.

"I asked you to lift up your skirts a wee bit higher so that we might have a good look at your legs, lass."

"Iain, have you and Parlan lost your minds?" Sesi asked, her voice an example of outraged femininity at its finest.

The men exchanged conspiratorial looks.

"Be still, luve. We mean no harm," Parlan said.

"Come now, show me your legs, Leeanne," Iain cajoled, ignoring his sister's protest.

"You've got to be kidding!"

"No' in the least. You see, we have desperate need of a vigorous runner, lass. And I'm thinking you might be the edge that will give Sesi's sweet bairn a head start in the world. An established herd of beef could mean the difference between an education at the university or no'."

"It could also provide some of the amenities Sesi requires to make these sad bachelor quarters into a proper home," Parlan added.

Leeanne glanced at Sesi. Hope had replaced the uncertainty and outrage in her delicate blue eyes.

"I hate to say it, but they're absolutely correct in everything they've said," Sesi confessed at last.

Head erect, shoulders squared, Leeanne said, "They haven't really told me anything. Exactly what are we talking about here?"

"*Camanachd*," Iain said. "The entire clan plays . . . young, auld, rich, poor, male and female alike."

"Divided into permanent opposing forces, they are," Parlan added.

Leeanne laughed out loud. "I get it now! We're talking winter sports, aren't we?" A harmless game of something known to the Highlanders as *camanachd*, Leeanne reasoned.

"Well what did you think we were talking about?" Sesi asked with interest.

"Oh, I don't know. Something else, I suppose." Something barbaric.

Iain placed his elbows on the table, making a steeple with his fingers. "Well, are you or aren't you, lass?"

"Am I or am I not what?"

"Going to cooperate and lift your skirts?"

To be perfectly honest, she was really quite proud of her legs, Leeanne thought. Smooth-muscled and physically fit, they were one of her best assets. And it wasn't as if she didn't display them to the world each time she danced. Besides which, even if she were a prude, which she wasn't, she considered her classic black tights modesty in motion.

"This is crazy, but here goes," Leeanne said, boldly lifting her skirts mid-thigh to display long, shapely legs.

Posturing like a Ford model, she gave them an eyeful from every conceivable angle.

Iain sat a little straighter in his chair. "As leggy as any thoroughbred," he said, his voice slightly husky. He cleared his throat. "What do you think, Parlan?"

"I think we've got our edge," Parlan said, drawing Sesi into his lap, bestowing a kiss on her upturned lips.

Iain took a deep breath. "You may lower your skirts now, lass," he said firmly. Reaching for his cup, he took a healthy swig of claret.

Leeanne raised her eyes to find Iain's watching her over the rim of his cup.

"Are you sure?" she asked.

For a moment, Iain seemed not to have

heard her. It was then that Leeanne realized he was recalling ministering to her cold feet, her ankles, the sensitive calves of her legs. Something sensual stirred within her, something she was entirely unprepared for—the acute desire to be back in Iain's cottage, with his strong hands moving upon her legs . . . to her thighs . . . and then higher still.

For a fleeting instant, Leeanne was so intensely conscious of Iain that it hurt. She found herself wondering what it might be like to throw caution to the wind and consummate her marriage to Iain. The answer was easy— nothing short of glorious, she decided.

"I said," Iain reiterated in an even voice, "drop your skirts, lass." Leeanne glanced at Iain's lap, thrilled and yet appalled to see the bulge that told her the attraction between them was mutual.

Leeanne abruptly dropped her skirts. Their gazes caught, and she realized that Iain knew exactly what she was thinking, for their minds were traveling in tandem.

"Have ye ever been to a *camanachd?*" Parlan asked, innocently breaking the spell that had momentarily bound her and Iain.

Leeanne responded to Parlan's question with the first thing that popped into her mind. "Can Highland ponies fly?"

Parlan frowned. "I do na ken what ye're saying, Leeanne."

Iain actually smiled. "See how merry she is

on her feet, Parlan. To prove it, quick as a wink she's rolled one of her witty English come arounds off her tongue."

Leeanne couldn't stop herself from returning Iain's smile. "Comebacks," she said softly. Her voice sounded strained. It surprised her.

"Aye, I stand corrected," Iain said. "Now, will you agree to play today in Sesi's place or won't you?"

Leeanne loved sports . . . gymnastics too. And because she'd missed her regular morning practice routine, her muscles felt tight. Some honest exercise might help to cool the turbulence within her, she decided. Besides which, to an adventuresome woman who had white-water rafted down the Chattahoochee River, sky-dived in Chester, South Carolina, and camped in the Arizona desert, a Highland *camanachd* should be a cinch.

To top it all off, Leeanne felt she owed Parlan something for covering for her during breakfast, for smoothing over a potentially explosive situation when he'd suggested the black bun, for keeping the peace "in the family."

And she made it a policy to pay back her debts.

"I suppose you can count me in," she said.

"Perhaps you should bring Leeanne a wee dram of claret after all," Iain told Sesi.

Sesi nodded as if Iain's suggestion made perfect sense.

Leeanne blinked involuntarily.

"You were adamant. No alcohol. I can't believe the honorable Iain MacBride is bending the rules of a bet."

"You've given me good cause to change my mind, lass. A cup or two of liquid courage never hurts. Especially before a *camanachd*."

Leeanne accepted the cup of wine with mixed emotions, wondering how difficult a simple game of *camanachd* could be. Wondering once again, with her limited knowledge of social customs and Scottish life-styles, what the heck she'd gotten herself into.

Chapter Five

What she'd gotten herself into was as alien as time-travel itself, Leeanne thought for no less than the tenth time.

In a Highland pasture wrested from a conifer forest, with bonfires blazing on four corners of the lengthy field, Leeanne watched as Iain unleashed the energy she'd sensed in Sesi's cottage, learning all she ever wanted to know and was afraid to ask about *camanachd*. The game resembled bits and pieces of several modern sports events all rolled into one, Leeanne thought. With Alasdair Macdonald acting as referee, two opposing teams endeavored by means of a club that resembled a tire tool to drive a golfball-sized ball down a football

111

field to a hockey-style goal.

It was the most incredible thing. . . .

By high noon, during what she considered half-time, when the pipers played their mournful bagpipe tunes and more claret along with barley bread and cheese was passed around to team members and sideline spectators alike, Leeanne finally realized the *camanachd* rules were questionable. Perhaps even changeable. The one factor she could count on, however, was Iain's initial promise to her.

"No matter what happens, you must run the way I point, lass," he'd said. "Do no' look back. Do no' worry about me. I vow, they will no' touch a lovely hair on your head as long as I'm guarding your back."

Though he now reminded her more of a battered, beaten, and bruised quarterback at the end of an NFL season, Iain had been true to his word. Each time the ball passed her way, she ran free and clear to a decisive goal against John Macdonald's astonished *camanachd* team.

Nerves taut and excitement high, Parlan's players now huddled to discuss the final strategy of the afternoon. A play designed to lead the team to the thrill of victory rather than the agony of defeat. Iain, the brains behind the brawn, coached them.

"The snow's grown slovenly, but no more so than our opponents' tactics. We've got them where we want them. I'm thinking you should feint to the left, Parlan, as if you're assured of receiving the ball. And you will receive it, for all of a single heartbeat."

"Aye. I'm following ye so far, Iain."

"As soon as John's cutthroats start to bear down on you, pass the ball down the line of women until it comes to me. I'll be down near our goal. Just before they pounce I'll send it on to Leeanne. The other men must cover her."

His gaze riveted on Leeanne. "Lass, you'll need to be behind me."

"Behind you?" Leeanne asked, attempting to follow Iain's line of reasoning.

"Aye. Only in that manner can we take John's braggarts by surprise. Even though they have a stronger force than we do, they'll never guess I've planned for you to run around me in the melee that follows."

"You don't think they'll catch on?"

"I'm counting that it will no' be before it's too late for them to save themselves."

Leeanne couldn't help noticing that one of Iain's eyes was almost swollen shut. The knees he'd gone down on in the snow with her in his arms to secure their bet looked as if a wildcat had used them for a scratching post. His soft linen shirt was ripped open at the shoulder seam, displaying a muscular biceps through the ravaged edges of the material; his dark blond hair was tousled from the Highland breeze whipping across the field.

He seemed nothing less than magnificent, Leeanne thought.

"Are we ready then?" Iain cried.

"Aye," the team members yelled in unison.

Caught up in the excitement, the clanship and camaraderie, Leeanne cried, "Right on! Go for the gold, you guys."

"Ye mean go for the bull, do ye na, Leeanne?" Parlan asked.

A warm smile parting her full lips, Leeanne agreed. "That's it. Go for the bull!"

"We're ready then?" Iain asked.

"To be sure," Parlan said.

"Nothing less than victory!" Iain said.

Though the team dispersed, Leeanne remained poised near Iain.

"What is it, lass?" he asked after a moment.

"I'm not sure how far behind you I'm supposed to be," she explained.

Iain motioned toward his sister, standing on the sidelines near one of the bonfires. "Start toward Sesi and do no' stop until you see the sett of my kilt blurring. That should be about right."

Leeanne stepped beside Iain to assess the way he pointed. When he lowered his hand to his side, his fingers brushed her arm. She started, her heart skipping a beat.

"Are you all right? No' getting chilled, are you?" he asked, reaching out to test her cheek with the back of his hand. His touch only served to stimulate her more.

114

"I'm fine . . . not too cold." *Just ultrasensitive where you're concerned,* she marveled.

"Good," he said, admiration lacing his voice. "I've said it before and I'll say it again. You're a brave, bonnie lass. There's no mistaking that. I do no' know many women who would put themselves out for a man's sister . . . and an impudent young thing at that."

Blushing at his compliment, caught between her burgeoning desire for Iain and a pressing need to return to her own time, Leeanne tried to focus her racing thoughts. She glanced across the field to Sesi, baby-sitting Iain's claymore for him while he played *camanachd*.

First things first! Leeanne admonished herself. Now was hardly the time to dwell on the sword and its unique potential. Not if she wanted to carry the day. And strangely enough, she did—mainly because of its importance to Iain.

"I don't mind. The afternoon has turned out better than I expected."

"Aye. It has indeed," he agreed softly.

"I . . . I guess I'd better go."

"I suppose you must."

"Yeah, well . . . I'll . . . uh . . . be waiting for the ball."

Leeanne sprinted into position across the iron-solid ground in thick-soled boots borrowed from Alasdair Macdonald's wife. Iain waved to her and she tugged her tartan shawl closer about her body, consciously hiding her

115

neon pink save-the-whales T-shirt from view.

Get on your mark, Leeanne thought, hitching up her skirts. Pushing her shoulders down. Straightening her body. Tightening her stomach muscles.

As she watched, Parlan passed the ball through the women players to Iain. Too soon, a mob of sports-crazed Macdonalds charged down the field toward a solitary man—Iain MacBride.

Get set, Leeanne told herself, sliding into a series of ballet *glissades* as if she intended to steal home base.

Iain waited until they were almost upon him before he aimed. Then, azure eyes glittering with determination, he swung his club with all the force left in his powerful body. Like a hole-in-one, the ball landed precisely at Leeanne's feet.

A man that reminded Leeanne of *Rocky* elbowed Iain in the side. Another, an ancient version of *The Terminator,* barreled into Iain's chest. A third, an impish thirteen-year-old with rowdy red curls who'd been introduced to Leeanne as Iseabal, tackled his legs.

Leeanne watched in horrified fascination as, with a loud "umph," Iain went down beneath a mass of flailing limbs.

For a split second, she considered racing to his defense and battering off his assailants with her club. Then Leeanne heard Iain's deep, muffled voice.

"Run, lass!" he gasped out before a wall of clansmen, intent on protecting her from the opposing team, closed Iain from her sight.

Go! Go! Go with the flow!

Leeanne leaped sideways in a brief *pas de chats*, pivoting from the cat-step and batting the ball before her as she dashed down the field like the exhilarating breeze that whipped at her unbound hair. Concentrating on the game, she ran for the joy and the freedom of it, for Sesi and for Parlan, but most of all for Iain, pinned beneath the stifling crush of bodies.

She ran so hard she thought her heart would burst through her chest, that her lungs would collapse, that her contacts would freeze to her eyes with the passage of the wind.

She ran until she could run no longer. Until she was close enough to see the goalie's astonished expression, until she could shoot the ball past him into the rawhide net with a minuscule probability of failure.

A cheer rose behind her, and her spirits lifted higher than they ever had before. Higher than after any dance performance she could recollect.

She was dirty and exhausted and totally out of her element, yet her spirits soared.

Adrenaline pumping hot and heavy through her veins, she felt positive that her joy could never go higher.

Until Iain disengaged himself from the pile of human flesh and bone to limp down the field toward her. Until he placed his arms around her waist and lifted her against his hard body. Until he spun her around and around, hugging her tightly to him while her hair sailed out in a sable cloud around them.

Until Iain MacBride slowly set Leeanne on her feet and claimed her trembling lips with his, she'd mistakenly believed it impossible for her spirits to soar any higher.

"We did it!" she breathed into his mouth, tasting the saltiness of his split lip.

"Aye, we did. You managed your claret well today," he teased.

"I'm thinking it's because I'm growing accustomed to the spirits hereabout, lad," Leeanne said, mimicking Iain's Scottish brogue.

Mouth to mouth, they laughed at the sheer delight of their triumph.

And then the contact underwent a subtle change. His tongue slipping between her lips, the kiss deepened as his tongue contacted hers. When she did not recoil, he continued in a slow circle the tentative exploration of the tender inner recesses of her mouth.

Her equilibrium taking a nosedive, Leeanne gasped faintly, clinging to Iain, reveling in the shared intimacy.

"I fear we're teetering on the precipice of something neither of us is prepared for," he breathed, his voice husky as he gathered her so closely to him that she felt her breasts flatten against his pectoral muscles.

Threading her fingers through the soft strands of Iain's fair hair, Leeanne wished she dared tell him she felt the same thing. That she was developing a severe case of the hots for him. And that it frightened her because she didn't belong in his century. That she had a life of her own—a world waiting for her beyond Glencoe. But all too soon, they were interrupted by a crowd of chattering clanspeople surging around them, jostling them apart in their enthusiasm.

Iain allowed the separation; seemed almost to welcome it.

Drawing a shaky breath, battling the unfamiliar tightness in her throat, Leeanne understood completely. One of them had to be sensible. It might as well be him.

A man disengaged himself from the crowd—John, a younger, more agile version of his father, Alasdair Macdonald. Leeanne detected anger in his sharp movements even before he spoke.

"A word with ye, Iain," John said.

"And what would that word be, John?" Iain asked, brushing at the dirt on his clothes.

"The word would be cozened."

Resting his hands on his hips, Iain looked John squarely in the eyes, querying with characteristic aplomb, "I take it I'm being charged with something?"

"Ye are. Nothing less than shrewd trickery."

An immediate hush fell over the crowd. They watched the men intently, but no one tried to interrupt the confrontation. Leeanne realized with a start that it must be because winters in the Highlands could be dreadfully dreary without radio and television, without books or magazines, without personal-improvement classes sponsored by the local community college, swimming at the YMCA/YWCA, and forty-hour-a-week jobs to take up the slack. A good fight might be considered just the thing to enliven an otherwise dull afternoon—barbaric, but highly probable, Leeanne deduced.

"How so?" Iain asked, rather calmly for a man being accused of cheating in front of an assembly of his peers, Leeanne thought.

"Ye allowed the lass here to play when ye knew she was no' of the permanent team."

"The lass you're speaking of is my *bride*," Iain enunciated carefully.

"Reluctantly, so I heard."

John was baiting Iain, and Leeanne knew it. She soon realized, so did Iain.

"She was reluctant this morning, to be sure. Who's to say she's no' had a change of heart since then?"

Iain caught Leeanne's fingers and tugged her through the crowd to stand beside him.

"Handfasting tis no marriage," said John.

"'Tis as true as the auld chief's judgment o' it," Parlan interjected, his ruddy complexion brightening with anger.

" . . . unconsummated," John grumbled.

Parlan lunged forward. Iain raised a muscular arm, blocking the attack.

"Hold back, Parlan," Iain advised. "John's no' questioned your honor. Only mine."

Iain cocked an eyebrow at Leeanne. "How can you be so sure the marriage is unconsummated, John? I do no' recall your presence in our cottage this morning."

"Because I ken ye, Iain MacBride. Ye want a woman replacing yer first wife about as much as I want to lose my prize bull! That's why ye went for the handfasting. Because the marriage will be over and done within a year and a day."

Several gasps went up in the crowd. One of them had Leeanne's name on it.

"John, your mouth is dashing along ahead of your brain," Iain warned.

With a sinking feeling, Leeanne realized that John wasn't going to accept his losses gracefully.

"I'll wager ye have no' even thought to give the woman a bride's gift to seal the ceremony. And if ye have no' done that, well then, I see no reason to turn over my bull into Parlan's keeping."

Leeanne glanced around at the faces in the crowd. Obviously the bride's gift, or lack of it, was a serious oversight on Iain's part. A steadfast tradition, something along the modern lines of old, new, borrowed, and blue.

She could see Sesi sniffling from the edge of the crowd, probably visualizing the loss of her "proper home," Leeanne mused. Perhaps even regretting being the cause of so much trouble for her brother. Or for agreeing that Leeanne should play in the games in her stead.

Her mother had always told her to look before she leaped, Leeanne thought. But she just didn't have the time. Too much was at risk! What would happen to Iain's sword if he was killed at the hands of John Macdonald? And in turn, what then could she expect? A lifetime spent trapped in the past? At the mercy of a group of Highlanders whose life-style, code of conduct, and moral values were as different from hers as leg o' lamb was from tofu?

It was a cinch she couldn't carry on without Iain's help. In the back of her mind, Leeanne realized without surprise that she wouldn't want to.

Speaking in a strong voice that carried to the fringes of the group, Leeanne interrupted John in Iain's defense. "But Iain has given me a bride's gift."

The attention of the group shifted to her, but it was Iain's attention, watchful, questioning, expectant, that mattered the most.

It was like having your dance costume sent to the cleaners by mistake and being forced to perform in a borrowed one that was two sizes too large, Leeanne thought. But she'd done it before; she could do it again.

Decision made, Leeanne did what she'd been trained from early childhood to do: give it her best shot.

"An excellent bride's gift," she improvised. "One I happily accepted . . . as my due."

"I'll have to ask that ye be more specific," John said, suspicion in his voice as he visibly wavered.

"He's offered me his friendship, and his protection, and I've officially accepted them. What more could a woman want?" Leeanne asked, silently admitting to herself, though it came as a rude awakening, that neither friendship nor protection would ever be enough for her with a man like Iain MacBride.

At that point, Alasdair Macdonald intervened.

"They've outsmarted us, John. Ye can no' fault them for that. Now give over the bull and have done with it. My auld bones are pleading that we retire to the warmth of the hearth. There'll be other *camanachds*."

The clanspeople surrounding them nodded in agreement. It was obvious that the chief's word carried the weight of the law. Leeanne felt the Macdonalds enfold her as one of their own, as Iain's wife, as a permanent member of the team. It was both gratifying to be accepted, and frightening because in her heart she knew she didn't belong. How could she? She was like a hothouse flower among giant oaks trees.

"Aye, there'll be other *camanachds*," John agreed finally.

"To be sure," Iain added, much to Leeanne's relief.

"'Tis only that it took some daring to rustle that bull from beneath the Campbells' noses."

"I know," Iain said.

John lowered his eyes, studying the toes of his deerskin boots. "How could I have forgotten? Ye were present that night."

"Sesi did na want me to go exposing myself two weeks before we were to be married," Parlan muttered. "I explained that the profits from the raiding were a necessary way o' life, but she would have none o' it. Pitched a rare fit, she did; set Iain up as my shadow. I was black angry at the time, but na later. Na when my life flashed before my eyes."

"A rare misadventure—Parlan and my younger brother, Alastair, almost got their necks stretched more than mere mortals can accommodate," John explained for Leeanne's benefit. "I was unaware they'd been captured by the Campbells until it was over and done with."

"Aye and aye again," Alasdair chimed in. "I've heard that the Lowlander nearly took your head off with his blunderbuss when you freed them, Iain."

"Robert Campbell was drunk. He did no' realize what he was about."

"Set on hanging them by the neck to make an example out of them, according to Alastair,"

Alasdair said. "Still blames the Macdonalds for putting Achallader Castle to the torch, I'll warrant."

"Even Robert Campbell would no' have murdered his niece's husband. Now Parlan Macdonald, that's another story."

Feeling as if she were listening to a soap opera, Leeanne couldn't stop herself from directing a question to Alasdair. "What's Achallader Castle?"

"'Twas once a Campbell stronghold of some merit."

"And your son Alastair, he's married to a Lowlander, to a Campbell from Achallader Castle?" It was common knowledge that Highlanders and Lowlanders didn't mix. Even she knew that.

Alasdair smiled indulgently. "Aye. She's Robert Campbell's niece and a pretty wee lassie if ever I've seen one . . . only half Campbell. The superior part is Stuart. And she's given me a strapping grandson I'd like ye to meet. He's a brilliant young laddie as infants go." There was no mistaking the pride shining in his eyes.

"If no' for ye, Iain, Alastair's son would have no father today. . . ." Looking sheepish, John left the sentence dangling.

Alasdair filled in the lull. "That's exactly what I've been saying. Those canny Glenlyon Campbells are trouble enough without fighting amongst ourselves. Besides, if truth were told, Iain has rescued ye and yer brother from enough scrapes over the years to deserve the bull outright. Now, have done with this, son," he said, his voice stern, his orders irrevocable.

Alasdair's breath wasn't wasted on John.

"I suppose Iain has, at that," John said begrudgingly. "Parlan, ye may pick the bull up at yer convenience."

"I'll see to it before dusk," Parlan replied.

The chief turned to Iain. "We're planning a *ceilidh* this evening . . . perhaps some music . . . dancing. Ye and Leeanne of Green Gables are invited to the main house at Carnoch."

Leeanne was suddenly so tired she couldn't see straight, much less laugh. Which was exactly what she felt like doing at the mention of Green Gables.

But the inclination to laugh quickly evolved into a sobering thought. Not only had she learned that the trophy she'd played so exuberantly for was stolen property, rustled from some Lowland family named Campbell, she'd also inadvertently discovered that she wasn't Iain's first wife.

The notion bothered her. It also added a new and unexplored dimension to the Highlander with whom she was handfasted. And like the smoking bonfires on the *camanachd* field, fuel to the unanswered questions blazing in Leeanne's head.

Chapter Six

"Are you sleeping, lass?" Iain questioned.

Stretched out on the bed, head turned in his direction, lashes lowered so that her eyes appeared closed, Leeanne answered, "I'm only resting."

She was fast becoming a consummate prevaricator, she thought. It was impossible for a woman to rest when watching Iain MacBride sponge-bathe. Firelight and shadow playing across his skin, he splashed water from the washbasin onto the abrasions marring his upper torso. With his shirt on, he was impressive. Stripped to the waist, he was absolutely beautiful, pure poetry in motion, Leeanne mused.

Iain paused to study Leeanne for a long

moment before asking, "Then, if it's no' too much trouble, I'd like you do something for me."

Her eyes fluttered fully open. She wanted to do something for him all right! Had the man read her mind?

He laughed softly at the expression on her face.

"I assure you, it's nothing drastic. I would have asked Sesi. . . ."

Leeanne relaxed. Iain wouldn't ask his sister to do what she'd been thinking of, so she supposed her innermost thoughts were safe enough from him.

"What is it?" she asked, realizing that Iain's physical appearance only enhanced his appeal on a more fundamental level. The genuine attraction, unlike so many of her male acquaintances, was that under the charming smile and bulging muscles, Iain possessed not one superficial bone in his body.

"Would you mind cleansing the chaos on my back? I can feel it, but I can no' reach it and I do no' look forward to the festering as a result."

Leeanne sat up, swinging her legs over the side of the bed. "No, I don't mind," she said, thinking that although she didn't plan to remain a permanent fixture in his life, Iain's kindness to her should be rewarded.

She reached for the linen cloth he'd dropped into the tepid basin. Wringing out the excess water, she folded it into a neat square.

"Hunker down on that stool and angle your shoulder away from the fire so I can see to swab the irritated area," she said, pointing to the fireside stool.

"As you please," he said.

The instant her hands contacted firm warm flesh, Leeanne experienced a moment of forbidden delight. The sensation spread until her fingers seemed to move of their own accord, gliding over Iain's shoulder blades, tracing old scars, learning through touch the padded column of vertebrae that disappeared into the belted waistband of his kilt.

Closing his eyes, Iain relaxed back against Leeanne's hands. "Och, lass. How did I ever live without you?" he murmured.

Was it her imagination, or did he sigh? Leeanne couldn't be certain. As lightheaded as she felt, the sigh might well have been her own.

Tongue darting out to moisten her lips, she finished with his back, circling his elbow to stand facing his chest. Slowly she dipped the cloth into the basin, wringing it, placing her forefinger in the center of the material, allowing the folds to fall about her wrist.

He opened his eyes. Leeanne watched his expression as she leaned toward his split lip.

"I'm sure you managed quite well before I arrived on the scene," she said rather briskly to counteract the effects of his nearness.

Leeanne hesitated a moment and when Iain

said nothing, she dabbed at the dried blood disfiguring his lips, remembering their demanding tenderness, the sensual surge of energy that had rippled through her body when he'd kissed her on the *camanachd* field. The incredible sense of desire she'd almost lost herself to.

"That feels nice," he commented.

God, had it felt nice! But she had to be sensible, Leeanne warned herself. His hard body invited her; and she was liberated enough to acknowledge that she wanted him more with each passing hour they spent together. Common sense, however, made physical association unwise.

"Iain," she began slowly, "I wish you would tell—"

Intrigued, Leeanne wanted to ask him what had happened to his first wife. Why he felt so personally responsible. Why his friends and family had so forcefully encouraged their handfasting.

It was as if he saw it coming and interrupted her on purpose.

"Lass, as much as I'd like to converse with you, we must no' tarry," he said. Capturing her wrist and forcing her hand from his lips, he surged to his feet.

"Why not?"

"Alasdair will be awaiting our arrival," he said. Plucking the cloth from her hand and tossing it beside the basin, he entwined his fingers with hers for a moment, giving them a quick squeeze before repositioning her hand firmly at her side.

Presenting his back to her, Iain reached for his clean shirt, and Leeanne couldn't help wondering what he was hiding from. Then it dawned on her that if her touch affected him as his did her, he might need a moment to calm down before facing her. She wasn't sure in her present state whether that was good or bad.

But as the ache within her slowly subsided, Leeanne reflected that she was almost relieved she hadn't grilled Iain after all. He would probably have cut her off with one of his scowls, an expression reminiscent of blue-gray storm clouds gathering on the horizon. And right now, she didn't think she could bear his displeasure.

Instead, she asked, "Do you Highlanders spend the entire winter like this?"

Iain shrugged into his shirt, tucking the tail into the waistband of his kilt. "What do you mean?"

"In a social whirl—first Sesi's wedding, then the *camanachd*, and now this . . . this *ceilidh* thing."

"You'd rather have slept?" he asked, gathering up the washbasin.

She was accustomed to working fourteen-hour days. She wasn't accustomed to playing so hard.

"A little shut-eye never hurt anyone." *And I'm beginning to feel the absence of my multivitamin*

131

bottle too. "But no, I can sleep anytime."

Iain opened the door, stepped outside, tossed out the dirty water, and refilled the bowl with snow.

"I'm thinking that if you ate meat, you would no' tire so easily."

Following him to the door, Leeanne almost stuck out her tongue at Iain. "If I had a snowball. . . ."

Iain twisted from the hip to glare at Leeanne. "If you had a snowball, lass, I'd advise you to keep it to yourself. There is no' one wee patch of skin on my body that does no' feel the affects of *camanachd.* Even my ears hurt."

Leeanne winced. His poor eye was puffy and swollen shut. A spreading purple bruise branded his cheek. He looked as if he'd gone three rounds with Smokin' Joe Frazier, Leeanne thought.

"Then why are we going to Alasdair's *ceilidh?* We could stay—" Leeanne almost said home. She quickly opted for another word, trying her best to keep matters in perspective. "—at the cottage."

Iain shouldered past her, closing the door and placing the basin on the hearth near the fire. Within minutes, the snow had melted. "Did you no' hear the tone of Alasdair's voice? The invitation to join him in his home was tantamount to a royal summons. Now, if you'd like to refresh yourself, we'll be on our way," he said, handing her a clean square of linen from the open strongbox beside the bed.

"I missed that somehow." *Probably because I was more concerned with your well-being than what Alasdair was saying,* she thought, accepting the cloth. Dipping it in the water and scrubbing at her face and hands, she wondered if Iain would faint if she asked for a full-body bath in the dead of winter.

She decided he probably would and that she better not.

"Alasdair asked us to the *ceilidh* because I suspect he's going to request that you dance," Iain informed her.

Leeanne's heart leaped into her throat as she handed the damp cloth back to Iain.

"The Blades of War?" she croaked, trying to keep the excitement from her voice, wondering if a tub bath might be closer at hand than she'd imagined.

Iain spread the cloth across the stool to dry, depositing his into the flames of the fire.

"Perhaps. Alasdair was rather impressed with your stirring rendition last evening. Everyone was."

Iain removed Leeanne's cloak from the peg, shook it out, and settled it about her shoulders.

"Well, imagine that. A repeat performance. How simply marvelous," she said.

"You like to dance," Iain stated, ushering her from the cottage and out into the snow.

"I live for it—to teach it, to perform it,"

she said as they traversed the broad expanse of winter-white marking the distance between Iain's home and the community center.

"Do you know you're an odd lass, Leeanne? Most women live for their families. For procreation. For the perfect marital association. But you, you live for entertainment?"

Leeanne stopped dead in her tracks, almost losing one of her mules as she slid to a halt. "You're not the first man who hasn't understood my affinity for the arts," she said, readjusting her slippered foot into the wooden shoe. "It takes ten grueling years to make a mature dancer. I started with my parents' ballet company as soon as I could walk. I've based my life on my profession."

"Is that so?" Iain kept walking.

"Yes, it is."

Finally, he stopped, rounding. "I've no' heard you speak of your family before. Where are your parents? It would be only right and proper for me to inform them of our marriage."

"There's no need for that." Blinking, Leeanne glanced at the ground, then back up at Iain. "They passed away last year." In a sailplane accident. That's how she'd inherited the company and the financial difficulties that went along with it.

"Aye. Mine as well. Twelve years now. Sesi was only seven."

Leeanne was stunned that Iain was actually opening up to her voluntarily.

"So that's why you're so close . . . said you'd brushed her hair more times than you cared to count. You raised her."

Iain smiled his charming, lopsided smile. "I'm thinking that's the problem with the sassy wench. She's no' had a women's hand to gentle her, as the headmistress at the finishing school in England was quick to point out. To hear her tell it, Sesi was a mischievous *bodach*, sent to bedevil the teachers at the school. She lasted all of a fortnight before the headmistress wrote that I should come and retrieve her."

Think fast! Iain imagines you were one of those bedeviled teachers from Sesi's finishing school.

"I'm sorry. I didn't know about Sesi's childhood. Perhaps if I had, I could have been of assistance."

It was true. She taught one free class a week for underprivileged children. She maintained an empathy for them, along with a firm belief that occupying any child productively acted as a deterrent to the all-too-prevalent alternatives—drinking, drugs, and sex.

"I do no' fault you personally, Leeanne. Sesi witnessed our parents' trial and execution at the hands of a band of drunken soldiers who imagined they were doing the Highlands a favor. My mother was Presbyterian; my father Anglican."

"They were murdered for their religious beliefs?" *How barbaric!*

"That and their political views, I suspect.

135

Mother was always voicing her support of the English crown. Loudly and in no uncertain terms."

"It seems she would have been wise to keep her own counsel."

"Aye, but she was that exuberant about her heritage. Sesi's locked our parents' death inside her. She speaks of it to no one."

Once again, Leeanne wanted to ask Iain about his first wife. Ask him why *she* hadn't given him a hand with Sesi. Ask him where she was and what she was doing now. Ask him if divorce was legal in Scotland during his time. If the christening gown she'd seen in the strongboxlike trunk belonged to Sesi's unborn baby or one of his own children.

She didn't because she didn't want to disrupt the moment, jeopardize the lines of communication unfolding between them like the velvety petals of a delicate violet.

"If you do no' mind me asking, what would this ballet you're speaking of be? I've heard of it, but I've never seen it."

Iain's question brought Leeanne full circle back to the subject of dance. It dawned on her that ballet had officially blossomed around 1581 when Catherine de' Medici produced the *Ballet comique de la royne* in honor of her sister's marriage. Which meant Leeanne had landed in the past sometime following that year. But how long afterwards?

"Iain, where did you hear about ballet?"

"There's a professional ballet school called the Royal Academy of Dance in France. I learned of it when I visited Paris."

Here was her chance to discover the year she'd danced her way into without being overly obvious! Grasping at straws, Leeanne reached far back into history with her mind's eye.

"Let me s-e-e. Didn't Louis XIV found the Academy in 1661?"

Iain fell right into her hands. "Thirty-one years ago? Aye, I imagine it's been that."

Leeanne did a quick mental calculation.

1692!

She'd landed in 1692? How in the world?

"Lass?" Iain prompted.

"Aye . . . I mean, yes?"

"What's the matter?"

I've just learned that I've managed to travel three hundred years into the past without a time machine. Dr. Who, watch out! Leeanne Sullivan's got you beat by a country mile.

The moon shining on the snow made the night seem almost like day. Leeanne watched as Iain backtracked to face her.

"You look as if you've got a chunk of that lamb Parlan served up this morning lodged in your throat."

"I do? I'm sorry. Now where was I? Refresh my memory." *And then slap me, because I think I'm going off the deep end here.*

"We were speaking of the Academy of Dance in France."

Get a grip on yourself! Leeanne told herself. Clearing her throat, she attempted to continue their conversation without stuttering.

"Oh, yeah. Well, you see, the ballet master at the Academy, Pierre Beauchamp, formulated the structure of classical ballet as I know it. It evolved from the pavane, the minuet, the jig, and the rigadoon."

"Rigadoon is no' familiar, but the others are. They're nothing more than court dances."

Leeanne's thoughts were diverted by gradual degrees from the year 1692 by the expression on Iain's face.

"I can tell you've danced a few of those yourself," she found herself saying.

"A few."

"At court?"

"Aye."

"Which means—"

"Which means once upon a time my mother was a lady in waiting."

"Gosh!"

"Do no' get any high-handed notions, lass. I relinquished that portion of my heritage when I chose to live in Scotland."

"I only meant I'd never been to court."

"I assure you, you've no' missed much. I'd rather spend a day in the Highlands knowing my life would end at sunset, than a year of sunsets at court."

"You feel that strongly," Leeanne marveled aloud.

"I do. Pray continue your recitation on ballet."

"Ballet is a takeoff of the french word *ballaire*, which means to dance. It's a theatrical art form that uses music and scenery to convey a theme. The dance itself is done with light, flowing figures and lots of predetermined leaps and turns."

Iain lifted Leeanne's chin to gaze down into her eyes with his one good one.

"You're beginning to sound like a teacher."

"And I believe you're beginning to see the light."

"You're quite serious about this, are you no', lass?"

"Dance isn't only entertainment, Iain. It's a higher art form. A way to express your innermost self. If you look closely enough, you can actually see the state of a person's soul shining through their dance."

"I think you must be correct. I can see your soul shining in your eyes at this moment, and you're only speaking of dance. What must it be like to watch you perform your ballet?"

He linked his arm through hers, walking along beside her as he said, "Now come along, lass. It's cold out here."

They'd almost reached the door of the main house when it flew open. The cheerful light of a dozen candles spiked in picket candlesticks, accompanied by the sound of music, spilled from the portal as Sesi stepped out into

139

the glistening snow with Parlan close at her heels.

Hand postured on her hip, Sesi said, "Ah, there you are. Alasdair is growing impatient. I was about to come over to the cottage and find out what was keeping the two of you."

Sesi acted as if she expected a verbal excuse for their tardiness. When none was forthcoming, she spun around, motioning for them to follow her inside.

As soon as she crossed the threshold, Leeanne realized that what she'd assumed to be a community center was in actuality Alasdair Macdonald's home. She glanced overhead, observing the medieval-style tapestries. Fanned by the heat rising from the wattle-and-daub fireplaces burning at either end of the room, the embroidered canvases fluttered like human hands waving in welcome.

The night before, she'd somehow failed to notice that the house was two-storied with concealed stairs leading to the upper floor. Studying the plank-and-timber ceiling, Leeanne decided that the chief and his family must live upstairs and entertain below.

Her gaze traveled to the scattered groupings of tables and chairs accentuated by a steel mirror in a painted wood frame, a gaming table inlaid with an ivory-and-ebony chessboard, and a tripod table with a piecrust lip upon which rested a set of wineglasses with roses and thistles engraved on them.

"Where did all this come from?" Leeanne asked in surprise, hardly realizing that she'd spoken her thoughts aloud.

Iain leaned toward her. "Would you be speaking of the furniture, lass?"

Leeanne nodded, thinking that the arrangement reminded her of a quaint, unassuming dinner theater.

"The chief's wife pushed it all to one side of the great hall to accommodate Sesi's wedding. We thought it bonnie of her to go to so much trouble."

"Yes, it was."

"Smile now, lass. The lady herself is making her way to greet us."

Leeanne lips curved upward as she reminded herself *not* to extend her hand.

The laird's wife sailed up to them, chattering an exuberant Gaelic welcome to which Iain responded in kind. Peering over the small woman's head, Leeanne recognized many of the families that had participated in the *camanachd*. Freshly groomed. Neatly attired. Feet tapping. Obviously enjoying themselves.

It seemed a subdued, more intimate party than Sesi's wedding had been—a more select gathering of friends, Leeanne thought. On the tail of that thought came another. As odd as it seemed, she felt increasingly at ease with the people of Glencoe, experiencing an expanding sense of familiarity as one after another followed their lady's lead, making it a point of

141

hospitality to personally say hello. To congratulate her on her marriage to Iain, and on her triumph at the *camanachd*.

The sea of faces parted as Alasdair Macdonald strode through the group, a cherub perched on his arm.

"I'm glad ye saw yer way clear to attend the *ceilidh*, Iain," he said.

"It's my pleasure."

The chief's gaze feel on Leeanne. "Yer bride's looking lovely tonight."

"I can no' disagree with that."

"Ye're a lucky man."

Iain only nodded.

"Leeanne, I'd like to present my grandson, young Alastair. He's one year old today."

His attention returning to the baby, he said, "Alastair, this is Iain's new bride, Leeanne of Green Gables. Go ahead, laddie. Do yer duty."

Waving a chicken leg in one chubby hand, the child leaned over and planted a dutiful, if somewhat greasy, kiss on Leeanne's check.

"Nice to meet you," Leeanne said, accepting the chicken leg the toddler offered her.

Alasdair chuckled. "What's this now, giving lassies presents already, and at yer untarnished age. What a rogue ye'll be when ye've grown to full manhood."

"I imagine he comes by it honestly . . . a regular chip off the old block," Leeanne said with a smile, replacing the chicken leg in the baby's outstretched hand.

A momentary hush fell over the room. Leeanne felt Iain shift his weight from one foot to the other, and it occurred to her that she'd said something amiss.

Then Alasdair laughed outright, and the atmosphere relaxed.

"Aye, my grandson does, at that. 'Tis common enough knowledge I've maintained a boisterous career for nigh on fifty years, one that William of Orange seems bound and determined to tax me for of late."

As if agreeing, the baby grinned, pulling at his grandfather's beard.

"Here now, none of that nonsense," the chief said, nose wrinkling as his attention shifted to his wife. He disengaged his beard from the baby's hand. "Woman, take this wee laddie to his mother. I've a notion his breeches need changing, and 'tis past his bedtime as well."

The chief's wife hurried to his side, swinging the baby up in her arms. Cooing to the child, she excused herself to disappear upstairs.

"When my wife returns, I'll be asking that ye dance for us, Leeanne."

Iain had been correct in his assumption. At least the chief didn't beat around any bushes, Leeanne thought. In this instance, she didn't intend to either. It was her first chance at Iain's sapphire-studded broadsword since nosediving into Glencoe.

"Iain warned me beforehand," she said.

"He did, did he?" Alasdair asked.

"Yes, and I'd be more than happy to dance for you and your guests."

"Yer're a braw lassie to humor an auld man."

"Not so old," Leeanne said almost flirtatiously, feeling light-hearted at the idea of returning to North Carolina—1992.

"No' so young either, but still kicking. And for a long time to come, the good Lord willing."

"I think you've made a conquest, lass," Iain interjected.

"Aye, aye. I've always admired a lassie willing to speak her mind," Alasdair said, moving off across the room to mingle with a group of men clustered around the fireplace.

Red-haired Iseabal, the teenage imp who had tackled Iain and knocked him to his knees during the *camanachd*, took the chief's place.

"I saw ye dance last eventide," she said, cutting through the polite chitchat. "His lairdship says ye're a teacher," the girl said, her eyes large and bright and inquisitive.

Leeanne glanced at Iain. He winked at her.

"I see word travels like lightning around here."

"Aye. To be sure. And there's na much that goes on that I do na ken," she bragged. She linked her hands behind her back, rocking on her heels.

"I can believe that," Leeanne said, thinking a teenager was a teenager in any language, in any time frame. They all had big ears.

"I heard his lairdship say ye'd be dancing for us again tonight. Will ye be doing that, do ye think?"

Leeanne's glance darted to Iain again, to the pommel of his broadsword peeking over his right shoulder as he turned to converse with Parlan and Sesi.

"I told Alasdair I would."

Iseabal nodded toward the chief's wife, who had returned from upstairs. "She's already agreed to play for ye in the piper's place."

Crestfallen, Leeanne glanced at the salt-and-pepper-haired woman as she seated herself before an angular harp.

"She's very good. Really she is," Iseabal said hurriedly.

"But I was under the impression I was to dance the Blades of War," Leeanne said, thinking, no bagpipes. No "Gillie Chalium." Therefore, no chance of returning home. Not this time, anyway.

"That would've been grand. But the piper sprained his ankle at the games and has begged off tonight. The chief gave him leave to rest."

"I see." *Can you see that I feel like crying? That fate is dangling opportunities in front of me and snatching them away before I have a chance to act on them?*

"Isn't there something ye might do against the plucking o' the harp? We've so been looking forward to it."

Nothing that will get me home. "I don't

145

know . . . I'll have to think about it."

"Why no' show us a wee bit of your ballet," Iain suggested, surprising Leeanne. She hadn't realized he'd been listening.

She'd choreographed for years. And impromptu performances weren't anything special because she had a great imagination. It might even help alleviate her disappointment over The Blades of War, Leeanne thought, though performing on point was definitely out due to the rigidity of the stone floor.

"I suppose I could so something abstract."

"Ab . . . stract?" Iseabal asked.

"Make up something as I go along."

Iseabal's face still looked blank.

"There's no plot in an abstract performance. You just dance for the sake of dancing," Leeanne enlarged. "If you'll ask Alasdair's wife to select something and play a few measures for me. . . ."

"Och! That I understand," Iseabal exclaimed, practically dragging Leeanne to the harp.

The wind-chime-like melody the laird's wife played reminded Leeanne of "Ballerina," written by Bob Russell and performed by Nat "King" Cole—a tune common to many modern-day jewelry boxes. She owned one herself, a gift from a lifelong friend and compatriot in the dance industry.

Leeanne smiled almost wistfully, deciding that with a few slight modifications, the score would do nicely.

"If she could slow the pace down some, it would help. It should be more fluid, like . . . um . . . a stream tumbling over pebbles and stones. Instead of plucking the strings, the chords need to flow into one another so that the music is relatively continuous."

"Ye mean like Allt Coire Mhorair flowing into the River Leven and that into Loch Leven itself?"

"I suppose," Leeanne said, not even attempting to pronounce the Gaelic names for Glencoe's river system.

Nodding thoughtfully, Iseabal translated the necessary changes to the chief's wife and within minutes they were ready to begin.

"I'll need a few minutes to limber up," Leeanne said. "If I don't, I could pull a muscle, and no dancer wants to deal with that."

"May I take yer plaid for ye then?" Iseabal offered innocently.

Leeanne stubbornly clung to the tartan cloth. No one in the room had save-the-whales written in puff paint on their shirts, she thought. None of the clothes glowed neon pink—literally.

"That won't be necessary," Leeanne said quickly, unwilling to attract undue attention to her T-shirt. "I often dance in my plaid."

"Aye," Iseabal agreed. "I've been known to do the same during the winter months."

While Iseabal ushered the guests to their seats, Leeanne discarded her mules. Using the back of a carved oak armchair as a *barre*, she checked off her warm-up exercises, simultaneously counting the house. Thirty pairs of curious eyes—including a suddenly enigmatic set of azure ones—observed her every move.

The last time she'd participated in something like this had been in Balboa Park, in San Diego, California, U.S.A., Leeanne thought. She'd been visiting the zoo with her company following a daytime theater performance of *Swan Lake* and had stopped outside the gate to watch a street mime do his thing. Before she knew what hit her, she'd somehow been drafted into his pantomime.

But then again, that really wasn't quite the same thing. Her audience in San Diego had been familiar with ballet, as most Americans were. Unlike Iain, these people had probably never even heard the word. The Blades of War was one thing; what she was about to present was another altogether. How would they react when she twirled across the room, and executed a deep knee bend and a leap, or an *entrechat* in which she crossed her feet while in the air?

More importantly, what would Iain have to say about her performance? Would he be disappointed? Outraged? Pleased? Taking a deep breath and composing her expression, Leeanne decided there was only one way to find out.

She nodded to the chief's wife, and the melodious voice of the harp instantly filled the quiet room. Jumper skirt belling as she advanced to center stage, Leeanne counted softly in time to the music, "And one, two, three; and one, two, three. One, two, three. One. . . ."

Chapter Seven

He wasn't looking for a woman, Iain thought, but if he were, Leeanne would be the perfect choice. He'd never seen anything like her. One minute she was throwing snowballs at him with a passion, the next taking his side against John Macdonald on the bride's-gift issue. Her stand, after all she'd been through with the hand-fasting, had earned his immediate respect.

Besides being warm, keen, and quick-witted, she was a most comely lass. She had a vivacious mane of sable curls he ached to comb his fingers through and striking blue eyes that continually startled even as they intrigued him.

On further consideration, Iain suspected that even if she were bereft of her physical attributes he would have been drawn to Leeanne.

She possessed a freshness of spirit that touched something within his own soul.

His first wife, a MacGregor from Loch Lomond, had been young, a hard worker, and attentive. But she'd never learned to play. In that respect as well, Leeanne was a joy, Iain mused, watching her dance her abstract ballet with a zest for life that showed in the arresting intensity of her movements. He marveled at the way Leeanne gracefully rotated her hips outward, at her diligence as she executed the intricate steps, and at the ethereality she injected into something that was obviously a difficult and taxing skill.

Iain discreetly surveyed Leeanne's audience. The people of Glencoe appeared as enchanted by her as he was.

A sense of pride welled within him, pride he had no right entertaining, Iain reminded himself. Aye, they were handfasted, but Leeanne didn't belong to him—not truly. In a year and a day, she'd pass from his life of her own free will. She'd made that quite clear, and he'd condoned it.

After only two days in her company, the notion of losing her sickened Iain. Leeanne reminded him of the white orchids that grew on a whim along the shadowed slopes of Gearr Aonach, Gaelic words meaning slender, lithe one. Other orchids abounded during summer near the hills of the Three Sisters which back-grounded the River Coe—showy pinks and purples. But he admired none as much as the refined, three-petaled white orchids.

Iain glanced toward Sesi, at the way her swollen belly rippled when her unborn bairn stirred within her. He found himself contemplating the manner in which she postured on the edge of her seat, hands massaging her lower back. His gaze alternated to Parlan, who leaned to whisper something in Sesi's ear. Pursing her lips, she hushed him by patting his knee reassuringly.

The implications of their exchange made Iain shiver. He'd promised himself he'd never again be responsible for inflicting childbirth on a woman.

Aye, Leeanne was a provocative blossom, he decided. One he did not care to see in his sister's present condition. One he dared not pluck for that very reason.

No matter how badly he yearned for the taste of Leeanne's sweet lips. Or the impossibly tender sensation of her hands upon his skin. Or the tempting softness of her silken thighs.

The music ended and Iain rose abruptly to his feet. Weaving a path through the audience, he crossed the great hall toward the center of everyone's undivided attention—his *sassenach* wife.

A deafening silence followed the conclusion of her performance, and Leeanne knew a genuine moment of concern as the clanspeople turned to stare at one another, conversing in low, unintelligible whispers. Though dancing before an audience made her feel more like herself than she had in days, she couldn't have been more nervous if she'd been awaiting a crucial Sunday-morning review in the newspaper, Leeanne thought. Any second she expected to be pelted with rotten tomatoes, or the seventeenth-century equivalent.

And then the room in general seemed to sigh as Alasdair's guests applauded.

Grateful for their enthusiastic display of appreciation, Leeanne bowed, exiting stage left straight into Iain's waiting arms. They faced each other one on one, man to woman, a mere foot separating their bodies. It seemed like eons before he spoke.

"I'm thinking you were correct in your opinion of ballet," he said finally. "It does tend to show your soul. As well as your shapely legs. And the tender curve of your elbow. And the slender white column of your throat." A teasing note vibrated in his voice, but beneath the surface Leeanne sensed that Iain was as serious as a heartbeat.

Cheeks flushed, breathing labored, she asked, "Would you have me censored, Iain?"

A faint smile tugged at his lips. "Nay, lass. I would no' care to repress your unique talent. The consequences could be dastardly, especially in winter when there's snow on the ground."

Feeling extremely self-conscious and entirely

vulnerable, Leeanne mopped at the perspiration beading her brow with the edge of her plaid. "Then I assume I may take your comment as a compliment?"

"Aye, you should indeed, for that's the spirit in which it was intended," he replied honestly.

Then Iain smiled, and Leeanne's heart seemed to swell two sizes too large for her breast to accommodate the organ.

"What now?" Leeanne asked, her breathing oddly constricted.

Iain arched a fair brow.

"I mean, what do we do now? Is the *ceilidh* over or what?" Leeanne asked, watching her audience break off into groups—the men to their cards, the women to their gossip, the children to a circle congregating around an elderly gentleman toasting himself by the fireplace.

A servant dressed in course tartans of a single color and bearing a tray appeared at Iain's elbow. With a nod from Iain, he presented a glass filled with foamy white liquid to Leeanne.

"Milk?" she asked.

"I was thinking you would no' mind if I ordered you a bit of refreshment. It's frothed . . . good for a body after rigorous exercise."

Leeanne smiled, thinking Iain sounded like a spokesperson for the dairy industry. Accepting the glass, she sipped tentatively. It didn't taste like homogenized, but it was definitely refreshing. She turned the glass up and replaced it, empty, on the tray.

"Now, to answer your question concerning the *ceilidh*, it's only just beginning," Iain said with a satisfied smile, moving toward the group of children, Leeanne in tow. "There's someone else I'd like you to meet," he said, stopping before the man the children were clustered around.

"How are you this evening, Mangus?"

Mangus beamed a toothless smile, surveying Leeanne with sagacious eyes.

"As well as can be expected for a man restricted to porridge three meals a day," he said, acknowledging Iain's greeting. "But I've a better question for ye. How are *ye* doing, Iain MacBride?"

"What can I say, auld man, that you would no' see through?"

Mangus chuckled. "Ach, lad, young and lusty as ye are, I'm certain given time ye'll realize the rightness of this handfasting."

Iain said, "You sound like Alasdair."

"Aye. We're o' a mind, he and I," Mangus stated.

"Most of the time."

"In this instance withoot a doubt. Now, introduce me to the lass I've been hearing aboot since my arrival and then sit yerself doon."

"Leeanne, this is Mangus." Iain turned to Leeanne. "He resides at Achtriochtan."

"With the swans?" she asked, accepting the stool beside Mangus.

"You remembered," Iain said.

155

"Of course," she said, stretching her hands toward the luscious warmth of the fire. "I have the memory of an elephant."

"Of an elephant? Now that's an unusual comparison," Mangus commented.

"It's a saying they use often where I come from. It just means I have a long memory," Leeanne explained quickly, thinking how frustrating it was to be forced to keep tabs on her mouth.

"And how do they ken, these people where ye come from, that elephants have long memories?"

"Well, I'm not sure," she said, slightly surprised by the turn in the conversation. "Investigation I suppose."

"What sort o' investigation?"

"Scientific?" Leeanne hoped the term had been invented before 1692.

"I'd think with elephants that would be a most difficult thing to determine, scientific or otherwise."

Leeanne almost jumped when Iain, who had remained standing, rested a hand negligently upon her shoulder. She had the craziest desire to reach up and take hold of it as, leaning slightly from the waist, he said, "Do no' let his questions rattle you, Lass. Bards are lively thinkers and Mangus is one of the best. He's cornered all of us at one time or another."

Leeanne felt as if she'd inadvertently opened a can of worms and they were squirming away faster than she could scoop them up. In desperation, she attempted to reroute the conversation.

"So, Mangus . . . you live at Achtriochtan. How interesting. Earlier today, Iain said he'd take me there for a visit sometime. Didn't you, Iain?"

Iain grinned down at her, and Leeanne had the feeling he knew exactly what she was attempting to do.

"That I did. The bards have established a community near the loch," Iain elaborated.

Leeanne said, "By bards I assume we're talking poets."

"And storytellers like Mangus."

Sitting cross-legged on the floor atop an animal skin, Iseabal discreetly interrupted the adults' conversation. "Please, Iain, might Mangus begin? The younger children will be falling asleep before he finishes."

"What will it be, Iseabal? *Bodachs?* Or witches? Or giants?" Mangus asked.

"Tell us the one about the fairy dog," Iseabal suggested.

"I'm no' so sure I ken that one. Why don't ye begin it for us, Iseabal."

"Och, ye recall, Mangus . . . an auld shepherd lived alone in a cottage, his only earthly companion his dog. One night he heard scratching upon his door."

Iseabal looked to Mangus.

"And what happened next?" he encouraged.

"And thinking it his dog returned from an evening o' scouting, he opened the door."

Iseabal took a deep breath, scanning the rapt faces of the children gathered around her.

"What was it?" Sesi, who had quietly joined them, asked.

"A great green hound with golden eyes and ears o' crimson was the guest scratching at the shepherd's door."

A small child gasped, "What did it desire?"

"Cold and weary from its winter hunt, it desired the most common o' things—food and water."

"Did the shepherd give it those most common of things?" another child asked.

"Aye. It ate and drank and rested by the fire."

"Did it bark?" Mangus asked.

"Nay. It never barked, for that would mean certain death," Iseabal explained. "It only rested. And when 'twas done, it left in the manner it had come."

Iseabal paused.

A bewildered frown creasing her forehead, Leeanne pondered the strange folktale. Though she was enjoying the Scottish cultural lesson well enough, she didn't quite get the point of the story. "Is there more?"

"I'm getting to it by and by, mistress," Iseabal said.

"Oh, sorry," Leeanne said.

"The shepherd's dog got wounded fighting some black angry wolves. It couldna herd until it healed. Well, a hateful snow blew in and the shepherd went alone to dig his flock from the cold. The weather worsened and he thought he'd surely die performing his duty. But the fairy dog found him. Then he was sure he'd be eaten alive, but instead the fairy dog and his friends herded the sheep and sent them safely home with their master. Just before he left, the fairy dog licked the shepherd's fingers. The shepherd bent to pat the dog's head. But do ye ken what happened?"

Iseabal's gaze rested on Leeanne.

"No, what?" Leeanne responded.

Iseabal eyes widened. "The fairy dog vanished beneath his touch."

"And that's all?" Leeanne asked.

"What more would you have, lass?" Iain asked.

"Oh, I don't know. Something."

"Perhaps you've a *sassenach* story for us that has that added something you're searching for," Iain said.

"I've never seen a *sassenach* that knew o' fairy dogs and such," Mangus said, rubbing the stubble on his chin.

Leeanne agreed. "I don't know any stories about green fairy dogs, but I know a famous one about a headless horseman."

Several of the men who had been listening with half an ear, Alasdair included, adjourned from their cards. Drifting over, they joined the group by the fire.

"Come away with you now. A headless horse-man, you say?" Iain asked.

Leeanne nodded. "The main antagonists in the story are Ichabod Crane and Brom Bones."

Iseabal scooted her animal skin almost beneath Leeanne's elbow.

"Go ahead, mistress," she said. "Tell us this *sassenach* story."

"Does she have your leave, Mangus?" Iain asked, deferring to the bard.

"Aye, she does. I'm curious to hear her tale," Mangus said thoughtfully.

Leeanne wasn't quite sure how she'd gotten herself into this one, but she was willing if they were.

"Well, the story was written by Washington Irving and is entitled *The Legend of Sleepy Hollow*. But, I warn you, it's rather involved."

"We've all evening," Alasdair said from his chair.

"Okay, here goes. In a village known as Tarry Town . . ."

" . . . and that's the story of *Wuthering Heights*," Leeanne finished hoarsely.

"I like the one about Jack and the Beanstalk," the youngest child said between yawns.

"*The Scarlet Letter* gave me much to think on," Mangus said.

"*Hamlet* was no' so bad either," Alasdair said.

Though she'd read the play, Leeanne had recounted most of the Shakespearean work from her memory of Mel Gibson's performance in the movie version of *Hamlet*, which she'd recently watched on cable television.

"I've never met a female bard," Mangus said.

"Neither have I, but it would appear we have one among us now," Iain said.

"That's what I'd like to be," Iseabal said.

"I'm no' so certain the bards at Achtriochtan would appreciate that," Iain said. "It's traditionally been a man's profession. At least until now."

Leeanne sensed an underlying innuendo in Iain's words. Perhaps even a slight admonishment not to put fanciful ideas into Iseabal's head, that what was good for the gander was not necessarily good for the goose. But before she could comment on the issue of a woman's right to career equality, Sesi interrupted her.

"Iain, might I borrow Leeanne for a moment?" she asked, rising from the fireside stool across from Leeanne.

Iain nodded.

Sesi drew Leeanne off to one side.

"I didn't wish to miss the *ceilidh*, and now, as Parlan feared earlier, it seems I've waited too long."

"Too long for what?" Leeanne asked, thoroughly confused.

"Too long to retire to my own cottage. I was wondering if you'd be offended if I asked to retire to yours instead."

"To sleep?"

"Nay, to have the baby," Sesi said.

Startled, Leeanne gasped. "I'll tell Iain immediately."

Sesi forcefully stayed her by grasping her forearm. Her fingers bit into Leeanne's flesh.

"I have no wish to alarm my brother. If you would but help me to your cottage. . . ."

Leeanne wanted to balk. Like many contemporary non-mothers, she knew only the most basic principles of childbirth. The closest she'd ever been to an actual delivery was when she'd visited a friend at the birthing center of the local hospital—after the fact. But the look in Sesi's eyes and the tone of her voice told Leeanne this was not the time to argue.

Leeanne said instead, "Sure. But wouldn't you like some other woman to accompany us . . . someone you're closer to, like the chief's wife?"

"Her duty lies with her other guests. Besides, you're my sister-in-law. What woman should I be closer to than one of my immediate family?"

"But—"

"Don't worry, Leeanne. The baby will come of its own accord and in its own good time. Birth is as natural a thing as the tide at the seashore."

"What about an obstetric . . . I mean a midwife?"

"I don't care for that woman. Though the Macdonalds set great store by her, she's old and feeble and refuses to wash her hands."

"In that case, I can't fault you for your reluctance."

"And anyway, I've seen enough children born to know my way around the thing."

Leeanne confessed, "I'm glad you have, because you've overestimated my ability."

Sesi looked surprised. "You mean you haven't?"

"You've got that one right."

"How unusual."

"Maybe here in Glencoe, but not in my hometown." You simply go into the hospital, flash your insurance card around, pay your deductible, and stroll out with a newborn.

"If it will make you more comfortable, I'll ask Parlan to attend us as well."

Leeanne asked, "Does he know anything about this?"

"Naturally."

"And he'll take care of whatever needs to be done? Like cutting and tying off the cord?" Leeanne knew that had to be done. She'd learned it in a high school sex education class.

Sesi blinked. "Well, why ever wouldn't he?"

"I don't know many men who go for Lamaze in the extreme."

"Lamaze?" Sesi asked, rolling the *z* off her tongue as if it were an *s*.

"Lamaze is *sassenach* for childbirth."

"I see. And the men in your . . . hometown . . .

don't help with this Lamaze?"

"Some do. Most don't care to get involved."

"I believe you've known a strange class of men, Leeanne."

"Let's call them different."

"Different like my brother, perhaps," Sesi said thoughtfully. "He'd rather fight ten English soldiers barehanded than attend a birth."

Sesi's grip on her arm tightened, and Leeanne had little time to ponder her statement concerning Iain.

When the contraction passed, Sesi asked, "Can we please go now?"

Leeanne scanned the room for Parlan—without success.

"I don't see Parlan anywhere!"

"I was so absorbed in your stories, I suppose I didn't notice he'd gone. He must have slipped away to collect his bull. He was that determined to see it in our pasture before morning."

"Great!" Leeanne said, verging on panic, but determined to disallow herself the luxury for Sesi's sake.

Just then, Iain intervened. "What's this, Sesi?"

Without preamble, Leeanne blurted, "She's having the baby."

The color ebbed from Iain's face, leaving it ashen. "I was afraid of this. We have to get you to the cottage."

"That's just what Leeanne and I were discussing, my lying-in chamber. It seems Parlan has run off with John Macdonald to collect his bull, and I've underestimated the time it takes a baby to make its entrance into this world."

"God's blood! I'll wring Parlan's fool neck over that bull yet and save Robert Campbell the trouble," Iain vowed.

Sesi managed to smile. "You sound like Mother at her worst, Iain."

"You certainly know how to kick a man when he's doon, Sesi."

"It's all right, Iain. There are times when her English phrases slip off my tongue and from between my teeth before I can catch them."

"No one is infallible, sister mine."

"I don't mind it once in a while. Even though we decided to live as Father did, in the Highlands, I loved Mother too despite their political differences. And I miss them both equally. Sometimes it's comforting to hear you go so far as to forget yourself."

"Is that so, my lady? Then I shall endeavor to forget myself more often. Do not, however, let Alasdair catch wind of it. He'll swear I've lost my bloody mind and crossed over to the side of King William's court," Iain said in precisely formed English.

Leeanne recognized Iain's light banter for what it was, an attempt at stoicism. It was also obvious by the tremor in his jaw that he was failing miserably.

Touched by his vulnerability, Leeanne said, "Husband in attendance or not, I think we'd better get Sesi to the cottage, Iain. Unless we're prepared for her to give birth right here in the middle of Alasdair's *ceilidh*." Leeanne glanced meaningfully at the liquid puddling at Sesi's feet. "I could be mistaken, but it looks to me as if her water's broken."

At that point, the chief's wife hurried over, trying in flowery Gaelic to persuade Sesi to retire upstairs. Sesi proved adamant, insisting that she required the solitude of Iain's cottage over the busy house at Carnach.

The scene might have been comical, Leeanne thought, if not for the acute pain marring Sesi's face. Pain that soon transmitted itself to the crowd surrounding her.

Leeanne's control slipped. "All this is fine and dandy, but it isn't helping Sesi one tiny bit," she said above the Gaelic and English chatter. Her American accent cut through the noise like an electric knife through Jell-o.

In the end, impatient and seemingly at his wit's end, Iain lifted Sesi in his arms and carried her to his cottage much as he had Leeanne the night before. Scurrying along beside them, Leeanne had to admit that she was beginning to see where, in certain instances, force had its advantages.

Once inside the cottage, Leeanne stripped Iain's bed, replacing the linens with the clean set he retrieved from the strongbox. His back to Sesi, he stoked the peat fire into a warm blaze while she disrobed down to her eyelet shift. At loose ends, Leeanne retrieved the cloth from the fireside stool, dampening it from the basin and fashioning a compress.

"Everything's going to be just fine," Sesi moaned between the pains gripping her abdomen as she sank into the freshly made bed.

Leeanne couldn't help but notice Iain flinch.

"I hope to heavens you're right," Leeanne managed through gritted teeth as she smoothed the compress across Sesi's forehead.

"You don't have to remain with me, Iain," Sesi added as she settled more deeply into the feather mattress. "Leeanne will do nicely until Parlan returns."

Iain remained utterly, terrifyingly silent.

As Sesi's moans escalated in volume, Leeanne drew a shaky breath, deciding she'd never been so frightened. She'd considered time-travel traumatic. It paled in comparison to the difficult proposition of childbirth.

Who would have believed yesterday that she'd be actively participating in such a miraculous process! Leeanne thought as a natural sense of curiosity began to counteract her fear. Soon she found herself calming down, mainly because she had no alternative. Sesi needed someone, and for the time being, she was it, Leeanne told herself.

Running on pure instinct, she massaged Sesi's lower back and legs as her labor intensified, praying for Parlan's speedy return. Praying especially hard when, white-lipped and perspiring, Iain finally lost his hold on anxiety.

"Forgive me, but I'm thinking I need some fresh air," he mumbled.

"But you can't leave me alone in this predica—" Leeanne began before Iain cut her short.

"I need air *now*, lass. I can feel the floor coming up to greet my face."

Iain pass out? How absurd!

Though his features were composed, his eyes gave away his distress. "Go ahead then," she said softly, amazed to see a Highland warrior react so squeamishly to the sight of a little blood. But then, the blood belonged to Sesi. "We'll be fine," she added encouragingly.

"That's my fondest hope," Iain said, hastily excusing himself from the cottage, for the first time since her arrival leaving Leeanne entirely at the mercy of her own ingenuity.

Chapter Eight

Eight exhausting hours later, Leeanne couldn't believe she'd done and seen and heard the things she had. But as she placed little Miss Sibeal Elizabeth Macdonald in Sesi's arms, there was no mistaking that every grueling, tedious, and taxing second had been worthwhile. Inadvertently, she had also learned that the gown in the strongbox did *not* belong to Sesi's firstborn.

"She's beautiful, isn't she?" Sesi asked, hugging the unswaddled baby to her breast.

"She sure is," Leeanne responded. She covered a yawn with the back of her hand.

"And so tiny," Sesi said.

Leeanne smiled, marveling at the baby's perfectly formed hands and feet and the reddish blond hair molding her skull. "I don't think she's all that small. My guess would be about ten pounds."

"Aye, a healthy lassie," Parlan said proudly. The baby was making rutting noises, instinctively nuzzling at Sesi's breast with its rosebud mouth.

"I think she's more interested in food than how pretty we think she is," Leeanne commented.

Parlan bent to straighten the covers around Sesi's legs; then, moving toward the head of the bed, he leaned and planted a kiss on her lips. Leeanne took the opportunity presented by their intimate moment to grab her cloak, slipping discreetly outside and into the freshness of a new dawn.

Leeanne inhaled deeply, hugging her arms about her shoulders. She felt like an earth mother, a creature of nature, one with the universe. Wonderful! She'd never dreamed she could deliver a baby. But she had, with Parlan's assistance. And successfully too. Without being sick, or appalled, or self-conscious. That was the real clincher.

How many people had the opportunity to experience something so gratifying? Leeanne wondered. In her world, not many, she decided.

Through the rising mist, a movement caught the corner of Leeanne's eye and she rotated toward the flash of motion. Peering through the lilac-tinted light, she spied Iain standing beneath the shelter of the pony barn's covered walkway facing a waist-high plank table. Tying the cloak's sashes in a bow at her throat, Leeanne advanced toward him.

"When you didn't come back last night, I was worried about you," she called, a puff of steam erupting from her lips as her warm breath contacted with the cold outside air.

Worried was an understatement, Leeanne thought. She'd been frantic, wondering what could have happened to him. Imagining at best that he was asleep in the barn; at worst that ravenous wolves, or perhaps hungry Highland fairy dogs, had eaten him alive.

At the sound of her voice, Iain turned from the table.

"Did you go back to the *ceilidh*?" she asked.

"Nay. I did no'. I went down to the burn to do a wee bit of fishing." He held up the string of shiny trout that his body had concealed from her view.

Leeanne couldn't inspect the trout for staring at Iain. He looked terrible. His fair hair was disheveled as if he'd been repeatedly raking his fingers through it, and a day's growth of beard hollowed his cheeks, while the whites of his eyes blazed bleary with fatigue.

"Ice fishing! But you could have frozen to death in this weather, and no one would have known where to search for you. You should have told someone where you were going,"

Leeanne exclaimed, disturbed that her concern for him showed so readily in her voice.

He smiled his lazy half-smile, the one that made Leeanne's heart do somersaults.

"Ach, lass. The wind was low and it was a mild enough night for the first of February. Besides, I know how to take care of myself."

"Is that right?" she asked, trying hard to maintain some semblance of indignation in the face of his overwhelming charm.

"Aye, better than most. That's the notion behind the twelve yards of woolen tartan that Highlanders use in their kilts. We know how to protect ourselves from the cold. And I recalled you eat freshwater fish on occasion."

"You went fishing for me?" Leeanne asked, exasperated and touched at the same time.

"I imagined, after the rigors of last night, you might be in the mood to break the fast in a more hearty manner than oatcakes and green tea."

She *was* hungry. Incredibly so. "You didn't have to do that, but thanks for thinking of me."

Iain's expression suddenly became solemn.

"How's Sesi doing, lass?"

The point-blank question seemed torn from him. Leeanne watched as he squared his shoulders. It wasn't difficult to tell he was steeling himself for bad news.

"You can rest easy. Parlan arrived not two hours after you left. Sesi's fine."

"And the bairn? Is it sound?"

"She's absolutely adorable."

He sighed audibly, a smile curving both corners of his mouth. "A girlchild, is it now."

It was odd, Leeanne thought, how the little things in life had become magnified, were suddenly the important things—like the aroma of fresh fish, warm clothes and peat fires, sharp knives, a baby's first piercing cry . . . and Iain's happiness.

Iain slipped a trout off the string, retrieving the razor-sharp knife known as a *skean-dhu* that he carried sheathed in his right stocking. *Skean-dhu* was one Gaelic word Leeanne was familiar with due to her research of the historic Highland dress code. It meant black knife. Marveling at his mastery of the blade, she watched as Iain scaled, gutted, and decapitated the trout in two seconds flat.

"Sesi's calling the baby Elizabeth, after your mother."

Iain laughed aloud, dropping the cleaned fish into a wooden bucket at the end of the table. "Well, that capricious *bodach*." He reached for a second fish.

"She didn't think you'd mind."

"Nay. I don't. It's only fitting that our mother's name should be carried on by her grandchild."

He glanced up at Leeanne. "Do no' mistake me. I cared for our mother. It's only that I did no' trust her. She was a woman who dabbled in politics. Her dabbling ended in her downfall.

And she took my staid Highland sire down with her—it is for that which I can no' forgive her."

"Oh," Leeanne said, admiring his loyalty to his father. Wishing that his mother hadn't soured his taste for *sassenach* women.

"Do no' look so serious, lass. I did no' mean to steal the cheer from your eyes. It's a good thing I went fishing. I'm sure Sesi will be ravenous, with the baby and all. Perhaps we'll fry up some potato scones to go with the trout."

The "we" bothered her.

"Iain, I'm afraid I have a confession to make."

As was his habit, he raised an eyebrow at her in question, all the while continuing to clean the fish.

"I don't know how to prepare potato scones. As a matter of fact, I'm a horrible cook. My work has always been more important, and since I'm single . . . was single . . . unattached . . ."

She paused. How did you tell a man who didn't even own a stove that you leaned heavily on a microwave?

Turning, Iain set the fish aside to slowly scan Leeanne's face.

"No' everyone can be good at everything, lass."

"I'm afraid good is stretching it. I can't even boil water."

"But I can."

Iain's rough sense of chivalry was almost Leeanne's undoing. Her eyes teared, as much from emotional reaction as from the fact that her extended-wear contacts probably needed a good saline soaking.

At least she tried to tell herself that. Iain's next comment shot the saline theory full of holes.

"Lass, I want to thank you for last night," he said. His tone was reverent, almost humble.

It was the last thing she'd expected. And from a man his size, it was extremely disconcerting.

"It was nothing," Leeanne stuttered. "Far easier than I expected. Sesi and Parlan did all the work."

"I think no'. I came to the cottage door once or twice before going for the trout. It was your calm voice I heard coaxing Sesi to pant and to push. Your voice humming a bittersweet ballad to ease the passage of her desperate hours."

She had been singing "The Twelfth of Never."

"It seems I'm eternally in your debt for the well-being of my sister and her wee bairn," he said, wiping his hands on something that reminded Leeanne of an orange shop rag.

"No, really."

"Aye, really," he said in an even voice.

Iain backhanded the soiled cloth onto the table beside the fish, and once again Leeanne knew beyond a shadow of a doubt he intended to kiss her. With a thrill of anticipation, she unconsciously swayed toward him. But instead

175

of the searing contact of the *camanachd*, instead of what she realized she desired most in the world at that moment, his hands remained at his sides while he dropped a light kiss on her forehead.

Leeanne swallowed her disappointment as Iain turned to resume cleaning the trout. An awkward silence fell between them, punctuated only by the sound of birds cawing somewhere nearby.

For a moment, he worked lost in his own thoughts. And then he pivoted, his gaze wandering somewhere over Leeanne's head.

"What is it?" she asked.

"Hush a moment, lass," he said distractedly. Head erect, jaw tense, he fixed a stare on the main house, which could be seen in the distance.

"Lass, look and see if you think those are ravens perched on Alasdair's roof."

Leeanne squinted through the rapidly vanishing haze. "I'm pretty sure they are. I thought I heard them a few minutes ago."

"Black as the devil they are." He glanced at his own rooftop. "I don't see any on the cottage."

"Neither do I," Leeanne agreed, somewhat bewildered.

"Thank the Lord!"

"Why get so excited about a few ravens?"

"Because, lass, in the Highlands the raven is considered a bird of ill omen. If you sight two hunting in the sky, it's unlucky. If one settles on your home, like as no' someone within is going die."

Leeanne couldn't stop herself from laughing. "I never would have believed it. Iain MacBride, you're superstitious."

He frowned at her.

"There are some things in nature that it's best no' to question. I've learned from experience the settling of ravens is one of them. They can smell death. Now, if you would no' mind finishing these fish for me, lass, it's imperative I go over and speak with Alasdair."

Glancing at the fish heads piled on the table, Leeanne was about to protest when a shout, followed by a low whistle, shattered the peaceful dawn. Startled, the ravens arched in a wave from Alasdair's roof, flying off toward the nearby rocky crags. Their raucous cries could be heard long after the birds themselves had vanished.

"What was that?"

"A warning. It means we have company coming and that you can forget about the trout for a moment." Iain made the statement as he withdrew his sword from its sheath, planting it point-first in the ground before him.

Stunned, Leeanne eyed Iain. More than ever, he reminded Leeanne of a Norse warlord preparing to do battle.

"What sort of company?" she asked apprehensively.

"The troublesome sort." He pressed the hilt of his silver-mounted *skean-dhu* into her hand, then with a firm pressure positioned Leeanne slightly behind him.

The hilt was still warm from his use. She found comfort in it as she clutched the dagger tightly in her palm.

"Stay put now, lass. They'll be appearing around the bend any second. And I'd rather you were no' the first person they see."

Leeanne assessed the way one of his hands rested casually on his hip, the other cupping the pommel of the broadsword. She felt a slight shiver run down her spine—a bad feeling—as she stood breathless, watching the bend for what she wasn't sure.

Then she heard the rattle of harness. And then she saw the company of soldiers outfitted in varying shades of green tartan, mounted on horses much larger than Iain's Highland ponies.

As the red-coated soldiers drew nearer, the man leading the entourage emerged clearly visible. Iain emitted what Leeanne assumed was a Gaelic expletive.

Filled with a strange foreboding, Leeanne asked, "Who is he?"

"That, my bonnie lass, is Captain Robert Campbell of Glenlyon."

Her mind veered instantly to Parlan as she hastily added two and two together. "That's the man that almost hanged Parlan before you rescued him."

"One in the same."

"They haven't come for the bull, have they?"

"I'm thinking no'. They're coming into the glen far too casually to be in search of the bull."

The oily smell of damp wool and horse sweat preceding him, Leeanne silently watched as Robert Campbell reined his horse before Iain. He slowly dismounted to stare past Iain at Parlan, who had quietly joined them. Arms akimbo, the redhead stood staunchly before the closed doorway of the cottage.

Iain and Parlan exchanged knowing glances.

Parlan wagged the blunderbuss resting in the crook of his arm at Iain.

A sense of confidence, of resolve, of raw power emanating from him, Iain nodded and tapped the pommel of his sword with his forefinger.

This must be how the Earps and the Clantons felt during the gunfight at the O.K. Corral in Tombstone, Leeanne thought, her stomach tensing. She passed from wanting to be kissed to looking for a hole to jump into and pull in after her. Only Iain's steely presence kept her from bolting.

"Well, well—Iain MacBride. I was told I would find you wintering with the Macdonald clan, and here you are."

His voice strong and sure, Iain said, "And I'd heard you'd joined forces with William of Orange. I'd considered the rumors only *clish maclaver* until now."

"You haven't changed a bit, have you, MacBride? Still the forthright rebel of Killiecrankie fame."

"I know you did no' come here to pass the time of day with me, so kindly state your business and be done with it," Iain said drily.

"There's no need to be hostile," Robert Campbell said, rubbing the side of his nose with his index finger. "I can assure you, I mean no harm." His finger traveled from his nose to the corner of his lip, giving Leeanne the distinct impression he was lying through his teeth.

"You've got a lively force of Williamites backing you, Campbell, for a man with peace occupying his mind."

Leeanne agreed. She didn't know whether it was the hundred or so men attempting to take her measure, or because she was unaccustomed to the presence of an armed troop company, or perhaps because her intuitive senses had immediately gone on alert, but the soldiers made her decidedly uncomfortable. Most particularly their leader. Her gut reaction told her the man spelled trouble with capital letters.

Warily Leeanne studied Robert Campbell. She judged him to be about Alasdair's age, with wavy hair rippling just above his shoulders, framing a long face. His fair skin possessed what Leeanne suspected to be a perpetual flush—as if he enjoyed his drink almost to a fault. He was a fastidious dresser, with an intricate tie encircling the starched ruffles at his throat, and close-fitting trousers that peeped from beneath a tiered greatcoat.

Her gaze traveled to his eyes. She was a people watcher. Body language and facial expression constituted a major part of her life. And though it might have been her imagination working overtime, Leeanne decided his eyes were as crafty as any snake's; his aquiline nose only enhanced the impression.

A shiver scurried down Leeanne's spine. She sensed that Campbell was a man capable of violence, and she hated violence. That was the main reason she avoided watching the evening news.

Campbell's horse snorted, stomping as if impatient to be on the move, or perhaps it smelled feed in the pony barn, Leeanne thought. Whatever the reason, it brought her attention back to the conversation at hand.

"Actually, we were searching the vicinity for some escapees from Edinburgh prison, and I thought I might stop for a short visit with my niece and her family. Her neighbors informed me that she could be found at the main house."

"Now that's for me to know, isn't it," Iain said, his tone bordering on sarcasm.

"Perhaps I should go at this in another manner," Robert Campbell said, eyes narrowing to slits. "As you can plainly see, my men and animals are done in and hungry."

"I was under the impression the King's coffers kept his army wanting for nothing. What happened in your instance?"

"Nothing more than a small misadventure, I assure you. A guard fell asleep at his post two nights ago. I'd forgotten how bad the wolves can be in these Godforsaken mountains during winter. They drove off our pack animals."

"Loaded?

"Fully loaded."

"You could no' track them?" Iain questioned, displaying an arrogance Leeanne hadn't seen before.

"A light snowfall covered their marks before daybreak. Therefore, I'm afraid we are at your mercy." Campbell extended his hands, palms up.

Iain's face remained devoid of expression.

"We seek nothing more than a few days' sanctuary from the elements here in Glencoe. Is that too much to ask?"

"That's no' for me to say," Iain responded.

Robert Campbell's jaw tightened and his callous eyes grew even colder as he lowered his hands to his sides.

The only other time she'd witnessed such an emotionally charged atmosphere was just before Hurricane Hugo hit the North Carolina coastline, Leeanne thought as she waited for one of the men to back off, or advance, or something.

Finally Campbell said, "Then I suppose I must speak directly to Alasdair for permission to remain in Glencoe."

"Aye. That you must."

"It looks as if, unfortunately enough for me, you're standing in the way of that, MacBride."

"Alasdair does no' care for surprises, as you should well know from your past association with his lairdship."

"Then he should construct himself a castle from which he might view travelers well in advance."

"Glencoe is a natural fortress unto itself."

"Are you saying you knew we'd arrived well in advance?"

"Aye, and so shall his lairdship, if he does no' already," Iain said candidly.

His gaze unflinchingly directed on Campbell, Iain said over his shoulder, "Lass, take a wee stroll for me over to Alasdair's and ask him to accompany you back to the cottage. Tell him unexpected travelers have arrived, begging the kindness of his hospitality." His glance told her something she'd already decided to add: *Tell him too that there's a potential for violence here, although Campbell states otherwise.*

"By the by," Robert Campbell said, giving Leeanne pause. "The escapees we seek are members of the MacGregor clan. In our search, we passed by your manor house near Loch Lomand. I believe your retainer is a MacGregor, as is your housekeeper."

"Aye, they're man and wife," Iain said warily.

"A fine old couple."

"Aye."

"Though understandably reluctant at first, in the end they were most hospitable concerning the King's business."

Eyes narrowing, Iain said, "Go on."

"There's no easy manner in which to relay the news, so I suppose I must be blunt. It seems fire has destroyed the west wing of your manor house, MacBride."

Leeanne saw Iain's fingers tighten on the pommel of his sword. So did Robert Campbell's.

"Here now, I assure you my men and I had nothing whatsoever to do with the fire. It happened days before we arrived on the scene. If you'll allow me a moment, I have proof."

His face a carefully blank mask, Iain nodded.

"Hamilton, front and center," he commanded in a resounding voice.

A young man with sandy hair, blunt features, and a gaze that fell almost wistfully upon Leeanne guided his horse to the forefront of the troop companies, dismounting to stand beside Robert Campbell.

"This is my aide-de-camp, Charles Hamilton. Perhaps you've heard of his second cousin,

Lieutenant-Colonel Hamilton of Fort William?"

"By recounting his bloodlines, do you hope to impress me, Campbell?"

Robert Campbell drew himself up to his full height, handing the reins of his horse to his aide-de-camp.

"Just like your sire before you, I doubt the devil himself could impress you, Iain Raonull MacBride. That, however, was not my purpose. I meant only to imply that Charles is a reliable source and will corroborate that your retainer stated the fire which consumed the west wing of your manor house was of accidental origin. And that my men were not involved."

Reaching beneath his greatcoat, Robert Campbell extracted a letter from the breast pocket of his jacket.

"I explained to MacGregor that I planned to be in this area. He requested that I deliver this missive to you."

"Ah, a man of hidden virtue—how magnanimous of you to honor a Highlander's request," Iain said pleasantly enough, though Leeanne detected more than a hint of sarcasm in his tone.

"Do not mistake me, MacBride. I would not have done so had it been out of my way."

Iain reached for the letter, broke open the seal with his thumb, and hastily scanned the contents.

"This is Gabhan MacGregor's handwriting. The last few lines are illegible, however." Iain's statement bordered on an accusation.

"Smudged are they? How irksome," Campbell said airily. "I suppose the Highland dampness seeped through the letter as it has my clothes."

His face grave, Iain refolded the piece of parchment and tucked it inside the breast pocket of his own jacket, glancing at Leeanne as he did so. As if surprised to find her still there, he said, "Run along, lass. Fetch Alasdair from the main house."

Leeanne's heart went out to Iain. Obviously the news of the damage to his property was hard to take, as it would be to anyone without homeowners' insurance, Leeanne thought.

Unable to help herself, she asked, "Are you going to be all right?"

Iain's expression momentarily softened. "Aye, I'll be fine. Now, be off with you."

With an odd sort of detachment, Leeanne did as Iain asked, thinking what an amazing creature the Highlander was. He wasn't hesitant to be tender, as in the instance of her hair, or frightened, as he'd been for Sesi, or courageous in the face of danger or personal loss, as he was being now.

For that Iain got a gold star in Leeanne's book.

And for almost single-handedly defying a company of King William's soldiers, he won her undying admiration. In her day and age, it was difficult to find someone to stand up to a mugger on a street swarming with able-bodied men.

Twenty minutes passed before Leeanne returned with Alasdair Macdonald plus a backup party of twenty armed clansmen—overnight guests from the *ceilidh*.

After a few minutes spent in serious conversation, Alasdair relented, offering Captain Campbell and his men shelter from the Highland winter.

As they moved off toward the main house at Carnoch, Leeanne asked in a low voice which echoed the fear she felt inside, "What do you suppose they really want, Iain?"

Leeanne opened her palm, relinquishing Iain's *skean-dhu* into his capable hands. It was then she realized the ravens were back, perching on the main house roof for all they were worth.

Iain shifted his weight, resheathing his sword and replacing the knife in his stocking while watching the Redcoats walk their horses toward Alasdair's home. "I'm afraid only time can tell us that, lass."

Leeanne found herself wondering if time could also tell her how, after a short three-day association, she'd fallen head over heels in love with Iain *Raonull* MacBride.

Chapter Nine

Over the flame in the cottage's fireplace, Iain cooked the trout to an aromatic golden brown, showing Leeanne how to make mouth-watering scones from flour, salt, and mashed potatoes. The four of them ate their meal in silence, each lost in their own thoughts with nothing more than a carefully covered belch from Parlan to break the monotony. Finally, Leeanne could stand it no longer. Collecting the trenchers and scrapping the trouts' skeletal remains into the fire, she decided that if no one else was willing to broach the subject, she must.

"It's obvious that no one wants to discuss this, but I need to know a few things. I'm not sure how to behave with an occupying army in the village. I've never had one to deal with before. I mean, does this happen often? Do I need to walk softly and carry a big stick? Are we going to be murdered in our sleep? What, for heaven's sake?" she asked, taking a seat on the fireside stool.

"They're not an occupying army, Leeanne," Sesi said, cooing gently to the baby cradled against her breast. "From what Parlan says, they're Alasdair's guests. He's offered them the protection of bread and salt."

"What does that mean?" Leeanne asked, hoping her voice betrayed none of her trepidation.

Iain explained. "It means that they've taken a meal at Alasdair's table by now. It means they've been given quarters in twelve of the homes in the glen, including the main house at Carnoch. It *means* they may no' be asked their business again for a year and a day."

"It sounds like the clan is handfasted to Robert Campbell!" Leeanne said.

"In a manner of speaking, it is, lass. The sacred law of hospitality is an auld and dear one. It can no' be broken. The shame the clan would bear should there be a breach of honor would prove intolerable. They'd be shunned from Argyle to Orkney and back down to Edinburgh by Highlander and Lowlander alike."

"They why did Alasdair do it? Why offer them his hospitality?"

189

Iain looked grim. "That, I'm afraid, you'd have to corner Alasdair to learn. I've no' quite figured it out myself."

"Mayhap 'tis something to do with Campbell's niece," Parlan interjected thoughtfully. "Mayhap she suggested they be allowed to visit awhile in Glencoe so she might show off her bairn. Alasdair's that proud o' his grandson."

"Pride goeth before a fall," Leeanne mumbled.

"Speak up, lass," Iain said.

Leeanne repeated more loudly, "Pride goeth before a fall."

Iain said, "I sincerely hope no' in this instance."

Leeanne threw up her hands, exclaiming, "This is beyond me."

Something was building inside her, something very close to rupturing. She had a sixth sense that the majestic glen itself was somehow in sympathy with her, that the soldiers had not only disrupted the peaceful morning, they'd disturbed the atmospheric tranquility of Glencoe as well.

"You Highlanders seem oblivious to the fact that the Campbells have a personal vendetta against the Macdonalds," Leeanne said, visualizing the bull with extra-long horns that Parlan had described.

"I can no' say that I blame you for being concerned. I'm no' a dogfish. I have my reservations as well," Iain commented.

"A dogfish?" Leeanne asked, the bull's image fading into that of a trout with a collie's head.

"Don't tell me you've never seen a dogfish," Sesi said.

"We have dogs and we have fishes in Ameri . . ." Catching herself, Leeanne switched phrases in midstream. " . . . where I live, but dogfish are a new one on me."

"It's something like elephants' memories, Leeanne. You see, dogfish are blind," Sesi explained.

"And, unlike elephants' memories, we can prove it without scientific investigation," Iain added with a playful wink toward Sesi.

Leeanne smiled for the first time since the soldiers had descended on Glencoe. "You two . . ." She shook her head. "How you can make light of the situation is more than I can fathom."

"Are they no' a pair, always making sport," Parlan said. "Ye should be forced to live with them on a regular basis," he added, obviously without thinking how it might sound. When he realized what he'd said, he had the grace to blush to the roots of his red hair. "Sorry, Leeanne."

Leeanne shrugged.

To cover his blunder, Parlan quickly reverted back to the subject of the Campbells.

"The history between the Campbells and Macdonalds goes back over two hundred years, though at the time o' Robert the Bruce, the clans were compatriots. The first sign o' dissension came aboot when the Campbells attempted to swallow up land that didna belong to them."

Great! Just what she needed! She'd landed in the middle of a Scottish hundred years war, Leeanne thought as Parlan continued.

"My great-great-grandfather had a hand in rescuing Donald Dhu from Innis Chonnel, an island fortress on Loch Awe."

"Donald Dhu?" Leeanne asked, thinking their past almost as difficult to understand as their present.

"Have ye na heard of Donald Dhu?" Parlan asked, astonished.

Leeanne shook her head, realizing that Donald Dhu must be legendary—the Scottish version of George Washington, or Patrick Henry, Attila the Hun . . . or King Arthur.

"He represented the last surviving Lord of the Isles and was a fast cousin to the Macdonalds. Needless to say, the Campbells didna care for the interference," Parlan explained.

King Arthur, Leeanne thought.

"And my great-grandfather, well, he was one o' the thirty-six Glencoe Macdonalds hanged by Mad Colin Campbell o' Glenlyon."

"For rustling, I suppose," Leeanne mused out loud.

Parlan smiled. "Ye've just met me and already ye ken my bloodline all too well, Leeanne of Green Gables."

This time she had no trouble holding her laughter—the joke was growing less and less humorous. How long did time intend for her to remain Leeanne of Green Gables in the Glen of Coe? Slowly, insidiously, she was being absorbed into the past. Her position reminded her of Stéphane Mallarmé's sonnet on the swan that stayed too long swimming in the winter lake, Leeanne thought. The lake froze. Ice collected around its feet and it was trapped.

She was the swan, the Highlands the winter lake, and time the ice.

As Iain picked up the family history where Parlan left off, Leeanne turned her attention back to what he was saying rather than dwell on her predicament.

"During the Civil War, the Macdonalds were Royalists. Alasdair's father fought with the Marquis of Montrose in an effort to reinstate Charles I as king. He even assisted Montrose in finding a shortcut over the Devil's Staircase to attack a Campbell constituency from behind. Over two thousand Campbells were killed that day. It was an overwhelming victory for the Macdonalds of Glencoe."

Leeanne had an insane desire to blurt out the truth. To tell Iain that she was a time-traveler and that she didn't understand their reasoning, their life-style, their rules of hospitality, or their casual reference to the deaths of two thousand men in a single day of fighting as if it were nothing out of the ordinary. But she held back, fear of being labeled a loony and subsequently tossed out into the snow stiffening her resolve to bide her time.

With a loud pop, a burning peat brick crumbled in the fireplace. Leeanne jumped as if she'd been shot.

"I sure could use a stiff drink," she said, surprising even herself. She hadn't meant to say that. She rarely drank and when she did she usually kept it to a glass of zinfandel. But now that the shock was wearing off, she realized just how much the unexpected appearance of Redcoats had rattled her cage. She felt wound up tighter than a ball of kite string.

Iain's eyes were riveted on her face. Enduring his stern perusal, Leeanne knew the full force of her precarious position.

She dropped her gaze from his.

"I—" she began. She wanted to explain that no matter what he imagined, she wasn't a lush.

"Think we all need a wee dram, to celebrate the birth of Sesi's baby," Iain finished for Leeanne, rising from the armchair. "I've a bottle of brandy I've been saving for a special occasion."

"Imported brandywine, I presume?" Parlan asked.

Iain smiled. "Aye, French, and expensive too."

"My favorite kind," Parlan responded from where he lounged at the foot of Sesi's bed.

"Every kind is your favorite, be it claret, brandy, or Scotch whiskey," Sesi said in a sleepy voice. "Admit it, you're a reiver and a braggart, Parlan Macdonald."

"Aye, I'm a reiver, and I'm a braggart, Sesi," he said, love shining in his eyes. "I'm surprised Iain finally allowed ye to talk him into granting permission to marry me."

"Iain knows that when I've set my mind to something, there's no changing it. You're my very own choice, and I love you regardless of your wild and boastful ways . . . and so will your daughter," Sesi predicted, while Iain searched through his strongbox, finding and extracting a brown, corked bottle.

"Here it is," he said, displaying the bottle.

Sesi leaned over the side of the bed to peer into the strongbox. "Do bring out Mother's book of poetry, Iain. It would please me greatly to hear you read a few passages from it aloud."

"I'm out of practice, Sesi," he said.

Sesi grimaced. "That's only because it's been packed away for so long."

"Aye, that it has," he said.

"You have too many grievances hidden in the deep, dark recesses of that strongbox, Iain. 'Tis time you rescued at least one of them and brought it out into the full light of day."

For a moment, Leeanne thought Iain was going to ignore Sesi's request, but finally he retrieved the velvet pouch. Placing the book on the bed beside Sesi, he uncorked the bottle, pouring a cup of brandy for each.

Iain handed Leeanne a cup, his eyes transmitting more than mere words could. Their sky blue brilliance told her he understood her concern over the soldiers. But that she must contain her fears as best she could, for Sesi in her vulnerable state didn't need to be reminded of the Williamites billeted in Glencoe.

Holding up his cup, Iain said, "A toast to wee Elizabeth. May her life be charmed and charming, may the Highlands always smile graciously upon her, and may she grow to be as fair and lovely as her young mother."

"Aye, aye," Parlan said, seconding the toast. He lifted his cup to click against Iain's.

Iain followed the same procedure with Sesi, and finally Leeanne. Their eyes met briefly over their cups as they tasted the brandy. Leeanne was the first to glance away, marveling at her growing affection for Iain's small family. Acknowledging, even though it sounded crazy, how lonely she'd been, with only her work to fill her hours since her parents' death. Wondering why no other man had ever moved her quite like Iain MacBride did.

The conversation lagged, and after a few moments Sesi picked up the book of poetry. Fondly smoothing the pouch, she said, "Iain, if you don't care to read aloud, perhaps Leeanne will agree to do so." She passed the book to Parlan, who handed it to Iain, who relinquished it into Leeanne's hands.

"I imagine I could read to you a little while, if it would make you feel better," Leeanne said hesitantly.

"Oh, I assure you it would please me well," Sesi said.

Leeanne gingerly slipped the leather-bound volume from the drawstring pouch. Opening the book, she placed it in her lap, thumbing slowly through the pages. It took only a moment to establish that she couldn't read it, aloud or otherwise. The typeface was so heavily angular and condensed that it might well have been Greek instead of Old English.

Leeanne shifted uncomfortably, flipping to the front again, hoping to discover something legible. Her search proved futile.

"I'm sorry, but I don't think I can . . . that is, to put it bluntly, I can't read this." She continued to turn the pages rather than look up.

"Do na feel badly, Leeanne. I've never learned to read either," Parlan said.

Leeanne glanced up, alarmed by the puzzled expression on Iain's face. She knew exactly what he was thinking, that she was supposed to be a teacher, and teachers knew how to read even though over two-thirds of the populace in his world probably did not. And if she didn't know how to read, she couldn't possibly be a teacher, no matter what she'd told him.

She had to cover her mistake, and fast!

Leeanne spoke directly to Iain. "It's not that I can't read, it's that I have an eye condition

197

called farsightedness. I can see perfectly at a distance. It's the close work, like reading or sewing, that bothers me." *When I don't have my contacts in, book-sized print is only a garbled blur, but that doesn't exactly apply in this instance.* "I . . . uh . . . didn't realize that the letters would be so closely set," Leeanne said, thinking she wouldn't be a bit surprised to have lightning strike her at any minute.

With a thoughtful frown, Iain retrieved the book from Leeanne's lap.

"Do no' let the black letter trouble you then, I'll do the honors," he stated, setting aside his cup.

It took only a page or two for Leeanne to understand why Sesi enjoyed hearing her brother read poetry. Obviously well educated, he read beautifully, his voice deep and vibrant and soothing after the recent chain of events.

As she listened, Leeanne sipped her brandy, savoring the heat of the apple-flavored alcohol as it seeped into her blood system, easing the burden that time had placed on her shoulders. Before she was completely finished, she began to feel the full effects of the drink, realizing how tired she really was. She supposed that Iain did too, for he closed the book, replacing it in its velvet pouch and depositing it into the open strongbox.

Taking a step toward her, Iain accepted her empty cup, placing it on the hearth. She watched as, without a word, he hastily prepared a pallet on the floor, vividly reminding Leeanne of the night of her impromptu arrival.

"Why do you no' lie doon, lass, and get a little of that shut-eye you were speaking of before the *ceilidh*. You've earned it. My reading has put Sesi sound to sleep, and Parlan has plans to slip over to their cottage and collect a fresh gown for her. He's only been awaiting the opportune moment."

As if to prove the validity of Iain's statement, Parlan tiptoed to the door, eased it open, and left the cottage.

Leeanne allowed Iain to guide her over to the pallet, wishing she could see her way clear to love this man without regret. She couldn't, but a platonic relationship with him would be no less difficult, she decided. The considerate things he was continually doing for her, without asking for anything in return, tugged at her heart strings.

"I guess it couldn't hurt if I slept for a little while, though I rarely take naps during daylight hours," she said, eyeing the pallet.

"Rare or no', I'm thinking you could use one. The wear and tear of your stay in Glencoe is beginning to be evidenced in your thinning disposition."

A frown creased Leeanne's brow. "Are you calling me a grouch?"

Iain smiled a lazy half-smile. "I'm no' sure. What would that be?"

"An irritable person."

"Aye then, I'd be calling you a grouch, lass."

Her frown disappeared. She'd met so many men who said whatever seemed convenient at the time, or what they thought a woman wanted to hear. Iain's honesty struck Leeanne as acutely refreshing.

"You sure aren't one to mince words," she commented.

"I see no advantage in that. It would just be wasting good breath," Iain reasoned, walking Leeanne to one side of the pallet.

He ran his hand down the back of her head, smoothing her hair, cupping her neck as if he might say something more. The contact instantly sent Leeanne's teetering equilibrium spinning out of whack. She stumbled on the edge of the deerskin coverlet; he caught her waist to steady her, drawing her against his muscular physique.

Leeanne fought the desire that welled within her, denying the pleasure she knew Iain MacBride could provide, because to succumb to his charm would be to accept the trick that time had played on her. She'd based her life on dance because she'd never really known anything else—she'd always been a dancer first, a professional second, and a woman third. With Iain, she just didn't know any longer. That was how much his nearness caused her to forget herself. That was how confused she'd become.

Iain drew a long, shuddering breath. "Lass, for the life of me, I sometimes do no' know what to do with you." His nostrils filled with her unique scent, and he experienced a pressing urge to make her his wife in fact as well as name.

The longer Leeanne remained with him, the more the vision of her slender figure pressed against his body plagued him. He'd noted during her ballet at the *ceilidh* that she was flexible and firm. Surely a body like hers was made for passion, he mused.

But he dare not allow irrationality to gain the upper hand, Iain warned himself. Passion was no guarantee that a woman could cope with the possible consequences—child bearing. The christening gown in his strongbox had been specifically included to remind him of that.

"You're not alone," Leeanne said. "Sometimes I don't know what to do with myself."

His thoughts on the way her dark tresses curled softly about her lovely face, Iain said, "You're an odd lass."

What Iain wanted to tell Leeanne was that her lips held an aura of promise that was driving him to the brink of distraction. That he wished to make her his blushing bride without further ado.

And he knew he could have her. If only he took the initiative. He could see it in her eyes, as bold as the Highland spring after a bleak and lonely winter.

Iain's sense of fair play disallowed taking advantage of women placed in vulnerable positions. His guilt over his first wife added restraint to his personal code of conduct.

"You've told me I was odd before and I didn't deny it," Leeanne reminded. "I won't now."

He kneeled with her on the pallet. Hearing his own heart pounding in his ears, he was thankful that Sesi shared the room with them. Otherwise, it might not be so easy to contain himself where Leeanne was concerned.

"As you wish, lass," he said in a strangely husky voice.

Leeanne glanced around the room, realizing that Iain had used all the available coverlets to make her hard bed soft. "You look as if you could use some shut-eye yourself," she said, her mind suddenly fuzzy with fatigue. The pallet felt so luscious, so inviting.

"Later, lass," he said.

Leeanne knew that Iain could bed down in the barn for a nap, but then Parlan and Sesi would realize the unconsummated state of their relationship.

"If you'd like, I could . . . I could share the pallet with you," Leeanne said in a quiet voice, careful not to awaken Sesi.

"Is that an invitation?" Iain whispered back. A formidable glint waltzed in his eyes.

"I was thinking of your sister," she said quickly. "She and Parlan will know about our pact of a platonic relationship if we avoid sharing a pallet while she's staying at the cottage. Considering how determined Sesi is for you to have a wife, it could get . . . complicated. And further unsolicited interference in this handfasting is the last thing we need."

"You've a point there, Leeanne. Sesi can be a meddlesome chit when she puts her mind to it."

"Then share the pallet with me."

"Aye, I suppose it would be the wisest choice."

Without further debate, Iain stretched out beside Leeanne on the pallet. Though he made a point not to touch her, Leeanne was deliciously aware of his hard body reclining next to hers. If she wanted to, she could actually reach out and touch *him*. . . .

"Rest well, lass," he said abruptly. He turned on his side away from her, hands pillowing his head. Within minutes, he was snoring softly.

Leeanne stared at Iain's back for a moment, then beyond him to the sword hanging on the peg beneath his fleece coat. The broadsword, not Iain, was her ticket to the twentieth century, she reminded herself. The sword, not the man, was her prime objective.

For her own good, her head told her that innocent sleeping arrangements and friendship were the most she should ever allow herself to share with Iain MacBride.

A heated battle raged between her heart and her head until Leeanne finally drifted off into the comforting arms of slumber.

Chapter Ten

Leeanne awoke to find the man of her dreams lying next to her, a mere six inches separating them. He was resting on his side with his head propped on his knuckles, tickling her lips with her own hair. Raising her slumberous eyes to meet his steady gaze, she smiled up into Iain's mischievous face.

"Rise and shine, lass," he said softly. "I promised you a trip to Loch Achtriochtan. I've decided today's to be the day of the swans."

Leeanne immediately sensed there was an ulterior motive. Stretching, she asked point-blank, "Are you up to something?"

Iain arched a brow at her. "Now why would I be up to something?"

"I don't know, but I have a feeling you are."

Iain twined the curl around his finger, scrutinizing its resiliency. "You can see clear through me, can you no', lass?"

Leeanne tugged the curl from his fingers, tucking her hair behind her ear. "Only when you smile."

"Ach, is that so?" he asked, recapturing the curl.

Leeanne's stomach suddenly felt as if a flock of butterflies were battering at the walls in an attempt to escape.

"Yes, it is. When you smile, the skin around your eyes crinkles. It's an indicator."

"An indicator of what?"

"Of what you're thinking. You see, body language is my specialty. I can read it like a book . . . as long as it isn't printed in black letter, that is."

His almost-but-not-quite smile appeared. "You're an odd—"

"Lass," Leeanne finished. "I know that already. What I don't know is why we're going to see the swans today." She stifled a yawn, arching her arms over her head and rolling onto her side to better view Iain's face.

He twisted and sat up abruptly.

"Because Sesi and Parlan could use some time together. She will no' be ready to move back into their cottage before tomorrow."

"And?"

"And because I'm thinking you might welcome a respite from the soldiers."

Iain rose to his feet, extending his hand to her. Leeanne accepted it and he lifted her to her feet. The firm pressure of his fingers sent an exhilarating spark of electricity surging through her sleepy body. Leeanne was suddenly wide awake. Alive.

"Are you always so considerate?" she asked, making a display of shaking out her jumper skirts.

"When it suits me," he responded.

Iain sounded so grave that Leeanne glanced up, tracing with her eyes the way his hair fell gently away from his regal brow. A faded scar bisected his forehead from his right temple to just above the bridge of his nose. She'd failed to notice it before, probably because his hair normally covered it, Leeanne decided. She had an intense desire to reach up and run her fingertip the length of the thin white ridge, to learn its contour along with the planes and valleys of his face and in doing so commit his features to memory.

"And sometimes when it doesn't," she found herself saying as she grappled with the impulse.

"Ach, lass, do no' make me out to be a saint. I fear you'll be sadly disappointed. The truth is, I could use a respite from those Redcoats myself. Mangus is heading back to Achtriochtan at noon. I'm thinking we could escort him and see the rest of the glen in the process. You've no' seen much of the glen, and since the weather is holding uncommonly fair. . . ."

206

He left the remainder of his sentence wide open for her acceptance or rejection.

Actually, a grand tour of the glen sounded rather intriguing, Leeanne thought. Now that she'd become reasonably accustomed to the idea that she had somehow transcended time and space, she felt a nagging desire to learn more about her immediate surroundings.

Call it curiosity. Call it a basic pioneering spirit. Or downright boredom. Leeanne wasn't sure which, but anytime she visited a new town and found time on her hands, she made a policy of soaking up some of the local color. Why should this be any different? Leeanne reasoned.

"You've talked me into it. Give me a few minutes to freshen up and I'll be ready to go."

"Aye, I'll just step outside and give you a wee bit of privacy."

"Thanks." Leeanne glanced around.

"By the way, where's Parlan?"

"Doon at the main house." He winked at her. "Never fear. I'll make certain he does no' come in on you."

"Thanks again."

"It's my pleasure," he said. He collected his jacket from the peg by the door and shrugged into it.

Leeanne watched as Iain opened the door and stepped outside the cottage. The minute the door was closed behind him, her attention was caught by his broadsword, left hanging on the peg. She gazed at the yellow sapphires winking at her like cat's eyes, encouraging her to remove the weapon from its sheath.

What's wrong with you? she asked herself. *This is the opportunity you've been waiting for. Are you going to just stand there like a knot on a log and let it pass you by?*

Don't be stupid!

Leeanne stood staring at the sword for a second longer.

Why are you hesitating? Don't you want to go home!

Leeanne took a tentative step toward the broadsword.

So you're in love with Iain. The love isn't reciprocated. Are you willing to sacrifice everything you've ever known, everything you've ever worked for, for a one-sided proposition in a place where you'll never fit in?

Unconsciously holding her breath, Leeanne eased the remainder of the distance to the sword. Reaching out, her fingers closed over the cool solidity of the metal pommel. Oh so carefully she began to inch the broadsword from its leather sheath.

"Lord, aren't you and Iain the polite ones."

The voice came from behind her. Exhaling in a rapid gush of air, Leeanne snatched her hand from the sword, pirouetting toward Iain's bed.

"Sesi! You little sneak. Why didn't you say something? You just scared me out of a year's growth!"

208

Sesi kissed the crown of her sleeping baby's head. "And ruin a perfectly good opportunity at eavesdropping?" she asked innocently. "Why would I do something as foolish as that? I might miss something important."

Busily gathering up the covers of the pallet, Leeanne made a big production of spreading them across Sesi's feet, thinking there was no doubt about it. Iain was right—his sister was a capricious *bodach* of the highest order.

"So I suppose you heard we've decided to escort Mangus back to Achtriochtan?" Leeanne said, smoothing the covers out and securing them beneath the mattress with the neat hospital corners she'd learned as a volunteer candy striper.

"I did and I think it's a perfectly marvelous idea. Go with my blessing. Take the entire day. Take the night. Take the day *and* the night."

"I didn't expect you to be so enthusiastic. I'm more than a little surprised. To tell you the truth, I wasn't so sure you'd appreciate us leaving you on your own so soon after Elizabeth's birth."

"If you'll recall, I have a husband to see to my needs—Parlan will take up the reins of responsibility quick enough when others are not about to do it for him. He only needs a gentle nudging; Iain recognizes that. I imagine that's one of the reasons behind the excursion to Achtriochtan." Sesi paused for a moment, obviously deep in thought. "On the other hand, his reasoning may be twofold," she said finally. "Loch Achtriochtan has always been a special place to Iain. I'm of a mind he would decline to share it with just anyone."

"What do you mean?"

A smug smile gracing her cupid's-bow mouth, Sesi replied nonchalantly, "That, dear sister-in-law, is for me to know and you to find out."

Thirty minutes later, Mangus, accompanied by Iain and Leeanne, left the cottage for Achtriochtan. Riding the sure-footed Highland ponies, they followed a meandering path that led northwest as best as Leeanne could tell. Mangus seemed disposed to quiet meditation, so they rode in silence for the better part of an hour. Leeanne was content to trail the men, gazing about her at the bleak, yet dramatic and ethereal beauty of the land—prominent peaks and gullies, rock formations of massive proportions, snow-caped ridges and rocky buttresses against an imperial sky. Glencoe was a veritable rock-climber's paradise dotted with conifer forests and patterned with babbling, peat-colored streams that only added to the breathtaking beauty of the region, Leeanne thought.

Finally Iain dropped back to speak with Leeanne.

"Are you staying warm enough, lass?"

"You know, I hadn't thought about it, but I'm not a bit cold. This place must be growing on me."

Iain nodded. "Aye, it'll do that. Grow on you, I mean. When I was a lad, I spent five years here with Alasdair. In turn, his oldest son, John, spent the same amount of time with my father."

"Why?"

"Why what, lass?"

"Why do that? Why trade off sons?"

"Ach, have you never heard of fosterage, lass?"

"No. They don't do that where I come from. In fact, I think they'd probably frown on it."

"It's a common enough practice in the Highlands, an act of faith, you might say. The son of one sept is exchanged for the son of another. They're generally cousins, you see, and it's a way of learning about the family at large. It also exacts devotion and respect for the chief. I came to Glencoe at the age of thirteen, and no matter where I travel, I always carry a part of the glen with me. I would imagine John feels much the same way about the MacBride estates near Loch Lomond."

"Do you always winter here, at your cottage in the glen?"

"Nay, I do no' spend as much time in Glencoe as I'd like. I'm here now only for Sesi."

"Her wedding, you mean?"

"Aye. I met Parlan during the first summer of my fosterage. We became fast friends, though his scruples were questionable even back then. Last spring, I made the mistake of asking him doon to Loch Lomond. He'd been in some trouble, you see, and Alasdair thought it best if he made himself scarce around the glen. Anyway, Sesi had heard me speak of Parlan long before they met. I had no idea she harbored girlish fantasies of him. I had no idea Parlan would act upon them. He did; she relished it."

"And Elizabeth is the result."

"Aye."

"But you only just recently consented to their marriage. Why did you wait so long?"

"I intended to protect Sesi from the rough life that Parlan had to offer. I thought her better off without him. I discounted Sesi's determination in the matter. She ran away to Glencoe. I followed her here to confront Parlan."

"I can guess the rest—she defended him."

"In no uncertain terms. She said I'd have to go through her to get to him. He went wild and said that she should listen to me and go along back to Loch Lomond peacefully, that it was for her own good that I opposed the match. Finally, ignoring me altogether, they began to argue."

"It must have been quite a scene."

"Looking back on it now, it seems rather humorous—it was no' then."

"I can imagine."

"I would have been forced to carry Sesi off kicking and screaming. That wouldn't have been good for her, or Parlan."

"Or the baby," Leeanne added.

"Exactly. That left me only one choice. Needless to say, I finally realized Sesi and Parlan truly loved one another. At that point, there was nothing left for me to do but give them my blessing."

"What about the woman you mistook me for?"

"It's common knowledge that before he met Sesi, Parlan had many women. One of his more impetuous English paramours, enamored of Parlan's devil-may-care attitude, threatened to disrupt the wedding. I vowed to Sesi I would no' tolerate her interference. I still can no' quite figure out how you got caught in the middle of it all."

Fate, Leeanne thought. It was as good an answer as any.

She sighed. "And so here you are."

With an answering sigh, Iain conceded, "And so here I am."

Handfasted to a woman from the future— namely me, Leeanne finished in her own mind.

If Iain had been in Loch Lomond, would she have landed there instead of Glencoe? Leeanne wondered. It seemed logical, since she was now convinced that his sword was her medium for travel. How different things might have been if only. . . .

Leeanne had no time to engage in further speculation, for with a wave of his hand, Mangus gained their undivided attention.

"This is where I leave ye," he said, pointing down a narrow track that led to a distant croft.

"Will we be seeing you at the main house again soon?" Iain asked.

"Nay. I can no' say I care for the company Alasdair is keeping at the moment."

Iain shrugged but did not deign to comment as Mangus reined his mount down the path.

Clucking to their ponies, Leeanne and Iain continued on through the quaint valley until they reached the flat shores of Loch Achtriochtan. Shimmering vivid blue in the weak winter sunlight, the loch was patrolled by a sentinel of cliffs Iain called Aonach Dubh.

Leeanne sat for long moments gazing out across the water, the only sound that of her pony nipping at the tall blades of dry winter grasses rising above a thinning blanket of white. Patches of ice shimmered on the loch like irregularly shaped sheets of glass.

"How lovely," she said finally, savoring the beauty. "Sesi said you were fond of Achtriochtan. Now I can see why. It's a wonderful place to come and think. Peaceful."

She was finally growing accustomed to the sound, or lack of it. No alarms clocks. No telephones. No car horns. No jets flying overhead, breaking the sound barrier. No unnatural noises.

"Aye," Iain agreed. "In the spring green grasses grow right up to where the shoreline begins. It makes a nice, easy stroll."

"I imagine there's a lot of wildlife."

"Besides the swans and ducks, there are herons and sandpipers that frequent the loch."

"Those are seabirds," she said, and he smiled.

"We're near the most northern and seaward entrance of the glen, lass, known as Meall Mor. The children even profess to having witnessed a sea monster living in the loch. They say it must have flown in like the seabirds and then later lost its wings because it preferred the water to the air."

Leeanne immediately thought of the Loch Ness monster, wondering if all the nearly landlocked lakes in Scotland had their share of legendary sea creatures.

"The beast is called Tarb Uisge," Iain continued. "It's supposed to be a most timid monster, bothering no one, no' even the water fowl. I'm thinking the water horse is a lot like you, lass."

Leeanne couldn't help herself. Her mouth curved into a huge, even-toothed smile. "I hope by that you mean a vegetarian."

His smile grew to outshine hers as his eyes lingered on hers. "Aye, I must, for I've no' found you to be timid in any way, shape, or form."

Leeanne turned back toward the water. It was weird, but the picture-perfect loch reminded her of something. She frowned in concentration. Something from a book on wetlands? That would make sense. Or the tidal marshes at Wrightsville Beach near Wilmington, North Carolina. Or perhaps a dream? But no, glancing at Iain, Leeanne acknowledged it was all far too real for any dream she'd ever had. He made it as vivid and compelling as love at first sight.

"It's so funny. I've lived my life without ever having experienced this place, but now that I have, I wonder how I could ever have been complete without seeing it, just once. Do you know what I mean?"

Her gaze shifting from Loch Achtriochtan, Leeanne met Iain's perusal.

His voice deep and somber and slightly husky, he said, "I'm thinking I know exactly what you mean."

It took Leeanne only an instant to realize they weren't speaking of the same thing. While she had been contemplating the water, he had been checking out her profile. Now, she understood that when he had agreed with her that Loch Achtriochtan was lovely, he had been referring to something entirely different—namely her.

Leeanne felt curiously gratified to learn that she moved Iain. It wasn't vanity, but a certain sense of feminine power which made her lift her chin ever so slightly and turn her face toward the light so he could view her features to better advantage. She'd never been so aware of a man as she was of Iain MacBride. He was the button that regulated her switches, the flame that warmed her heart, the pulsating impulse that tweaked her exposed nerve endings.

He was also the pool in which she would find herself drowning if she wasn't more careful, Leeanne cautioned herself.

She had the impression he was about to say something profound. Then he changed his mind, dismounting his pony and dropping the reins on the ground. He knelt down and picked up a pebble from the shore. Holding it between his thumb and forefinger, he rose, turning slightly at the waist. Eyes in direct line with the water, he let it fly.

The pebble bounced three times across the loch before quietly sinking to the bottom.

"The bards have a fanciful notion that skipping a stone across the loch will bring you good luck."

Leeanne dismounted as well, dropping her pony's reins so that they dragged the ground in imitation of Iain's pony.

Bending at the waist, she selected a ball-like pebble.

"I can use all the luck I can get, fanciful or not," Leeanne said, haphazardly sailing the pebble over the water. It arched high and promptly sank with a loud *plop* without ever bouncing.

"Oh, foot!"

"It's clear you've never skipped stones."

Hands on her hips, Leeanne said, "Don't you dare laugh at me."

"I'm no' laughing at you, lass. Do you see me laughing?" he asked, his hands held out, palms

217

up, in a supplicatory gesture.

"I *feel* you laughing."

He dropped his hands to his sides. "Do you now?"

Leeanne nodded.

Without further comment, Iain silently picked up a flat-sided pebble and deposited it in Leeanne's hand, closing her fingers around the smooth surface. She almost gasped when he stepped behind her, sliding his right arm snugly around her waist and extending his left arm to hold her hand lightly in his.

"Are you open to a few wee suggestions, lass?" he asked against her ear, sending tantalizing tingles scurrying along the sensitive side-column of her throat.

"Always," she said, her voice sounding strangely winded to her.

"Well then, you hold the pebble thus." He adjusted it between her fingers. "And you draw back, leaning ever so slightly to the left." He maneuvered her into position against his hard body. "Then you squint your eyes against the surface of the water and take aim." He glanced down, his lips almost against her cheek. "You're no' squinting your eyes, lass."

Leeanne squinted.

"Turn your hand just so . . . and shoot it out across the water with a certain strength of purpose. Like this!"

The pebble bounced three times and disappeared.

Leeanne beamed up at Iain.

He lowered his arm, but he did not release her. "Now that one was for good luck, lass," he said, slipping his free arm around her waist, resting his cheek against the crown of her head. She leaned into him, gazing with Iain out over the calm blue water of the loch, enjoying the rush of feeling his proximity provoked.

Intellectually, Leeanne knew it couldn't work between them. They were far too different. They hardly even spoke the same language and were as dissimilar in upbringing and ethics as her 1992 America was from his Scotland of 1692. Three hundred years separated them, and yet emotionally . . .

On an emotional level, and for the moment, they were as one.

"I thought swans lived here," Leeanne said, draping her arms over the muscular ones that held her securely against an even more muscular physique. She knew eventually she would have to deal with her feelings for Iain—but not now. No, not now.

"Aye, they do. I would no' lie to you. But I suppose we'd have a better chance of seeing them if we returned in the spring."

Spring! Would she still be in Glencoe in the spring? Leeanne wondered, torn between hope and panic at the sheer thought of what an extended stay might entail. There was no doubt in her mind that her dance company would fall apart without her supervision—all those years of work down the tubes. Another thing: she'd be forced to deal with the alien Highland ways that alternately appalled and fascinated her. How long could she hold up under the strain of juggling the past and the present, watching her every word, weighing her every move, judging her every thought?

And then there was the handfasting. What would happen if she and Iain maintained their platonic relationship for a year and a day, and at the end of that time he no longer wanted her complicating his life? In her own world, she would have no trouble fending for herself. Correction, *had* no trouble, Leeanne thought. In Iain's, she wasn't so sure it would be all that simple.

Iain must have felt her stiffen, for he slowly extracted himself from the embrace.

"Since we've come this far, there's something else I'd like to show you if you're in the mood for a wee more riding," he informed Leeanne.

Anything to take her mind off spring in the Highlands, she thought.

"By all means. Lead on."

Iain assisted Leeanne back into the saddle and together they turned their ponies northwest once again, toward Loch Leven and Eilean Munde Island. When they reached the banks of Leven, Iain pointed out a chapel established by an Irishman known as St. Mundue. With a sweep of his hand, he encompassed the island, explaining how it was used as a burial ground for the Macdonalds of Glencoe.

Fascinated by the history of the Leven Islands, Leeanne listened as Iain described the largest one named St. Serf. It bore the ruins of a priory, Iain told her, while Castle Island, much smaller than the rest, boasted the castle where Mary, Queen of Scots had signed her Deed of Abdication over a hundred years before.

Though she was thoroughly attentive to Iain's words, the weather eventually caught up with Leeanne. She did her best to hide it, but, unaccustomed to exposure to the elements, her reddened nose erupted into a series of sneezes which by the end of the tour were accompanied by a dry cough. Though for a spell she successfully muffled it in the collar of her cloak, the cough finally betrayed her.

Iain cornered Leeanne without hesitation. "You are no' feeling well." It wasn't a question, or an accusation, but a straightforward statement of fact.

"I'm fine."

Brow furrowed in concentration, Iain asked, "Why did I no' see it sooner?" Reining his pony parallel to hers, he reached out to test her forehead. She drew away before he could do so.

"What's there to see?"

"Do no' play games with me, Leeanne. And I'll have no riddles and no comebacks either," Iain said sternly. "Why did you no' inform me you were catching a chill?" His eyes challenged hers.

Disconcerted by the budding anger she saw reflected there, Leeanne defended herself. "Because I was being selfish and perhaps the least little bit overindulgent. I'm not normally that way, but I've had a great time and I didn't want you to cut the day short on my account."

She could explain that she was a workaholic, rarely taking a day off to enjoy the more simple pleasures in life, but she wasn't sure Iain would understand. Instead she said, "I apologize."

The anger in his eyes cleared substantially, to be replaced by obvious concern on his part.

"When I informed Alasdair of my plans for today, he offered me the use of his summer house, Gleann-leac-na-muidhe. It's located between here and Achtriochtan. I'm thinking it would be wise if we take him up on his offer and remain there overnight rather than push for home."

Leeanne sneezed again. The force of it caused her throat to burn. "I suppose you're probably right," she said.

Recognizing the warning signs, she could have kicked herself for postponing the surgery her doctor had recommended after her last bout with strep throat. Of course, she hadn't anticipated being placed in such an inconceivable situation. She'd imagined she had plenty of time to make a decision. *Humph!*

The day ended with Leeanne wondering what she was going to do if her cold turned into something worse—tonsillitis, for instance. How *did* one manage without a family physician, a prescription for antibiotics, and the handiness of a friendly neighborhood pharmacy?

Chapter Eleven

"Here, drink this," Iain said, intensely aware of Leeanne, bundled as she was in a soft lamb's wool blanket with nothing except bare skin beneath. It was becoming increasingly difficult to remain indifferent to her. If ever he had been, he thought.

Observing Leeanne gave him pleasure, something he'd denied himself for a long while. He caught himself doing it more and more often—watching her when he thought she wasn't looking, and recently, even when he knew she was. Assessing her smile, the graceful manner in which she traversed a room, the way she blinked when she didn't understand something, the furrowed lines of her brow when she was perturbed. Mentally evaluating her individuality of spirit.

Leeanne was rare indeed, not flawless, yet beautiful in ways she didn't seem to realize. Iain kept telling himself he neither needed nor wanted a woman to ease his guilt-ridden heart. That feminine companionship was the last thing on his mind. That he abhorred the idea of remarriage.

Might he be fooling himself?

Somehow, he'd imagined his pain still too private to share. Now he was beginning to seriously wonder if he'd locked himself in a self-imposed prison because he was in reality a coward, because it was easier to deal with life on an unemotional level than to meet it full force as Leeanne did.

"What's this?" Leeanne asked, accepting the wineglass from him only to sniff suspiciously at the murky contents.

Her bluer-than-blue eyes grazed his momentarily before she glanced back down at the liquid.

Iain had no idea what was in the concoction, though he'd tasted it before offering it to Leeanne.

"It's no more bitter than thin green tea. It reminds me of claret, with crushed rose petals, a dash of sage, a pinch of cloves, and a hint of bog wood smoke thrown in for good measure. Mangus made it," he informed her.

"So that's where you went while I bathed—to the croft at Achtriochtan."

"Aye. Mangus is wise in the ways of roots and herbs. Many of the people of Glencoe seek his advice when they're feeling unwell."

"A medicine man, huh?" she said.

Iain responded by reciting a Gaelic phrase Mangus had instructed him to repeat in Leeanne's company.

"Do I dare ask what that was all about?"

"It's a charm, lass. Mangus informed me it works well in conjunction with the brew."

"You've got to be kidding."

"Kidding?" Iain mimicked. He was even growing accustomed to the peculiar style of communication they shared.

"Teasing."

"Now, why should I be teasing about something as serious as this? Go on now, drink up and make Mangus's effort worth his while," Iain said, nodding toward the glass.

Sometimes Leeanne reminded him of an inquisitive child, saying the most unpredictable things, asking the most astonishing questions, Iain mused. Mystifying and captivating him at the same time.

Iain watched her dutifully sample the aromatic brew. Her cheeks puffed out as she rolled the liquid on her tongue. With a brave smile that could just as easily have been a grimace, Leeanne swallowed, though he imagined she'd rather have spit the concoction out.

"Not too bad," she pronounced finally. "Soothing actually."

"Mangus vows that if you partake of it, your ague will be greatly improved by morning."

Leeanne drank a second swallow. And then a third.

With an acute sense of relief, Iain noted that her color already seemed better, though he surmised her recovery had started the instant she'd discovered that Gleann-leac-na-muidhe, a smaller yet impressive version of the main house at Carnoch, possessed a bathing room. Nothing would do but she must avail herself of the hipbath. *Immediately.*

Now, clothes industriously laundered in that same tub and spread out to dry by the fireside in her bedchamber, her alabaster shoulder peeking enticingly from the blanket, he was reminded of a sculpture he'd beheld in Florence, carved by the same artist who had decorated the ceiling of the Sistine Chapel. Well-traveled, Iain had done and seen many things, met people from all walks of life. He'd found nothing and no one to compare with the Highlands. Until now.

Heart of his heart, the Highlands were more real to him than reality itself. They were a solitary place, yet all that much more spectacular for their loneliness. Ever changing, they could be quiet and sparkling one moment, glowering and defensive the next. Difficult to love and impossible to hate. And above all, never, ever dull.

Leeanne was like that.

Iain experienced a pressing urge to weave his fingers through the candlelight-kissed tresses of her shiny sable curls, and he dared not. He dreamed of holding her slender, scantily clad body against his and exploring the delicate curve of her waist and the flare of her hips, and yet he resisted. He wanted to gaze into her startlingly potent eyes and tell her things he'd never told another woman, not even his first wife. Something held him back, something more than his past, something more than self-control, which he normally prided himself on and which he felt sadly lacking where she was concerned.

Physically, Leeanne stirred him as the parade of Highland lassies he'd met in the last year did not—one a week since Sesi had decided it was in his own good interest that he remarry and settle down. He wasn't being arrogant in thinking that his sister's acquaintances chased him. They did. He was a prime catch: the son of a nobleman with extensive holdings, a prosperous manor house, and formidable connections. And of all of the women, he was attracted to one who had become handfasted to him by pure accident. A woman who knew nothing of his assets, and, he suspected, would not be overly impressed if she did.

A *sassenach*.

Of all things!

Wouldn't his father be beside himself if he was alive? Wouldn't his mother be pleased?

And was not life ironic . . . and damnably inconvenient at times? Iain mused.

Thoughts of his parents brought reminders of home and duty. He had to break the news to Leeanne. All day he'd known he must, and yet he had purposely delayed.

"There's something we need to speak of, lass. I've put it off long enough," he began. He took a bowl of porridge from the hob projecting from the side of the fireplace. Taking her partially drained glass, he replaced it with the steaming bowl. Simultaneously she rocked forward to tuck her feet beneath her in the settle, and for a moment they were nose to nose.

Leeanne's breath smelled of roses, her freshly washed hair of heather honey soap, her cheeks of the goat's milk and sweet flower lotion Mangus had provided her, all combined with the heady base scent that was uniquely Leeanne's. Iain had never wanted to kiss her as badly as he did now.

He straightened away from her to prove to himself he could do it.

"Mangus wanted to send beef broth to strengthen your blood, but I explained you would no' eat it," he said, swirling the liquid in the wineglass. Mangus had not only supplied the medicine and lotion, but the oatmeal for Leeanne and the meat pie he'd supped on as well.

Leeanne inclined her head.

"Would you care for a raised shortbread cake

with your porridge?" he asked abruptly.

"No, thanks."

Placing the glass on the table beside the settle, he hunkered down to add a peat brick to the already blazing fire. Then, rising to rest his arm on the carved stone chimneypiece, he stared pensively into the orange flames.

"I don't think food was the topic you had in mind a moment ago," Leeanne said solemnly.

Iain cast a sidelong look at Leeanne. "You're correct. It has naught to do with food."

"Did it have to do with me?" she challenged.

"Aye."

"Were you thinking of kissing me?"

Iain raised his brows. "Perhaps."

"This time we aren't at a wedding or on the *camanchd* field with a crowd of people to run interference. We don't have Alasdair presiding over the situation, or your sister sharing a room with us."

"Nay, we're alone. Does that concern you?

"It might. How about you?"

"In a manner of speaking. Largely because I hold you in high esteem."

"And that bars you from crossing over the platonic yellow line we've drawn with our pact, doesn't it?"

"What did Mangus put in that brew!"

"Maybe truth serum."

"What?"

"It's irrelevant. More to the point, you aren't going to allow either one of us to overstep the boundaries of friendship, are you?"

"I'm thinking it's for the best."

"What else can I say—ditto."

"I take it that you mean we're of a mind."

Leeanne replied with a question. "So, what *did* you want to talk to me about before I mistakenly started this nonsense?"

His attention returned to the fire. "I'll be seeing you back to the cottage at dawn, and after that I'm leaving for the manor house at Loch Lomond," Iain announced finally. His tone was more brusque than he'd intended. He softened it as he explained, "The missive Robert Campbell delivered was real enough in respect to the fire at the manor house. I must return to assess the damage and to instruct Gabhan MacGregor, my retainer, concerning the immediate reconstruction of the west wing."

Iain glanced up to gauge Leeanne's reaction.

Her eyes round and startled, he realized he'd caught her off guard. She said hurriedly, "Then I'll go with you."

Her reaction did not surprise him. Actually, for some strange reason, he'd expected it.

"I can no' allow that."

"I thought we were friends," she said, her voice cracking slightly.

Lacing his hands behind his back, Iain turned to face Leeanne. *His wife.*

"That we are, lass."

Even though she asked for no explanation,

she looked so hurt, so incredibly lost, that Iain felt the need to offer one. His reasoning was threefold. One: it was his responsibility to see to his manor house in Loch Lomond. Two: he hesitated to expose Leeanne to the harsh Highland winter on an extended basis. And three: he thought distancing himself from Leeanne might help him come to terms with the fire building in his loins and the slow awakening of feelings that had lain satisfactorily dormant until now.

Iain chose to share only the first two reasons with Leeanne.

"I'm no' abandoning you, if that's what you're thinking," he said, his calm voice masking his emotions. "The trip entails several days of rigorous travel, lass. I'll no' put you at the mercy of the weather for that majority of time. No' after today. I'm asking that you remain in my place and be my eyes and ears. You may sup with Sesi and Parlan if you have a mind to; he knows your preference for meatless meals. And there's a braw supply of peat bricks beneath the sheltered walkway if you run short of them in the cottage."

"What about Robert Campbell and his bunch?"

"I realize you're apprehensive of the man. But have faith, lass. Alasdair knows how to keep troops in line. Even ones that are no' of his own calling. Besides, Robert Campbell is no' daft. He would no' dare to cause trouble under the canopy of the auld chief's hospitality."

At the moment, no matter what Iain said, no matter what she told herself, she felt as if she were being abandoned. The mental image of fending for herself in Glencoe without Iain, of functioning against the backdrop of seventeenth-century Scotland and with the added duress of armed troops, intimidated her like no stage production ever could.

Leeanne didn't want to ask and yet she knew she must. "How long will you be gone?"

As they'd made their way to Alasdair's summer house, she'd thought Iain seemed preoccupied. Aloof. Now she knew why. All the while, he'd been plotting to ride out of Glencoe and leave her and the trouble she represented behind him, Leeanne thought.

"Less than a fortnight."

"Speak English, Iain!" she demanded, blaming the sick feeling in the pit of her stomach on Mangus's medicine rather than Iain's announcement.

Iain studied her curiously. "I am speaking English, lass."

"I'd be grateful if you'd give me the terms of this . . . this trip . . . in days instead of . . . instead of fortnights."

"Less than fourteen, I imagine."

Two weeks! A lot could happen in a day, much less two weeks. Iain would surely take his sword with him. And without it, there was no hope of her escaping the past. Worse still,

233

what if something happened to him and he never returned? Fate certainly wasn't cutting her any slack.

Beleaguered by doubts, she fought down a sense of desperation, coaxing herself not to panic even though she felt precariously close to blurting out her story in the hope he wouldn't leave her.

And then Leeanne realized that it was the absence of the man, not the sword, which concerned her the most. The implications scared her more than the thought of two weeks in Glencoe without a chance at the broadsword.

Attempting to master her uncertainty, she scanned Iain's shadowed face, studying his dampened hair and the muscular column of his throat above the white linen of his shirt. He had sensitive lips and strong hands, she decided. In combination, they played havoc with her imagination.

In addition, his forceful personality and natural chivalry almost made her forget who and where she was, what a fine chalk line she walked between his reality and hers.

She still couldn't believe he'd kicked up such a fuss over her bathing "during the deep set of winter and with the ague." She'd remained adamant, and finally he'd relented, building fires in each of the three fireplaces in Gleann-leac-na-muidhe. When the house was cozy and toasty warm, he'd filled the shallow oak tub with water heated in a hearth.

She'd luxuriated in the tub for nearly a quarter of an hour, marveling on how dependent she was becoming on the Highlander. Afterwards, he'd surprised her by using the tepid water to bathe as well.

"You must no' allow yourself to become too dependent on me, lass," Iain said with a rueful smile, breaking into her thoughts.

Now who was reading minds?

Leeanne refocused her attention on what Iain was saying rather than his body, taking his statement to mean he intended no extended commitments toward her—which was as it should be since they were only handfasted.

"You're right, of course," she agreed coolly. She had been leaning on him. Heavily. The woman who never leaned on anything or anyone. What a laugh!

The fact that Iain was dead on target made her angry, at him and at herself. She felt like crying. Instead of giving way to self-pity, she upbraided herself for a fool. She had two feet and she knew damned well how to stand on them. Independence was a state of mind; the last thing she wanted to be was a nuisance to Iain MacBride. She didn't know what had made her push the issue of their relationship.

Leeanne attempted to block her emotions, to pause them like a film clip on the VCR so she could examine and then regulate them to their proper place in the scheme of things. She failed.

Her parents had bequeathed her not only their competitiveness, but their knowledge of how to roll with the punches, Leeanne reminded herself. Changing internal tactics, she drew on that facet of her character to place her feelings temporarily on the back burner of her mind.

"Fine. I'll see you when you get back. And please, don't feel you have to rush on my account. I'm sure things will be just hunky-dory here while you're away," she said with forced bravado.

Now, Leeanne thought, all she had to do was convince herself that she believed what she'd told Iain.

Setting aside the untouched oatmeal, she rose with as much dignity as her woolen sarong allowed. "I'm suddenly extremely tired. I think I'd like to rest now. I'll see you in the morning."

Mouth grimly compressed, Leeanne crossed to the stairs that led to one of the comfortably appointed second-floor bedchambers.

"Lass?"

She paused.

"Watch yourself on the top tread. It's a tripping step, the riser installed higher than the rest to trip up unwary intruders."

She nodded over her shoulder, continuing toward the stairs and the tester bed, complete with a long-handled warming pan filled with live coals, which she knew awaited her.

"Leeanne?" he queried softly.

Iain rarely called her by her given name unless he had something serious to impart. She paused again, yet refrained from turning toward him.

His sincerity unmistakable, Iain said, "I vow I'd take you with me if I thought it prudent. But it's my belief you'll be better off here. With any luck, I'll be returning from the manor house at Loch Lomond before you've had time to miss me," he assured her.

Her lips trembled.

Leeanne realized that Iain was attempting to lighten her misgivings by teasing her about missing him. She wasn't in the mood for it, because in all honesty, she would miss him. More than she cared to admit, even to herself.

"I hope to God you're right," she said in a voice as strong as her sore throat and bruised ego permitted.

Slowly ascending the stairs and leaving Iain to his own thoughts, Leeanne found herself praying that skipping pebbles on Loch Achtriochtan did in fact bring good luck to the participants. Little did Iain realize that she was staking her life, her future, and very possibly her sanity, on his safe and speedy return to Glencoe.

The next morning, she and Iain parted on shaky terms.

The morning following Iain's departure for

the manor house at Loch Lomand, Sesi and Parlan removed to their own cottage on the River Coe while Leeanne conquered her fears, learning to carry on tolerably well without Iain constantly at her side.

The evening after that, at the main house at Carnoch, she attended an indoor wrestling match between a Macdonald heavyweight and a Campbell of comparable porportions.

The next day, she co-judged an archery contest open to male and female participants alike, celebrating when a woman won first place with claret served in one of Alasdair's engraved Jacobite wineglasses.

And in the ensuing days, Leeanne occupied herself by visiting Sesi, choreographing a production of the *Nutcracker* sponsored by Alasdair Macdonald, and insinuating herself into the enemy camp of Captain Robert Campbell of Glenlyon.

Chapter Twelve

Charles Hamilton was Captain Robert Campbell's aide-de-camp.

He was also a wrestler.

An archer.

An accomplished flutist.

And an Englishman.

But the most amazing thing about Charles was that he had no neck. His head seemed to rest squarely on his shoulders, reminding Leeanne of a box turtle with its head drawn partially into its shell. That, however, did nothing to affect his musical ability or his infatuation with her. Which served her purposes admirably.

Actually, Leeanne thought as she listened

to him practice her modified version of "The Waltz of the Flowers" which she planned to use in the final act of the *Nutcracker*, he seemed a veritable godsend. Without him, she couldn't have learned one-tenth the information she had concerning Robert Campbell.

She'd already seen for herself that he was a drinker and a gambler. What she couldn't see was that he despised the Glencoe men for their reiving ways which had led him to financial ruin and forced him into the military at an age when most men were home, spending time with their wives and bouncing grandchildren on their knees. As was Alasdair Macdonald.

With that thought, Leeanne glanced from Charles to the laird's wife. Motioning to her as if conducting a full-fledged orchestra, she said, "This is where you cue the children. Remember? Strum the harp softly, just like I showed you."

The gentle voice of the harp, like reverberating ripples in a still pool, filled the great hall of the main house.

"Now, Charles, this is where you come in," Leeanne directed.

The thrill of the woodwind joined the murmur of the stringed instrument.

"Speed it up just a little. That's it. You've got it! Perfect. You sound great together. Just remember that when I give the signal for the curtain to go up, that's also your cue to begin playing."

Naturally enough, Leeanne had found herself missing the things she took for granted in her own century. A hot shower. Frozen yogurt with pecan sprinkles. Electric lights. Books from the public library. Music at the flick of a button. Her dance studio. Her dance company. Therefore, when Alasdair had proposed a ballet, Leeanne had jumped at the chance to work again. She'd chosen the *Nutcracker* because there were a million versions and no set way to choreograph it—and she had the score memorized.

As principal player, she would be dancing the role of the Sugar Plum Fairy. The children of the glen, including Iseabal, constituted her cast and crew. Enthusiastic and more than eager to please, they'd been recruited on a voluntary basis and had proved a joy to work with.

"Didna ye promise I could play something here, mistress?" Alasdair's piper, Barr Macdonald, chimed in above the music. The harp and flute ensemble petered out on a disharmonious note.

The laird's piper, recovered from his sprained ankle, seemed determined to participate in the production as well. No amount of cajoling would deter him. And with Alasdair backing him up, it was virtually impossible to deny him his moment in the limelight.

If her company could see her now, choreographing the *Nutcracker Suite* with a flute, a harp, and a bagpipe, they'd throw in their towels—after phoning the funny farm and sending for the men in white jackets to take her away, Leeanne thought. Not to mention Peter Ilyich Tchaikovsky. The Russian composer was probably turning over in his grave. Of course he couldn't, because he hadn't been born yet. Which made her feel even more peculiar, since she was using music that hadn't been written and performed before 1892.

1692. 1892. 1992. Might there be some weird correlation?

Leeanne pressed her fingers to her temples and massaged. The only consolation in dealing with Barr Macdonald, unlike the laird's wife, was that he spoke English and she need not resort to sign language when her young interpreter, Iseabal, was otherwise occupied in practice with the children.

"I did say that you could play something, Barr." *At Alasdair's insistence.* "But not during the ballet. I'll think about it. Perhaps . . . perhaps I'll dance the Blades of War at the end of the performance. Would that suffice?"

The piper beamed. "Aye. I'd consider it an honor to play for that, mistress."

"Then that's what we'll plan on. I'll dance and you'll play and everyone will be happy."

"Aye. That we will."

"Okay, let's call it a day. I've asked the children to be here by four. I'd like to see the musicians back at the main house at five sharp. The performance starts at seven, and it would probably be a good idea to run through things once more with the cast before curtain time."

She got no response. Everyone except Charles remained as they were, the laird's wife smiling benignly and Barr looking as if he expected some sort of elaboration on her instructions.

Leeanne tried again. "At twilight," she said slowly. Nothing. "Dusk." Still nothing. "You know, sunset."

"Ach, gloaming, ye mean," Barr said.

"Gloaming then, just be here on time."

"It would be so much easier if there was a universal language . . . besides music," Leeanne muttered to herself. "Now I know how the alien that finds the Voyager's record of earth greetings is going to feel. . . ."

Lost in thought, Leeanne turned to leave and stepped chest first into Charles Hamilton. His flute clattered to the stone floor. He bent to retrieve it at the same time Leeanne did. They bumped heads.

Leeanne straightened, pressing the flute firmly into his hand. "I'm sorry. I didn't realize you'd moved behind me, Charles."

Sallow skin flushing scarlet, he stuttered, "Are you hurt, mistress?" He reached out a tentative hand as if he might rub the red spot on her forehead.

Unconsciously, Leeanne flinched from his touch.

"I should be asking you that," she assured him hurriedly. "I'm the one that stepped all over you, not the other way around."

"Yes, mistress; I mean no, mistress. That is to say, I didn't mind it a bit, mistress." He hesitated, as if he might say more.

"Was there something else?" Leeanne prompted.

He glanced furtively across the room at Robert Campbell, engrossed in a game of chess with Alasdair Macdonald, and judging by his self-satisfied smile, winning too, Leeanne decided.

"I'd rather not converse here," Charles said in a low voice, tucking the flute into his belt. "Might I escort you to the door of your cottage?"

It went against the grain to encourage Charles, and yet Leeanne was determined to find out what Robert Campbell was up to. He was crafty—too crafty. Even though he drank too much, he hadn't yet tripped himself up. Which was what she'd been hoping against hope for. It would have been so much easier on her if Robert Campbell spilled the beans himself.

But she sensed she was running out of time. That Glencoe was on the precipice of something earth-shattering. If only she could get Charles alone long enough to pump him for details, Leeanne thought.

"As a matter of fact, there was something I wanted to discuss with you as well," she found herself saying. "I never dreamed so many people would want to attend *The Nutcracker.* If it was summer, we could have an outdoor performance to accommodate everyone. But since it's winter and the main house won't hold them all, we've arranged to perform it twice."

"Alasdair has planned a hunt for tomorrow. Many of the men will be gone until evening. Mayhap even later."

Leeanne wrinkled her nose in distaste. "I know. Alasdair told me it was more necessity than sport with so many extra mouths to feed. That's why a matinee performance will be held the day after tomorrow. I thought tickets might help keep things in order. The children made them, and I'd like you to distribute a bundle to the men of your company who plan to attend one or the other."

Glancing once again toward Robert Campbell, Charles nodded. Acting the gentleman, he opened the door for Leeanne, allowing her to precede him.

Once outside the main house, Charles breathed a heavy sigh which Leeanne interpreted as relief.

"That bad, huh?" she asked.

Charles glanced at her, adoration shining in his nondescript eyes.

"I wanted to thank you for asking me to play my flute for your ballet."

"Well, I'm happy to have you. If not for Alasdair, I'd never have known you were so talented."

"When Captain Campbell heard you were planning a performance, he offered my services to the chief in hopes that we might attend."

"Interesting. Your captain doesn't seem the sort to patronize the performing arts."

"He thought it might be a way of alleviating some of the restlessness among the men."

"You mean they'd rather be off chasing those escaped convicts from Edinburgh than billeted here in Glencoe?"

"They'd rather complete the King's business so they might return to their own homes and families." He glanced up at the overcast sky, teeth worrying his lip.

"It's a pity the wolves frightened off your pack animals. I suppose you could be on your way if not for that."

Charles seemed perplexed for a moment. "Oh, that. Yes, I imagine we could," he agreed thoughtfully.

"But then, it gave Captain Campbell an excuse to visit his niece," Leeanne said, although she'd noted during the past few days that he seemed more inclined toward avoiding his niece.

As they reached the door to the cottage, Leeanne toyed with the idea of inviting Charles inside. But it seemed the glen had eyes everywhere, most of them directed toward her activities right now.

"Well, I suppose this is where I must leave

you," Charles said, saving her the trouble of a decision.

"I'll see you later this evening. And don't forget to bring your flute."

With a polite wave, Leeanne pushed open the door to the cottage.

"Mistress?"

Leeanne paused on the threshold. "Yes."

Charles half turned from her, his gaze roaming off across the expanse of partially melted snow toward the pony barn.

"What of the tickets?"

"Oh, yes. Thanks for reminding me. Wait one second and I'll get them for you."

Leeanne scooped from the bed a bundle of one hundred and twenty tickets counted out specifically for the soldiers.

"Here you go. You'll need to do this before you return to the main house for the opening performance. Each ticket is marked with a date. It's a tossup who will attend tonight and who will have to wait, but in the light of our unexpected popularity, it seemed the only fair way to do this. Alasdair distributed his lot by family. Perhaps you could have the soldiers draw from a hat and then exchange tickets if they prefer to attend with a friend."

Charles paused, his face a mirror of conflicting emotions.

"If you have a better suggestion, I'd love to hear it."

"It isn't the slips of admittance that concern

me. They'll do well enough. I'll simply have one company attend the first performance and the other attend the last."

"The music?"

"Not that either."

"The children's ability to pull this off after so little instruction? I must admit, I had my reservations about using them, but I'll be dancing the most difficult role and they've absorbed their parts like thirsty sponges. I've never seen a group more eager and willing to learn."

He shook his head. "It has nothing to do with the performance."

"What then?"

"Do I have your leave to ask a personal question?"

Curious as to where this might be leading, Leeanne nodded.

"Am I to understand that you're only handfasted to Iain MacBride?" he asked finally.

Though surprised, Leeanne immediately rallied. "That's correct."

"And that he's left you behind in preference for his holdings near Loch Lomond?"

Leeanne nodded again without comment.

"Do you have feelings for the Highlander?"

Leeanne gave what she hoped was a nonchalant shrug. "I hardly know him, Charles. Besides, as you said yourself, we're only handfasted and under most unusual circumstances at that."

Charles gave another great sigh. "I've heard

all about the handfasting and what led up to it
from the clanspeople."

"I didn't realize our arrangement was such a
popular topic for discussion."

"Have you ever considered leaving Glencoe
behind you? Leaving MacBride before a year
and a day is done?"

*Only about one hundred and fifty-three times
in the past ten days.* "Is there a reason that I
should?"

Charles kicked at the frozen earth with the
toe of his boot. "It's just that Glencoe is no fit
place for a teacher, and an English one at that.
The Highlands are not England. Winters here
can be . . . disastrous."

Leeanne's eyes narrowed. Charles was
attempting to tell her something without
saying it outright. She decided it could
only be one of two things. Either this was
some sort of offbeat proposal, or his way of
warning her of impending doom.

"Disastrous, dangerous, or deadly?" she
asked.

Hands behind his back, Charles clenched his
left wrist with his right hand. "Who's to say?
Possibly all three."

"You're telling me the situation is volatile?"

"I'm saying 'tis common knowledge that
Alasdair Macdonald has made some powerful enemies over the years. There are those
in London, as well as Edinburgh, who are
displeased with his tardiness in tendering his

oath of submission in January. Some feel, particularly William's Master of Stair, Sir John Dalrymple, that an example should be made."

She knew nothing of seventeenth-century politics or politicians, but names were important if she was to force Iain to hear her accusations against Robert Campbell.

"Dalrymple?"

"You would not think the Secretary of State for Scotland anxious to stir up more trouble in the Highlands, but he's being underwritten by the Earl of Breadalbane. John Campbell is ambitious, and the Scottish treasury is in poor condition. Since even the common man knows that further land taxation impossible at this time. . . ."

Leeanne was finally beginning to get the gist of things. Economics and concern over the national debt weren't new to her. Neither was property taxation. It was one of the things that most infuriated the American people.

"A rebel like the old chief does nothing less for the economy of Scotland than keep it in turmoil," Charles continued. "And even Alasdair must realize that King William's patience with the Highland chiefs is exhausted. He never would have expended the time and energy during harsh weather to take the oath of allegiance, late or otherwise, if he did not."

Presuming on his infatuation, Leeanne batted her eyelashes at Charles. "And?"

"And even though the English privy council seems divided, general governmental consensus is that the plundering by rebel forces must be stopped," he finished in a rush.

So, they'd come full circle back to the questionable acquisition of first James Macdonald's, and then Parlan's, long-horned bull.

"How is it that you know so much about this? Do you aspire to be a politician?" Leeanne asked coyly.

"Not I. I'm content being a professional soldier. 'Tis my second cousin, Lieutenant-Colonel Hamilton of Fort William in Inverlochy, that keeps up on the King's policy and government opinion in aspirations of higher office. Though he has a long way to go to catch up with Major Robert Duncanson, our immediate superior at the fort."

The cold had nothing to do with the shiver that ran up Leeanne's spine; the implications of Charles's ground-level information did. Whatever was going on, it seemed well plotted, far-reaching, and highly hush-hushed.

When she'd first arrived in Glencoe, she had heard Alasdair speak of Fort William and his oath of allegiance to the King. At that time, Alasdair had assumed that he'd sealed the fate of his people with his belated submission to the English king. Perhaps he had, but not in the manner he had intended.

Leeanne thought of Iain. Of Sesi, and Parlan, and newborn Elizabeth. Of Alasdair, his wife, sons, and angelic grandson, of lively Iseabal in the first bloom of womanhood, of the families she had met on the *camanachd* field who had offered her bread and wine, of Mangus the bard, and even of Barr, the laird's determined piper. What was to become of them?

Leeanne hugged her cloak more closely about her shoulders, her gaze following Charles's in a direct line toward the pony barn. It was then she realized he wasn't looking at the barn, but to something beyond it—a spot in the distance that Iain had pointed out to her during their tour as Signal Rock and the An Tor summit.

"How soon would you suggest that I find the means to leave Glencoe behind me?"

Charles worried his bottom lip with his teeth.

"My best guess would be as soon as possible following your final performance of the *Nutcracker.*"

Seventy-two hours!

Leeanne's mouth went dry. Here at last was what she'd been looking for, something more than body language and half-baked supposition. Something concrete and very nearly damning.

"I don't suppose you'd consider being a little more specific."

"To be any more specific than I already have been would be to commit treason."

"I see." What she saw was that he'd risked as much as he dared.

His right hand moved slowly to the sword belted at his waist. Charles fiddled with the sheath, flicking at the leather strap securing the pommel.

"Am I safe in assuming you will refrain from mentioning this little discussion to anyone?" he asked.

Leeanne realized that Charles Hamilton could prove a formidable adversary if it came down to protecting his own skin. Fear, like love, sometimes did strange things to people, bringing out the best *and* the worst in them. But the Macdonalds of Glencoe had been generous in their acceptance of her. Hospitable. Supportive. Extraordinarily kind under the circumstances. And the children she'd been teaching the past week were such dears. To add to that, she'd never been as close to another woman as she was to Sesi, due to her help in delivering baby Elizabeth!

In good conscience, she couldn't stand by and do nothing . . . and she wouldn't run. Not even if the sapphire-encrusted broadsword was at ready beneath her fingertips. Barring all the other personal bonds she'd formed, she loved Iain MacBride too much to let him walk blindly into Robert Campbell's blade.

"Charles, I wouldn't dream of double-crossing you."

How easily the lie slipped between her teeth and over her lips, Leeanne mused.

*   *   *

Later that evening the more influential clanspeople of Glencoe as well one company of Robert Campbell's soldiers congregated in the great hall of the main house at Carnoch to view the opening performance of the *Nutcracker*.

"It seems ye and Charles Hamilton have become fast friends over the last few days." Iseabal's voice was conspiratorial as she preened before the steel mirror in the great hall. They'd partitioned a small area near the entrance for a dressing room, and everyone was ready and waiting upstairs for their grand entrance, except the vivacious redhead.

"What in the world are you talking about, Iseabal," Leeanne exclaimed, tightening the sash around the teenager's waist and tying it in an intricate bow in the back.

"Just that. I overheard his lairdship tell Parlan ye were getting awfully friendly with Robert Campbell's aide, what with Iain away and all."

So her behavior was being discussed behind closed doors, Leeanne thought. She should have expected that.

"Iseabal, we have five minutes before curtain time, and by the way, you make a lovely Clara," Leeanne said, keeping her voice mild as she critically surveyed her protégée's garb.

"Thank you, but as I was saying, Charles—"

"I think you'd be a lot better off if you had put your energy toward rehearsing your dance steps rather than in listening to idle gossip."

"Then there's no mortar to the bricks of rumor? I mean, I wouldna have ye hurt Iain in retaliation for the handfasting, though I can see it might perturb you a bit, the way it was done and all. Still, even if ye did feel the need to light a wee spark beneath Iain, ye could do far better for yerself than a red-breasted *sassenach*."

Leeanne glanced up sharply. She was using Charles Hamilton, but not for what Iseabal implied.

"I'm a *sassenach* too, Iseabal."

"Nay, no longer, na in the eyes of the clan. You're a woman of the glen, and I'd wager the Macdonald men would line up to give Iain MacBride a run for his money," Iseabal continued innocently.

"Iseabal!"

"Well, 'tis as true as the day is long, mistress. Have ye na seen the way they gape at ye? Why, I'd give my hair up to my earlobes to have Niall Macdonald look at me the way he does ye."

Leeanne smiled as she tucked a wayward curl back into the bun at the nape of Iseabal's neck. She knew Niall Macdonald. He was the son of the smithy, robust and easygoing with the eyes of a poet and the body of a dancer, though his muscles had been achieved through manual labor. She could see how Iseabal might have a crush on the sixteen-year-old.

"Give yourself time. You'll have Niall eating out of your hand before you know it." *And somehow, I'm going to help give you the growing time you need.*

"Ye think so?"

"I know so. And you can stop worrying as far as Charles Hamilton and I are concerned. Our ballet needed some sort of music other than bagpipes. He plays the flute like an angel. So between Charles and the laird's wife . . ."

"We've got our music and that's all there is to it."

Leeanne honestly wished that was all. The people of Glencoe possessed an unpretentious goodness along with an unsuspecting suscep-tibility that warranted protecting. If only she could figure out how to accomplish the feat without landing in a world of trouble in rela-tionship to Alasdair and his Highland code of hospitality. It was a challenge, as was Iain, but Leeanne had a funny feeling that both were worth whatever the cost.

"Why don't you go and tell the children it's time for them to come downstairs? We've got a good box office, and I want to get this show on the road before our audience gets antsy."

"A good box office? Isna that stage talk for a full house?"

"You learn quickly."

"Now, that I'll na argue with ye aboot. Besides, 'twas na too difficult to decipher. The main house is fair bursting at the seams."

"You see, our days spent in stage planning are a success and we haven't even raised the curtain."

"Just wait until we do. I ken they'll be that surprised."

With that, Iseabal hurried off to collect the other children. Leeanne had barely enough time to complete her own exercises before they bounded down the stairs, dancing around her knees like energetic moppets, as anxious as she was to begin.

Leeanne clapped her hands to gain their attention. "Okay, hush now. Let's have a moment of silence. Everybody take a deep breath through your mouths. Exhale it through your noses. Now, places everyone. Ready. Set."

Leeanne signaled the stagehands to manually lift the curtain fashioned from yards of tartan cloth. The makeshift orchestra was watching for their cue, and the music started immediately.

"Let's go," Leeanne mouthed, dancing out onto the stage, which was little more than a corded-off section of the great hall. She was followed by a garden of petite Scottish attendants and one beaming, red-haired Clara.

Ordinarily, stage lights acted as blinders, diminishing audience visibility. In this instance, Leeanne could actually count heads all the way to the back wall of the great hall. What she saw leaning nonchalantly against that wall, haloed by the golden light of a flickering torch, filled her with anticipation.

Iain!

Acute self-discipline and strict training kept her from losing her timing.

How dynamic he looked with his bonnet positioned at a rakish angle atop his fair head, a half-smile playing on his lips, and the pommel of his broadsword peeping over his shoulder, Leeanne thought. How often she had dreamed of him in the last eleven days. How much better it was to have him back with her in the flesh.

With an added spring to her step, she danced "The Waltz of the Flowers" as if only he watched. Because for the time being, no one else mattered. With the graceful movements of her sinuous, double-jointed body, Leeanne welcomed to the glen the tall and dashing High-lander newly returned from his property near Loch Lomond, opening her soul to the music and to Iain MacBride.

At the end of the ballet, which was condensed in consideration of the younger children's endurance, the audience gave the Sugar Plum Fairy and her colorful cast a vigorous ovation. Leeanne could see Iain nudging his way through the crowd, could feel him watching her. Then the piper intervened with an announcement concerning the Blades of War, and for the first time in her professional career, Leeanne visibly faltered as the first tentative strains of "Gillie Chalium" skirled through the great hall.

How could she have forgotten her promise to Barr Macdonald? she wondered as the children took a final bow and scattered in anticipation of their teacher's solo performance.

Leeanne watched in horrified fascination as things escalated from that point on.

Halfway down the center isle, Iain extracted his claymore from its sheath.

Concern written on his face, Robert Campbell leaned over and said something to Alasdair.

Alasdair quieted his red-coated guest by hastily withdrawing and placing his own sword on the stage at Leeanne's feet.

Panic, harsh and nearly debilitating, welled within her. If Iain crossed his sword on top of Alasdair's, which was what Leeanne feared he intended, there was a ninety-nine-percent chance she'd return to her own time when she danced the Blades of War. And as nutty as it sounded, she wasn't ready to go yet.

Damn Alasdair's piper!

As if she hadn't seen Iain making his way toward her, Leeanne's gaze darted across the stage, falling on Charles Hamilton, sitting not five feet from her. With a sharp wave of her hand, she motioned for him to present his sword—quickly.

Without hesitation, Charles set aside his flute, rose, and withdrew his unimpressive weapon from its sheath. Sprinting across the stage, he crossed Alasdair's sword with his own.

A hush fell over the audience.

Iain froze.

Charles Hamilton's expression was reminiscent of Sylvester's when he held Tweety Bird captive in his mouth, Leeanne decided.

A scowl darkening his face, it appeared as if Iain might come and yank her off stage at any second.

Glancing from the Highlander to the Englishman and back, Leeanne belatedly realized she'd shamed Iain before an assembly of his peers. She found herself thinking how glad she was that Sesi had been unable to attend the opening performance.

Next, Robert Campbell weaved drunkenly to his feet, complaining loudly about women and misplaced affections.

Iain snarled something clipped and decisive in Gaelic.

Frowning at her, Alasdair turned toward Iain, retaliating in kind.

Leeanne could only assume it had been a command of some sort for, mouth grim, Iain acquiesced by slowly resheathing his claymore.

Just as slowly, she stepped into position between the crossed sword blades.

Captain Robert Campbell resumed his seat.

As the bagpipes swelled in crescendo, Iain continued down the aisle, passing the stage without acknowledging her as he exited the great hall.

Alasdair trailed Iain outside the main house at Carnoch.

Gritting her teeth, Leeanne forced her feet to carry on with the show. Dancing counterclockwise inside and outside the squares formed by the blades, she performed the Blades of War when all the while what she really wanted to do was cry.

Chapter Thirteen

"You're late, lass."

"And you're back three days early," Leeanne
said as she let herself into the cottage.

Iain was seated near the fire, his leg slung
over the arm of the chair, his back to the door.
Leeanne glanced at the empty bottle of claret
on the hearth.

"And no' a day too soon to my way of thinking."

God, his voice sounded good, even if his
accent was heavier and his words slightly
slurred due to the wine, Leeanne thought.

"What kept you at the main house?" he
asked.

"I stayed to help the laird's wife straighten
up."

She untied her cloak, hanging it on the peg beside his jacket and claymore—the infamous claymore that had caused her so much trouble, she thought, reaching out to trace the lacings of its sheath.

"Alasdair walked me to the cottage. He has something he'd like to ask you. He's waiting outside the door."

"Well then? Tell him to step inside out of the cold."

Leeanne waved her hand, signaling to Alasdair. He strode across the threshold, closing the door behind him yet remaining near the entrance.

"'Tis a sorry day when men as fond of one another as we are come to such an impasse, Iain," he said solemnly.

"Aye," Iain responded without rising.

It took Leeanne only a moment to realize that Iain was purposely giving Alasdair the cold shoulder. She wondered fleetingly what had passed between them outside the main house while she was inside performing the Blades of War.

"I'm of a mind that dissension is no' good for the clan," Alasdair continued.

"Nay."

"And that's why I'm here, to encourage ye to join me in the hunt on the morrow," Alasdair said.

"You're a brazen auld chief."

"Aye, and thrawn too as I recall."

"Aye, as obstinate as that long-horned bull Parlan was so determined to win from James."

Alasdair rolled his eyes at Leeanne and winked.

"Now, lad. You've a right to call me auld, and brazen, and thrawn—I'll admit to those quick enough. But to liken me to a brainless piece of beef, and Campbell beef at that, is a low blow indeed."

"Perhaps."

Leeanne could feel the tension in the room lessening as Iain's shoulders relaxed.

"Will Parlan be attending the hunt?" Iain asked.

"How could ye think he would no'?"

"And Robert Campbell?"

"Ach, no. The captain's already planned a day of chess with his aide-de-camp. He's no' one for the cold—'tis my opinion thin blood runs in the Campbell clan. Besides, he would no' care for the choice of glens we're to hunt in."

"I see the way of it now," Iain said. Rising, he turned to face Alasdair.

Alasdair smiled, twirling the ends of his curly moustache with his fingertips.

"You're a wise man for thirty summers, Iain MacBride."

"I've had the best of teachers, Alasdair Macdonald. I'll join you on the morrow . . . to keep an eagle eye on Parlan for Sesi."

Leeanne suddenly had the distinct impression that Alasdair was calling it a hunt, yet planning a cattle raid into Campbell territory. And right under Robert Campbell's nose! The incorrigible Macdonald clan had more nerve than a battalion of marines. And the strangest sense of humor—planning to feed the Redcoats their own cattle.

"I'll leave that between ye and Parlan, though I imagine he'll be on his best behavior with the new bairn and all," Alasdair said, redirecting his attention to Leeanne.

"My wife will be preparing tatties-an-neeps in the morning. She says to come over around midday and she'll send a bowl back with ye for yer repast."

Leeanne glanced at Iain, remembering that he'd mentioned Sesi preparing tatties-an-neeps for him.

"Does it have meat in it?"

"I'm thinking your English words for the dish are potatoes and turnips," Iain interjected.

Yah! Something other than oatmeal and soda scones, Leeanne thought.

"Please tell your wife thank you and that I'll be there at noon on the dot," she said, her mouth watering for a dish of vegetables she would have once refused as beneath her palate.

"Well, then, I'll be seeing ye at first light, Iain. We'll plan to meet here," Alasdair said.

Iain nodded. Alasdair returned the nod, ducking out of the cottage and into the winter night.

Iain's contemplative gaze fell immediately to Leeanne.

"I'd like to apologize," he began.

Leeanne blinked. "For what?"

"For no' remaining at the main house to see your performance through to completion."

"That's all right. You really didn't miss much," Leeanne said, feeling that his voice was deceptively mild, that he was really initiating a clever game of cat and mouse. The thing she couldn't figure out was why.

"Come, sit by the fire and warm yourself," he said. He offered her the chair he'd recently vacated.

"No, I'm—"

"Please, I insist."

Leeanne nodded, traversing the room to lower herself into the armchair. The seat was still warm from his body heat.

"I brought a gift for you," Iain said abruptly.

Before she knew what he was about, he reached inside his jacket and extracted from his breast pocket a parcel wrapped in white silk and tied with blue ribbons.

Rotating it over and over in his hands, Iain finally tossed the packet unceremoniously into her lap.

"What is it?"

"You'll never know unless you open it."

Leeanne untied the ribbon, unwrapping the silk cloth to discover a beautifully engraved pewter container about the size of a large compact. She lifted the lid, gazing down at the mound of brown powder it contained. For a moment, she thought it might be some kind of snuff, until the aroma hit her. She immediately recognized her mistake.

"Ground cinnamon?"

"I thought you might enjoy flavoring your tea with a pinch of it now and again. When I was at the manor house, I recalled my mother's fondness for drinking spiced tea."

"Did this container belong to her?"

"Aye."

Touched, Leeanne said, "You didn't have to do that."

"I'm aware of that. It pleased me to do so."

"Was it a long trip?"

"Long enough."

"Cold?"

"Aye, cold and bleak, and uneventful."

"How was the west wing of the manor house?"

"Burned to the ground. They'll be no rebuilding it until spring."

"Did you find out how the fire started?"

"As Robert Campbell reported, it seems to have been accidental."

"I wonder—"

Iain interrupted her.

"Let's put aside the inane conversation, lass. I've something of importance to discuss with you," he advised her, his voice crisp and authoritative. "Simply put—I'm asking that you stay away from Robert Campbell's aide."

Astonished by his blunt request, Leeanne was careful not to look into his eyes. Now wasn't the time to be wish-washy. Not in the face of male arrogance at its finest.

"I afraid I can't do that."

He arched a fair brow at her. "Can't? Or won't? Need I remind you it's no more than your duty to respect my wishes?"

"Is that so?"

He watched her keenly. Her response having had a rather curious effect on him, she watched him just as keenly. He was getting angry and she wasn't sure why.

"If duty will not stay you, then consider honor," he said harshly.

"I have my own sense of honor. I'm aware you don't understand it, but that's the way it is," she retaliated. "There are things going on here that everyone except me seems oblivious to." She hadn't been playing Jessica Fletcher, Sherlock Holmes, and Agatha Christie all rolled into one for nothing while Iain was away.

"He does no' love you, you know," Iain said lightly—too lightly.

"Who?" Leeanne asked, thoroughly confused.

"Robert Campbell's aide. The one with the flute and the gaze that would no' leave you be during the ballet. He lusts after you. I've been informed that you seem to harbor a similar interest in him, and that does no' reflect well on me." He paused as if carefully considering his next words. "Could it be that you did this to me for leaving you behind?"

"Someone said something to you," Leeanne said, shutting her eyes against the pain of the accusation, pain that was surprisingly intense. Almost unbearable.

"I have eyes, Leeanne. Campbell's aide nearly broke his neck scrambling to place his sword doon for you."

"Don't be absurd. Charles has no neck," Leeanne murmured faintly, unable to believe what she was hearing.

Iain continued as if she hadn't spoken.

"And if that was no' enough, Alasdair made a point of speaking with me after the ballet. Robert Campbell complained to him that you were corrupting his aide due to a lacking in our relationship. Would you care to guess what Alasdair feels is lacking?"

So, Robert Campbell was on to her! *And* he'd outsmarted her, causing trouble where there was none just to shake her off his scent. The one-room cottage seemed to close in on her, the aroma of peat cutting off her breath. She cleared her throat, but it didn't help much.

Pride rising to the forefront, Leeanne reiterated more firmly, "Robert Campbell's aide isn't my type. Charles Hamilton has no neck."

Iain frowned. "No neck?"

"Exactly. No neck. He reminds me of a turtle."

"The neck is no' the important part of a man," Iain replied evenly.

It was impossible to explain the moral dilemma she found herself in. Philosophically, she knew she shouldn't get involved, but there were forces beyond her control at work and she felt compelled to act.

"I'm not untrustworthy and I'm not vindictive. I've good reason for what I've done. Or at least what it appears to everyone I've done."

"And what might that reason be?"

Rising to her feet, Leeanne pressed the compact of cinnamon into Iain's unresisting hand. "Politics."

Iain laughed. The sound was not pleasant. "What would a teacher, and a woman at that, know of politics?" he asked, negligently tossing the compact onto the bed.

Spinning on her heels, Leeanne said in a strained voice, "I'm getting out of here."

Crossing the cottage in three strides, she grabbed her cloak from the peg and threw it around her shoulders.

"You can no' run from this," Iain said solemnly.

Intent on departure, Leeanne moved to the door, and tugged it open. Her voice no warmer than the outside air infiltrating the cottage, she said over her shoulder, "I'm not running. I've faced everything head-on since I arrived in Glencoe. I don't plan to handle this any differently. But it's obvious to me you're not in the proper frame of mind to listen, so I might as well stop wasting my time."

Leeanne could feel Iain staring a hole through her back. She squared her shoulders.

"Where do you think you're going, lass?"

She choose not to answer him.

It made her heartsick to oppose Iain, but she was convinced that fate had put her here for some higher purpose. She didn't know if she could rectify past mistakes, but she couldn't allow Iain to stop her from trying. It was as if she were meeting her destiny, not in a dance studio, but in the Highlands. And Robert Campbell wasn't going to get the best of her.

Grabbing her hand, Iain spun Leeanne around, slamming the door shut behind her. She hadn't even heard him cross the room.

"I asked where you're going, Leeanne."

She made the fatal mistake of looking into his eyes.

"I'm not making any headway with you, so I might as well go over to the main house and try to talk some sense into Alasdair . . . get this thing out in the open before time runs out," she said, bracing herself against the door.

"Have you gone daft?"

"I beg your pardon?"

"I said you're daft."

"Iain, can't you see that something is coming down here?"

"Coming doon?"

"Getting ready to happen."

"What are you trying to tell me, Lass?"

"That they've concocted something in London between the Master of Stair and the Earl of Breadalbane. And yes, I believe that possibly even King William is in on it. And I'm going to get to bottom of it if it's the last thing I ever do! If I could jump when you snap your fingers, I would. But I can't. I was raised to be independent. To stand up for myself. To put the brains God gave me to good use. But not to be unfaithful. I don't like being falsely accused. Not by Campbell or Alasdair . . . or you."

"Och, and I thought Sesi was stubborn! Her stubbornness is as pale as watered wine compared to yours."

"And speaking of Sesi, I think it would be a good idea in light of Robert Campbell's presence for you to talk to Parlan. One of you big, strong men should start making plans to get her and the baby out of Glencoe," Leeanne predicted.

"So now you're fey, are you?"

"You know, it's difficult to carry on a good argument with you when I don't understand what you're calling me."

"I'm no' calling you anything. I'm asking if you think you can see into the future."

Damn! Leeanne thought. Why hadn't she realized it before? It wasn't Robert Campbell and his body language, or Charles Hamilton and his advice, or even the English troops in the glen that worried her. It was a passage she'd skimmed during her research for her theatrical production of modernized Highland dance. Buried deep within her subconscious was something vital concerning Glencoe. And no matter how she racked her brain, she could remember nothing more than a colorful picture book retrieved from the oversized shelf in her local library.

"I wish I could," she said, a distant look in her eyes. "You see, that's the whole problem, Iain. It's not the future I can see into, but the past," she said softly.

The tension rippling through Leeanne's body transmitted itself to Iain. She'd had a lot to contend with recently, for a teacher accustomed to the tranquility and protection of a schoolroom, he decided. But to explain that he'd already challenged Robert Campbell and been banned by Alasdair from the main house for the remainder of the captain's stay would only aggravate the situation.

For a moment Iain hesitated. Then his face hardened. Leeanne didn't understand. Perhaps she never would. Perhaps it was too much to ask of a *sassenach*. But he had to try. He also needed time to consider all that she'd said, for Robert Campbell's continued presence in Glencoe disturbed him as much as it did her. He'd imagined that when he returned from Loch Lommond the soldiers would be gone. Perhaps the hunt would see them supplied with enough food to move on.

And if not, he must be the one to confront Alasdair with their suspicions, not Leeanne.

"The auld chief is a bonny man, but for you to barge into his home and charge a guest with deception and political intrigue would most probably *be* the last thing you ever did," he warned darkly.

"I can't believe you're just going to sit back and let Robert Campbell do whatever vile thing it is he plans to do to your family and friends," she said.

Courage replaced the look of distance in her miraculous eyes. Courage and defiance. If she could not compel him to act, she would do something rash, even if it meant flaunting convention and defying Alasdair Macdonald. She did not know the price of dishonoring a Highland chief, but Iain did. He'd witnessed men's heads rolling from their shoulders, their blood spilling to curdle on the ground, staining his hands and his clothes and the air with its sickly sweetness, for far less than she now proposed.

"I've tried to explain to you the traditional ways of blood brotherhood and fosterage, and the inviolability of Highland hospitality. But it seems you let my words go over your head without taking any of them to heart."

Leeanne knew he could be gentle, but Iain wasn't being gentle now. His fingers felt like steel talons gripping her arm.

"You're making a big mistake, Iain."

"Nay, lass. I'm keeping you from making one. I can no' allow you to insult Alasdair. The penalty for disrespect is too grand."

A stiff silence followed as they confronted each other.

"You can't stop me," she contradicted finally.

The silence spun out like a spider's web, entrapping Leeanne in its gossamer strands.

"Do you think no'?" His expression belied the mildness in his voice.

"Only with brute strength," she said, tilting her chin pugnaciously.

"If it takes that, then brute strength it shall be."

Leeanne didn't care for the ominous-sounding implications. "Please, let me go, Iain. You're hurting my arm."

He lessened the pressure on her arm though he did not release her entirely.

"I wish I could let you go—you do no' know how you press me, lass," he said, his voice dropping to a husky timbre. "Although I did no' think you had it in you to cuckold me, I was actually jealous of Robert Campbell's aide, of the time he undoubtedly spent in your company while I was away. Do you think I welcome these covetous feelings!"

Leeanne couldn't help but note the ring of possessiveness in his voice. Oddly enough, his abrupt change in attitude disconcerted her more than his display of anger had.

"But I didn't do anything with Charles Hamilton," she said.

"Do no' pretend innocence with me."

"I swear, I'm telling you the truth."

His gaze lingering on her lips, Iain exclaimed, "Och, lass. Do you no' realize what you do to me when you look at me with those dazzling eyes? You make me weak at the knees."

The same man who had stood before one hundred and twenty soldiers and virtually single-handedly defied their leader? Never!

Eyes wide, Leeanne could only stare at Iain.

"I'm tempted to compromise you and be done with it in hopes it will cool some of the ardor I feel inside."

He released her arm only to envelop her in an embrace that bordered on cruelty.

"Then why don't you?" Leeanne found herself challenging, wondering how their argument had taken such a contorted turn.

"You've made your feelings concerning the handfasting as clear to me as your penchant for vegetables. I do no' want to jeopardize your chances of leaving the glen after a year and a day."

"What is it with you? What did your first wife *do* to make you so skittish?"

Iain tensed. "You're being presumptuous, lass."

Seeing a combination of guilt and sadness, pain and anger revealed in his eyes, Leeanne suddenly realized what they were all about. She made him feel things against his will, and he didn't like the sensation.

Because she was already in more trouble than she knew how to talk her way out of, Leeanne decided to force the issue.

"Every time your first wife is mentioned, I see myriads of emotion reflected in your eyes. Each time I think we're coming close to something beyond friendship, you back off from me. It's the same way with your gallantry—polite courtesies enable you to distance yourself from me."

"Nay," he denied vehemently.

"Do I frighten you?"

He glared at her.

"I frighten you. Why is that?"

"I've never met a woman who did no' know when to leave well enough alone."

"Until now."

"Aye and aye and aye again!"

Loving Iain despite the differences that time had imposed on them, despite the desperation of their situation, and the uncertainty of their relationship, Leeanne smiled.

In direct response, Iain's demeanor softened slightly.

"Leeanne, do you no' know that a smile to a man is an open invitation?" he said, his anger disintegrating into exasperation.

Her smile broadened. Feeling suddenly impetuous, Leeanne closed the breathing space between them, her mouth finding his.

She could feel his surprise. "Damnation, but you're a challenge, lass!" he said against her lips.

Encircling his neck with her arms, Leeanne asked, "Am I now?" Unable to resist the undeniable electricity between them, her mouth moved tantalizingly upon his. He tasted of mellow red wine and the warmth of desire.

"Och, aye, a fantastic challenge. You exhaust my resolve, sending my self-control to rack and ruin," he groaned.

Leeanne's nipples swelled, growing hard against the fabric of her jumper. She knew Iain noticed. She saw his eyes register shock. And then sheer and undeniable pleasure.

"You aren't kissing me back," she murmured.

"That's as it should be," he countered, desire darkening his eyes. "True Thomas kissed the most beauteous Queen of Elfland and was lost to men's sight," Iain recited.

"For a year and a day?"

"And more."

Leeanne felt powerful; she felt wanton; she felt complete in Iain's arms. "I'm not your legendary Queen of Elfland, Iain. I'm just a plain old flesh-and-blood woman." *An American woman.*

"I'm no' so sure about that, lass. Somehow, you've bewitched me. I thought I would die with want of you while I was away at the manor house near Loch Lomond."

Leeanne knew she should get a hold on herself, but she couldn't. Instead, her lips further enticed his almost-willing mouth, demanding an appropriate reaction.

"Leeanne—" he said, drawing back to look down into her eyes.

"Iain—" she returned, her voice suddenly thready and breathless with anticipation.

"This is no' in your best interest."

"Neither is making you disappear, so you can relax."

Weary with resisting Leeanne's exquisite allure, Iain lowered his head and found her lips. His tongue darted between her teeth as he lifted her, positioning her hips against his.

"Are you no' going to close your eyes, lass?"

She shook her head. "I want to savor your face. It's . . . intoxicating."

He'd abstained so long. Perhaps too long when presented with a woman as incredible as Leeanne, Iain mused. Distancing was impossible at the moment. His need for her overrode his guilt over his first wife. Superseded and surpassed it in a way he'd never dreamed possible. Enchanted, his will was as nothing in the face of her blatant sensuality. She absorbed his every waking hour; she invaded his dreams at night, slowly breaking down the barrier of old guilt that stood between them.

In fact, making her his wife had become his most fervent of dreams.

Unconsciously, Iain hugged Leeanne closer. The intimate contact left her in no doubt as to the extent of his arousal.

Her pulse quickening gloriously, Leeanne marveled at how easily Iain had evoked a complementary passion within her. She'd fully intended to confess the truth, the whole truth, and nothing but the truth about herself before anything physical happened between them— that as outlandish as it sounded, she was a time-traveler from twentieth-century America.

Now, senses heightened, she couldn't think coherently enough to explain. She couldn't wonder. All she could do was feel a semisweet desire beat relentlessly at the heart of her being.

She loved Iain MacBride, and for the present that was enough to justify what they were about to do, Leeanne thought as she tugged his shirttail from the waistband of his kilt. Not only was their platonic pact a farce, it had been a bone of contention between them long enough.

They exchanged no words of love, but their bodies spoke of a universal need to be close, to love and be loved.

Iain brushed her cape from her shoulders. With a soft swish, it fell to the floor at her feet. Bending slightly, he pressed a hungry kiss to the tender exposed column of her throat just above her plaid. She arched her neck to accommodate him, stopping him only when she felt his fingers at the ivory *dealg* pin that held her plaid together.

"Stop, Iain."

He paused.

"Now, lass?" he rasped. "How can you ask that of me?"

"I didn't mean it the way it sounded. I meant, turn your back while I undress."

He took her request for an exhibition of shyness and she let him. In reality, she wasn't ready to reveal her contemporary clothing, most particularly her stretchy leotard and neon pink save-the-whales T-shirt. They could only result in more questions, and questions were the last thing on her agenda, Leeanne thought.

She stripped out of her things, neatly folding them and placing them in Iain's strongbox along with her gift. Diving into the four-poster bed, she scrambled beneath the mountain of skins and coverlets, sighing at their coziness.

"Lass?"

"Do I detect a note of impatience lurking in your voice, Iain MacBride?"

"Now that you ask, I'm fair bursting with it, lass."

Leeanne smiled to herself. For her, Iain's honesty was a unique portion of his charm.

"You can turn around now. I'm ready."

Iain slowly turned.

His gaze leisurely scanned the dark cascade of curls falling in waves about her bare shoulder, then her face. "Are you now?" he asked, his gaze dropping as he surveyed the covers clutched to her breast.

"Yes."

"No second thoughts?"

"Not a single, solitary one," she told him decisively.

"That's just as well. I fear I've gone well beyond stopping for second thoughts. Yours or mine."

Allowing the covers to fall to her waist, Leeanne opened her arms to Iain. "Ditto."

For the space of a heartbeat, Iain stood stone still, staring with acute admiration at her high, perfectly rounded breasts.

And then, as if fearful she might vanish, he strode to the fireplace. Lifting the armchair, he crossed the room to prop it against the door.

"This is one night I do no' care to deal with any uninvited guests," he said, hastily discarding his shirt. His boots and stockings followed. He concluded the unintentional strip-tease by adding his black-and-white kilt to the growing pile on the floor.

"So that's what a true Highlander wears beneath his kilt. I've always wondered," Leeanne said with a mischievous smile on her lips.

"Do you find it humorous?" he asked, a wicked twinkle in his eye as he removed his close-cut tartan trews to display his naked magnificence.

"Hardly," she said, staring without self-consciousness at him.

"Aye and aye again. That too is as it should be."

Iain slipped beneath the covers, pressing his heated "hardly" against Leeanne's thigh.

"All teasing aside, be forewarned that it's serious business we're about, lass." His tone was gentle and grave, full of consideration for her and the magnitude of the step they were taking. "I can no' promise you there will be no issue," he said, running a caressing finger down the tender flesh of her inner arm.

Leeanne silenced Iain with a moist kiss on the lips.

She had no intention of agonizing over her decision to share her body with him. She was a grown woman. She knew what she was doing. And she knew the consequences. She also knew she was deeply and irrevocably in love with the man and that their sexual bonding was healthy, and natural, and beautiful.

Iain responded by entwining his strong fingers in her hair and bending to press a potent kiss between her breasts. His eyelashes, like butterfly wings, brushed at her nipple, sending delicious sensory impulses coursing down toward the juncture of her thighs.

Iain inhaled deeply, exhaling on a sigh.

"You smell wonderful, lass."

"So do you."

He chuckled at her compliment. "I smell like a man."

"That's what I mean."

283

"You're delightful, lass."

"So are you."

"I take that to mean you think we make an incredible couple."

"More so than you realize."

"I'm thinking that's enough talk, lass. We have all the time in the world for that—afterwards."

I sincerely hope so, Leeanne thought, surprising herself. Less and less her thoughts turned to her own world while more and more she became involved in Iain's.

Where would it all end?

She knew the answer to that, at least as far as tonight was concerned, Leeanne decided as, with more of a sucking motion than a bite, Iain nibbled his way from the sensitive area just behind her ear down the column of her throat to her collarbone. He continued in a merciless path, zigzagging across her breasts to tease each rose-colored tip before proceeding to her navel, where he laved the indentation with his tongue.

"Are you teasing me, Iain?"

He glanced up, passion smoldering in the blue depths of his expressive eyes. "It's tempting you that I'm doing, lass."

"That's for sure," she said, tracing feather-light circles across the broad expanse of his shoulders, marveling that his muscles could be so firm and yet the skin encasing them feel so silky.

"I'm helping to prepare you for—"

"I'm more than prepared," Leeanne advised him in a breathless rush. Following an overpowering desire, she boldly shifted to her knees, forcing Iain flat on his back. Sliding low, she straddled his hips. Logic, along with sensibility and any feigned attempt at emotional detachment, took a flying leap out the window as Leeanne slowly eased herself onto the long length of him.

He rasped something in Gaelic which Leeanne decided must be a charm for spontaneous combustion, because all of a sudden her soul burst into flames. She couldn't think. She couldn't wonder. All she could do was feel. And feel. And *feel*.

"Ach, lass . . . speak of impatience!" Iain said with a sharp exhalation of breath. Rolling, he pinned her to the bed with his muscular body, finishing in a series of steady thrusts what she had started.

Their joining was fierce, wild, primitive. And right. Oh so incredibly right, Leeanne thought as, dehydrated and thirsting, she plunged into a liquid pool of fulfillment.

Long after Iain fell into sated sleep, his dark blond head nestled on her rib cage just below her breasts, his hand across her abdomen, Leeanne remained awake, thinking about all sorts of things. Comparing the similarities between agony and ecstasy. Marveling that in deference to her and the Highland code of handfasting, Iain had practiced the oldest form of birth control known to man. And lastly, and the longest, about the implications of soldiers in Glencoe.

With her fingers entwined in Iain's damp locks, it was after midnight before Leeanne joined him in slumber, Robert Campbell's potential for duplicity against those she loved foremost on her mind.

Chapter Fourteen

Iain awoke all at once. At least his body awoke. It was a moment before he could get his eyes to function. They felt as if lead coins weighed them down. He squinted, eyeing the empty wine bottle. His mouth tasted as if he'd eaten a fistful of unbleached lamb's wool, but his head was clear and his arms full—full of more woman than a man dared hope for in a wife.

Back pressed to his chest, rump against his loins, Leeanne slept soundly. For a moment, Iain considered waking her with a kiss and then proceeding from there. But he could see by the light filtering between the door and its frame that dawn was fast approaching. The hunting party would not be far behind the sun.

Iain reluctantly disengaged himself.

"Iain?" Leeanne asked in a sleepy voice without opening her eyes.

"It's all right, lass. Sleep on a wee while longer. I'll wake you when the tea is boiling hot."

"Sounds like a winner to me," she muttered, scrunching into a ball beneath the covers to compensate for the loss of his body heat.

Arranging the deerskin and woolen coverlets more closely about Leeanne's slender figure, Iain slid to the side of the four-poster and rose. Goose bumps blanketed his skin as he moved to stoke the peat fire into a friendly blaze of warmth. He scrubbed his face with water from the basin on the hearth, glancing at his clothes piled on the floor by the bed. No longer, in good conscience, could he wear the black-and-white tartan, Iain told himself. Rummaging through the heap, he shrugged into his trews and shirt, retrieving the kilt to roll it into a tight checkered bolt of cloth.

Quietly he crossed to his strongbox, easing open the lid. On top of his personal items rested Leeanne's. He reached to shift her clothing aside only to have his attention arrested by a sleeve peeping from the center of the neatly folded stack. He'd never seen so bright a color! Come to think on it, he'd never seen that particular color at all.

Glancing at the softly snoring form asleep in his bed, he shifted aside the jumper to better view the short-sleeved, collarless shirt. Odd, he thought, tracing the raised letters with his fingertips. He'd never seen anything like those either. It took a moment, but he finally deciphered the words.

"Save the whales?" he asked himself in a low voice, a frown creasing his forehead as he rubbed the supple material between his fingers, studying the precise stitches hemming the sleeve. What must possess a person to scrawl writing upon their clothing? It reminded him of one of the many stories Leeanne had recounted at the *ceilidh*—namely, *The Scarlet Letter*.

Leeanne said something in her sleep, and Iain hastily buried the shirt between her gown and undergarments, removing the Highland green and rust-colored kilt he'd retrieved from Loch Lomond. Placing the black-and-white kilt inside the strongbox, he refastened the lid.

With nimble fingers, he pleated the patterned, knee-length tartan, belting it about his waist, pondering whether or not Leeanne had woven the wondrous material for the shirt herself and if so, what she'd used to dye it.

Still marveling at the shirt, he made the tea, then turned toward the bed once again.

"It's time to rouse yourself, lass. The hunting party will be arriving at any moment."

Leeanne made a face and snuggled more

deeply beneath the skins, covering her head. "Five more minutes."

Her words were muffled, but Iain understood them perfectly.

"Nay, no' one more minute unless you want to take the chance of Alasdair catching us abed together."

Iain moved to sit on the side of the bed.

Leeanne uncovered her head, smiling up at him. "But you're already dressed."

"Aye. But no' for long if you continue as you are—tempting me to forget the hunt and come back beneath the bedding with you."

"Why don't you?" she asked in a seductive voice.

Their eyes met, and with a wistful smile, Iain growled, "You're an insatiable wench."

"When I find something I like, I hang on with all fours. It's one of my many character flaws."

As if he could no longer keep his hands from her, Iain playfully tweaked her nose. "To my way of thinking, it's no' a flaw."

"Is that a leer I see on your face, Iain MacBride?" Leeanne asked, a grin spreading across her lips.

Iain chuckled.

"Aye and aye. There's nothing I'd like better than to join you on all fours, but you know I can no'. I've given my word. Alasdair will be counting on me."

"I understand," Leeanne said, meaning it.

There had been a time when she might have looked upon Iain's stance as something other than what it was—incredible strength of character.

"Do you now?"

Her grin relaxed. "I think so . . . at least I'm learning to. It must be that some of your Scottish cultural values are beginning to seep into this lowly *sassenach.*"

He did not respond verbally, though Leeanne sensed his teasing mood at an end. Instead, Iain reached out once again to touch her, this time stroking her hair, her cheek, the curve of her chin, as if memorizing her features by heart.

"I want to thank you for last evening," he said finally, pressing a moist kiss in the hollow of her palm and sending a responsive tingle spiraling through her body.

When he released her hand, Leeanne cupped it to her heart, longing to tell Iain that last night had happened because she loved him. That she didn't want to and yet did, deeply and irrevocably. In her wildest dreams, she'd never imagined she'd find someone like him— someone who complemented her as he did. Through him, she'd experienced the sense of fulfillment lacking in her past relationships. Others had fallen by the wayside, and she'd never really known why she'd allowed them to. Why she didn't return their calls. Why she worked through dinner five nights out of six.

Why she stopped seeing them the moment they proposed.

Now she did.

Her life, though she hadn't realized it, had been marred by a missing puzzle piece—and that intricate piece was Iain. No other piece fit. Others had looked as if they might, but only he properly completed the picture.

Leeanne opened her mouth to pour her heart out to Iain when a knock on the door stopped her.

"Leeanne? Iain? Parlan didn't want to leave me alone and he didn't want to miss the hunt, so he's packed me up for a visit." They heard a muffled exchange, then Sesi's voice complaining, "I can't open the door, Parlan! It's secured from inside."

An ineffectual kick to the door followed.

"Wake up, Iain, 'tis as chilly oot here as your sister is o' an early morning!" Parlan complained loudly.

"Sounds like Sesi's in rare form," Leeanne said, scrambling toward the strongbox.

"Aye, she's never had a fondness for starting the day at dawn," Iain confirmed with a soft laugh. "I'll detain her outside for a wee breath while you make yourself presentable, though personally I prefer you as bare as the day you were born."

The teasing note in his voice was unmistakable. So was the appreciation shining in his eyes.

"Your birthday suit isn't so bad either," Leeanne said, a matching twinkle lurking in her eyes.

"Birthday suit is it now? You certainly have an intriguing way with words, lass," Iain said in parting.

When the door closed behind him, Leeanne sprang for the strongbox, dressing hastily and running her fingers through her rampant curls. A short time later, Iain stuck his head inside the door.

"Presentable?"

"Yep."

He ushered Sesi inside, placing the spinning wheel and bag of wool she'd brought by the hearth.

"What's this?" Leeanne asked, giving the wheel a twirl.

"I've brought my work with me," Sesi stated. "I thought since Parlan would not leave me alone to do my household chores, perhaps you could card while I spin."

"A woman's work is never done," Leeanne commented.

"Nay. Parlan needs a new shirt, and I dare say Iain could use one as well."

Leeanne could just visualize Iain MacBride in a shirt she'd made from scratch. The Macdonald men would laugh him out of the glen.

The image of Iain being put at a disadvantage because of her made her cringe. Sobering,

293

Leeanne asked herself, beyond the heavenly sex they shared, what kind of a wife could she hope to make for the Highlander? She knew how to balance a checkbook, how to check the oil in her car and the air in her tires, how to hook up an answering machine, to type on a computer, to dial long-distance, and read a road map. She could direct a dance company and make her own living, phone for in-home pizza delivery, and pass a driver's license test. But she wasn't much of a homemaker. She couldn't cook, spin, weave, or sew. She didn't want to spend her morning milking cows and cleaning house. And she knew little or nothing of seventeenth-century Scottish etiquette.

As a matter of fact, she could picture Iain functioning much more readily in her world than she did in his.

"The others are here," Iain said, rescuing Leeanne from her troubled thoughts. "I'll be going now, lass. Take care of Sesi and my wee niece and don't forget the tatties-an-neeps."

Leeanne tripped to the door. "I won't. Will you be away all day?"

"That's difficult to say. If I do no' see you before gloaming, you may count on tomorrow afternoon for certain. I've left the teapot warming on the hearth for you. . . ."

He winked at her, then surprised her by bending down to press a brief kiss on her lips before closing her in the cottage with his sister.

"Well now. I have a feeling things are looking

up between you and Iain."

"If you expect details, you can forget it," Leeanne said with a complacent smile.

"I don't need the details. I can see the way of things for myself. Iain has discarded his widower's tartan, declaring to the world he is no longer in mourning."

Leeanne felt as if the wind had been knocked from her. So that was what he'd meant when he had pointed out the bars and stripes of his kilt! He'd been speaking of the color of the sett. Of what it proclaimed.

"You need not tell me he hasn't explained about his first wife. I can see plainly enough I've spoken out of turn again," Sesi said, placing Elizabeth on the bed. She wore a *curraichd* of linen on her head. Unfastening the scarflike square from beneath her chin, she shook out her fair hair, leaning to kiss the baby's cheek. "Your mother has a way of doing that," she said to the cooing infant. "It's the nastiest of habits and something I'm determined you'll not acquire through watching me, little one."

Next, Sesi unbundled the baby, checking her diaper.

"Still dry," she said with satisfaction.

"Why all the mystery, Sesi? Why don't you just go ahead and recount the story of Iain's first wife? Get it all out in the open," Leeanne asked.

"Oh, I couldn't do that!" Sesi said over her shoulder.

"Wait a second. Don't tell me. Let me guess. It's Iain's place to tell me about her. Right?"

"That's correct. I fear he would disown me if I did the recounting for him."

Leeanne came to stand behind Sesi, peering down at Elizabeth over her mother's shoulder.

"Bethy, don't you dare follow in your mother's footsteps," Leanne said, "It's dangerous. I don't know how she made it this far without someone near and dear strangling her."

Sesi chuckled. "And never, never listen to your Aunt Leeanne. She's far too full of herself."

"Aunt Leeanne?"

Sesi scooped up the baby and deposited her in Leeanne's arms.

"Now what else would she call you if not Aunt?"

Leeanne gazed down at Elizabeth.

"I don't know. I guess I hadn't thought about it."

Would she still be in Glencoe when Elizabeth was old enough to talk? Leeanne wondered. What of her career? The friends back home in North Carolina who must be worried about her by now? Prior commitments?

She couldn't think about all that right now, Leeanne decided, rocking Elizabeth in her arms. She'd be like the famous Miss Scarlett O'Hara. She'd think about it later. Later would be much better.

"I've never seen such a pretty little girl. And I can't believe how much she's grown."

"My milk agrees with her," Sesi stated. "I'm proud to say she's a strong and robust child."

Elizabeth grabbed Leeanne's finger, wrapping her tiny hand around it. "You can say that again," Leeanne commented.

"By the by, I brought some *gruitheam* to break the fast. If you'd like some, I'd be happy to share."

"Gruitheam?"

"A butter and curd mixture. You haven't eaten, have you?"

"Maybe later," Leeanne said, thinking that the Highland diet certainly lacked the variety she was accustomed to. The tatties-an-neeps were sounding more and more inviting, though what she would really like was a quart of cranberry juice and a bowl of navel oranges.

Leeanne dug into her jumper pocket, extracting the gift Iain had given her. She handed it to Sesi.

"How about pouring us some tea and add a pinch of cinnamon to each cup?"

Sesi carefully examined the compact. "Iain gave you this?" she asked.

"Yes, I hope you don't mind," Leeanne said quickly.

"Nay. I'm happy for you. You've accomplished all I could have asked for and more."

"I'm not sure I understand what you're talking about."

Sesi pursed her lips together, glancing down at the floor a moment before answering. "You realize that I know you're not a teacher from that school in England where Iain sent me to learn the ways of a proper lady, don't you?"

"I suspected as much."

"Nor Parlan's ex-mistress either. She was reputed to be beautiful, and you certainly are that. But she was fair-haired, and I knew it."

"So why did you go along with the deception? I saw you glance up from the receiving line at the wedding. I have a funny feeling you could have stopped this whole thing before it got started."

For once, Sesi was choosing her words carefully. "Because, Leeanne of Green Gables, the how and why of your coming to Glencoe does not matter to me. You're a prayer answered and that's enough for me to know."

"I'm still not quite sure I understand."

"My brother was lost before you came here. You found him and brought him back to the land of the living."

"Oh, I don't know about—"

"But I do," Sesi interrupted. "You have no idea how I've despaired over him these past two years," she said firmly, handing Leeanne a mug filled with tea.

Leeanne took a sip, savoring the spicy flavor.

"You make a much better cup of tea than Iain," she commented.

"I doubt he would care to hear you say that."

"Iain has other attributes that I admire much

more than his way with tea."

Sesi smiled a knowing smile. "So does Parlan."

They passed the remainder of the morning in girl talk, something Leeanne hadn't done since her mother's death. Sesi taught Leeanne to card wool as they talked.

After cleaning and disentangling fibers from half the bag that Sesi had brought with her, Leeanne was more than ready for a break from the tedious job.

"I think I'll go on over to the main house and see about our lunch," Leeanne said, setting aside a thick square of leather spiked with bent wire teeth. She reached to collect her cloak from the peg near the door.

Sesi rose from her stool by the spinning wheel, stretching and massaging her lower back muscles.

"Now that's an idea," Sesi said. "I could use a brisk walk myself, and Elizabeth is sound asleep in her nest upon the bed. She won't be waking to nurse for at least another hour."

"You think she'll be all right alone?"

"She's too small to move to the edge of that big four-poster. Besides, I'm certain she'll be fine. I can see the cottage from the main house. And we won't be away long."

Leeanne nodded.

In companionable silence, they headed for the main house, traveling on foot through the unearthly mist that was so often synonymous with the Highlands. Outside the entrance, Leeanne reached up to knock. Sesi stopped her with a shake of her head.

"There's no need for that. Alasdair's wife is expecting you," Sesi said.

Leeanne eased open the door, glad after a moment that she hadn't knocked for she could hear voices—familiar voices, deep in heated discussion. The curtain partitioning off the stage's dressing room was still in place, concealing a good portion of the great hall from view. And concealing Leeanne from the view of those in the great hall.

Leeanne threw up her arm to prevent Sesi from brushing aside the curtain, placing her finger on her lips and pointing to her ear.

"Listen," she mouthed, determined to eavesdrop on the conversation.

"It's a good thing the laird's wife was called away to attend a sick child. Otherwise, she would have been here when the messenger arrived from Fort William with Major Duncanson's instructions," Robert Campbell was saying.

"But we've been here almost a fortnight!" Charles Hamilton argued. "The Macdonalds have been nothing but hospitable to one and all. They've billeted us in their homes, for God's sake! How can the major command this of us?"

"We are not expected to accomplish it alone.

300

The missive plainly states that Lieutenant-Colonel Hamilton will be bringing in reinforcements at five o'clock on the morning of the thirteenth. He is to arrive across the Devil's Staircase, and you, sir, will light the fire on Signal Rock to rally our troops."

"I'll not be a part of this! I would rather resign my commission than be associated with so foul a deed!" Charles hissed.

Robert Campbell glanced around, and Leeanne and Sesi retreated more deeply into the shadows behind the curtain.

"Keep your voice down, man!" Campbell shoved his chair away from the chess board, the legs scraping on the slate floor like fingernails on a chalk board. "Would you oppose your King over a sept of thieves?"

"This is nothing more than a letter of fire and sword, concocted, I dare say, by ambitious politicians!"

"You cannot deny the old fox deserves the reward he shall reap."

"But all those under seventy do not. Where is your sense of morality, Captain Campbell?"

"You have no choice in the matter! The orders come from far above our heads. And I'll be thanking you not to relay any of this to that MacBride woman, upon pain of my displeasure. Understood?"

Suddenly pale and hugging her stomach, Sesi slipped quietly back outside. Leeanne quickly followed.

Halfway to the cottage, Leeanne caught up with her. "Are you okay?" she asked.

"I think I'm going to be sick," Sesi replied.

"Well, don't do it out here! If we delay, they might see us. Here, let me help you to the cottage where you can stretch out on the bed," Leeanne said, taking Sesi's arm.

"If I had not heard it with my own ears, I would never have believed it, Leeanne. Do you realize what the English have done? They've supped with Alasdair. He's given them the protection of bread and salt. And yet they've invoked the letter of fire and sword against the Macdonald clan."

"What does that mean—fire and sword?"

Sesi turned her stricken gaze toward Leeanne. "Nothing less than murdering us all." Tears welled in her delicate blue eyes.

Appalled, Leeanne murmured to herself, "I knew it was something terrible!"

Once inside the cottage, Leeanne found she couldn't sit still. She paced the floor, wondering what, if anything, she could do to stop the soldiers. Pondering how to best protect the Macdonalds. It hardly crossed her mind that she too was in danger.

Leeanne glanced at Sesi, arms flung over her eyes, prostrate upon the bed beside sleeping baby Elizabeth.

First things first, Leeanne told herself, halting by the side of the bed she'd so recently shared with Iain.

"Sesi, we've got to get you and the baby out of here."

"What?" Sesi stuttered. "Would it not be better to warn the clanspeople?"

"I've already considered that. But you're thinking like a woman, Sesi, not like a man. The laws of Highland hospitality require that Alasdair be informed of the letter of fire and sword before anyone else. Besides, most of the stronger men, like Iain and Parlan, are away on the hunt. If we alert the others, it might produce an adverse affect. I think we're much better off to wait until the hunting party returns. From what Robert Campbell said, we have today and tomorrow before all hell breaks loose around here."

Sesi sat up on the bed. "You're probably correct in thinking that Alasdair must be informed first."

"I know I am. In the meantime, I think it would be a good idea if I saw you and the baby to Achtriochtan."

Sesi frowned in confusion. "Why Achtriochtan?"

"Because you'll be that much closer to Meall Mor and the northern entrance to the glen." Leeanne eyed Sesi's clothes as she would a potential stage costume. Dressed in a long woolen garment of tartan that reached from her neck to her ankles and fastened at the breast with a large brooch, Sesi should be warm enough, Leeanne decided.

"As soon as you're settled in, I'll return to the cottage and await Iain's arrival."

"But what of Parlan?"

Leeanne had learned a lot about the Scottish code of honor from Iain. Now in an attempt to manipulate Sesi, she played on that knowledge in conjunction with Sesi's maternal instinct. What she didn't tell Sesi was that she was hoping she could talk Mangus into seeing her on to the manor house near Loch Lomond and well out of harm's way.

"Right now, you have to put Elizabeth's welfare above everything else. It's your duty as a parent to see her to safety."

"But—"

Iain's absence proving a catalyst for her need to do something, Leeanne said sternly, "Parlan can catch up with you later."

"I suppose."

"I know so."

A faraway expression in her eyes, Sesi asked, "Did Iain tell you that I saw my mother and father killed by soldiers? It was a terrifying ordeal. I still have nightmares about it."

"Iain told me that you rarely talk about it," Leeanne said, sympathy evident in her voice.

A single tear rolled down Sesi's cheek. She dashed it away with the back of her hand. "I'll not have my baby's life tainted by senseless violence."

"Of course not. And that's why you're going to Achtriochtan." Leeanne took Sesi's hand and pulled her to her feet. "You bundle the baby up good and warm and I'll saddle the pony."

"It's fortunate that Iain left your mount."

"It's a good thing Parlan brought you here to spend the day with me," Leeanne said.

"I wish Parlan could read so I might leave him a note of explanation."

Leeanne could understand the sentiment. She'd like to leave Iain a note as well.

"I never thought I'd say this, but it's best that he doesn't. Someone else might find the note before I get back, and then the cat would be out of the bag long before we'd like it to be."

There were several things Leeanne hadn't counted on when she'd considered traveling to Achtriochtan—Sesi's need to stop and rest every half hour, and three-quarters of the way to the bards' croft, the appearance of predators.

From her research, Leeanne knew that the Highland light played tricks of color on the eye, but she wasn't depending only on her sense of sight. The first indication she had that they were being stalked was a rustling in the dark clumps of brush that lined the wayside. The second was the way the pony shied, rolling its eyes and shaking its head as she attempted to guide it up the rough hill road. The third was the musty odor borne to her on the breeze.

Hoping to make Achtriochtan without frightening Sesi, Leeanne tightened her hold on the reins, kicking the pony into a gallop. In the movies, people always headed for water to throw dogs off their scent. Leeanne decided it was worth a try.

They splashed down the bank of a rushing burn and up the other side.

"Leeanne?" Sesi asked in surprise. "The poor beast is doing its best, considering the double weight on its back. It's foaming at the mouth as it is."

Cold, yet perspiring, Leeanne snapped rather more gruffly than she'd intended, "Keep it down, Sesi!" The closest she'd ever come to wolves was the Columbia Zoo in South Carolina. And she wanted to keep it that way.

Fate saw it otherwise.

Because the pony was becoming increasingly skittish, Leeanne decided to dismount and walk beside its head.

"What are you doing now?" Sesi asked in dismay.

"I'm not accustomed to riding a horse. My rear end hurts. I'm going to walk for a while," Leeanne replied, attempting to keep her voice at a normal pitch.

Before she could grasp its halter, the pony balked, shying and wrenching the reins from Leeanne's hands. Alarmed, Sesi slipped to the ground and stepped away from the animal.

"Something is frightening her," Sesi gasped from the sidelines.

"I know it," Leeanne replied, attempting to restrain the mare. Before she could recapture the reins, the mare swiveled on its haunches, careening across the burn and back down the path in the general direction of home. Leeanne raced after it for a short distance, stopping at the water and throwing up her hands in disgust.

"Damn! Damn! Dammit!"

"What do we do now?" Sesi called, gazing after the rapidly receding pony.

Leeanne turned and retraced her steps. "We walk," she said. "It's not that much farther."

Leeanne assumed that the wolves would reject crossing the water and go after the pony, and that the mare was what they'd been interested in anyway. It was only moments before she realized she was caught in a comedy of errors. Only in this instance, there was nothing to laugh at. She hadn't actually spotted the wolves in the flesh, but she still sensed their foreboding presence. Lurking across the water. Watching. Waiting.

"Here, let me carry the baby for a while," she said, thinking that if they could make it to the shelter of the trees just ahead, they could perhaps lose the wolves.

Sesi relinquished the baby, glancing over her shoulder and into the underbrush.

"They hunt in packs, you know," she said solemnly.

So Sesi had figured it out.

Only too well, Leeanne could visualize the wolves with their cool topaz eyes. Hear the growl of their empty stomachs. Feel the gleaming, saw-edged sharpness of their carnassial teeth ripping at her flesh.

In her world, the wolf was an endangered species. She should be thinking of how to better protect them. All she could think of now was how to destroy one should it choose to show itself and attack.

A guttural growl fractured the stillness of late afternoon, and Leeanne imagined gray shadows converging on them.

"They must have crossed the burn," Leeanne said, trying to stave off terror.

"I'm afraid so. Their voices don't carry far," Sesi advised.

"I didn't think they hunted in broad daylight."

"They're hungry in winter. It makes them bold."

"You'd think that they would be more interested in the pony," Leeanne said.

"I fear they smell Elizabeth, and she doesn't have hooves to rend and bruise," Sesi said in a strained voice.

Nerves jangling, Leeanne hugged the baby more closely to her breast. Boy, she'd really put her foot into it this time with her bright ideas! She'd gotten them into this mess and it was up to her to get them out, because if anything happened to Sesi and Elizabeth, it would be on her conscience for the remainder of her life.

"Well, they won't get the baby! Or you either. Not unless they can fly," Leeanne stated, her gaze directed toward the treetops.

They'd reached the forest, and though the trees weren't tall, they offered a refuge from the wolves. The only problem was that the limbs were too far from the ground to reach without some sort of ladder.

No matter, Leeanne decided, making a snap decision.

Stopping at the base of the tallest evergreen in the copse, Leeanne momentarily returned a blissfully sleeping baby to her mother.

"Where I come from, there are animals called opossums. They're marsupials and they have an ingenious way of carrying their babies—in a pouch."

Yanking her plaid from beneath her cloak, she fashioned a carrier from the rectangle of cloth. Then, tying the hammocklike pack in a tight knot around her amazed friend's neck, she slipped Elizabeth into the deep folds of material and secured it with Iain's *dealg* pin.

Finally, Leanne cupped her hands like a sling in front of Sesi, ordering, "Now, play the opossum and climb, Sesi, climb!"

"But you can't remain on the grou—"

"Don't you hear them? They're right on our heels. We don't have time to argue," Leeanne hissed through gritted teeth. "This isn't the time for a display of your renowned stubborn streak! I said climb, dammit, and by heaven, I mean it! Don't make me pick you up and throw you up there." Leeanne grabbed Sesi by the collar of her cloak and directed her toward the tree as if she could really accomplish the feat she threatened.

Still, Sesi hesitated, eyes wide, mouth agape.

"I'm sorry, Sesi," Leeanne said, her voice softening to a whisper as she released Sesi's cloak. "I don't know what got into me. I'm a staunch advocate of nonviolence . . . was a staunch advocate. I've never manhandled anyone before in my life."

"You've been taking lessons from my brother, and he has always told me that desperate situations call for desperate measures," Sesi said with a wry smile.

At the mention of Iain, Leeanne cringed. "Please, Sesi. Do this for me," she said, a sense of urgency bordering on panic tingeing her voice. "Can't you see that Iain would never forgive me if anything happened to you and the baby? And there's no way I could live with myself afterwards."

With a quick peck on the cheek, Sesi relented, placing her foot in the sling that Leeanne fashioned with her hands.

"On three, reach for the limb and pull yourself up. Ready, set. One, two, three. Up . . . you . . . go. Reach!"

The tree swayed slightly, as if a breeze had passed through its boughs.

"I've got it!" Sesi said as her weight lifted

from Leeanne's hands, and she scrambled up into the tree, perching like a sparrow on a sturdy limb.

"We'll be all right," Leeanne assured her, though they both knew it wasn't true. Two of them might survive, snug in the tree. The third . . .

"Leeanne, this isn't your fault. I want you to remember that I came with you willingly. I would rather face a hundred beasts in the forest than remain in Glencoe and be slaughtered by Argyll's regiment. That's the honest truth."

"I appreciate that," Leeanne said in a low voice, squinting to stare out through the trees. "Now, no more talking. We don't want to give away our location too easily."

As if it mattered, Leeanne thought.

She could detect the sound of feet padding through bracken where the evergreens sheltered the forest floor from the snow. Stealthy. Menacing. Determined. Headed directly for them. Despite herself, she imagined the wolves working together like a team of trained bloodhounds hot on a scent.

Stay cool, Leeanne advised herself, searching for and discovering a fallen limb. Adopting the same arrogant attitude she'd seen Iain use against the soldiers when they had arrived in the glen, Leeanne braced her legs wide apart. Holding the club like an all-star batter, she waited.

She didn't have long to twiddle her thumbs.

The trio broke through the trees into the copse, then braked, posing like iron statues as they sized up their victims. Leeanne supposed the sight of a human waving a tree limb threw them off kilter.

But only momentarily.

The obvious leader, a muscular wolf with back bristling, advanced steadily into the copse.

Nose wrinkled over bared yellow-white teeth, the wolf licked its lips, pausing once again to study her with eyes that seemed far too intelligent for a wild animal.

Leeanne moistened her lips as well, wondering if werewolves existed outside the movies. Because if they did, this one with its black face and shaggy silver coat was a prime candidate.

Mastering the turbulence within her, Leeanne warned, "Look here, mister, if you think you're dealing with Little Red Riding Hood, you're sadly mistaken." She brandished the makeshift club threateningly, determined not to disgrace herself.

Snarling, the wolf backtracked a step, though Leeanne decided it was more her voice than the club that gave the wolf pause. She assumed that like most wild things it avoided man whenever possible. Then again, it was winter, and with food scarce, she doubted the pack could overlook even the slightest chance at a square meal.

For a good ten minutes, Leeanne managed a great imitation of a Mexican standoff, thanks to the fear-enhanced adrenaline coursing through her system. But then the wolves grew aggressive, edging further into the copse despite the increasing volume of her voice and the ever-present threat of her club.

Sesi leaned down from the tree. "Here, Leeanne," she said somewhat frantically. "Take my hand. Perhaps I can lift you up with me."

Leeanne spared a moment to glare up at Sesi. "Stop wiggling. Do you want to fall out of the tree on your head? I'm fine right where I am!"

Leeanne wished she felt as brave as she sounded. She marveled that she sounded as brave as she did. Her voice was as steady as a rock while her legs trembled like jelly. She'd never realized what a good actress she was. When she got too old to dance, she just might have to investigate an alternative career on stage.

"I put you up there and you're going to stay up there until morning if you have to." They'll take off eventually, after they've indulged in a bite or two of something, Leeanne thought to herself, shivering. Swallowing the knot of fear lodged in her throat, she pressed on. "Do you hear me? No matter what happens. Promise me you'll do as I say, Sesi."

Sesi shook her head, refusing to commit herself.

"I want your word of honor on it, Sesi," Leeanne insisted. When that didn't work, she instituted Iain's favorite technique to tip the scales in her favor. "Remember, it's your duty to protect Elizabeth. You couldn't come down if you wanted to—the baby's welfare is more important than anything else. Remember that. Once this is over and done with, you should be able to make Achtriochtan on foot."

As if she knew she was the main topic of conversation, Elizabeth began whimpering.

Finally, in a defeated whisper, Sesi said, "You have my word of honor, though I don't have to like this."

Elizabeth's whimper escalated into a full-blown cry; it was feeding time.

"No, you don't have to like it . . . only to see it through," Leeanne said. *Just as I do.*

The baby's voice brought Leeanne's reprieve to an abrupt end. Approaching in a semicircle, the wolves seemed done with waiting.

"Our Father, Who art in heaven—" Leeanne began in a husky whisper.

Chapter Fifteen

Iain could see Leeanne through the fading amber light, her sable hair falling in a wild tangle about her shoulders, her teeth clenched as she lifted her makeshift club and dealt the wolf a magnificent blow to the nose. With a yelp of pain, the animal staggered backward several feet, rubbing its snout with a front paw. Like water flowing around a rock in the bed of a burn, his accomplices skirted their leader, intent on moving in for the kill.

Iain glanced over Leeanne's head, into the tree top. Sesi was safe enough. Leeanne on the other hand was fully exposed.

Sheer desperation reinforced by anger drove Iain the last few yards into the copse. With an unearthly yell that had caused many a man to tuck tail and run, Iain drew his broadsword and launched himself between Leeanne and the wolves. Startled by the appearance of a seasoned warrior, the beasts scattered only to regroup at the edge of the copse.

Iain realized that killing the wolves was a last resort. The smell of blood would only send them into a frenzy, and he couldn't deal with more than one at a time. No, it was best to simply show them that man was the master of his domain.

"Come, you silver devils. Come if you dare, though I warn you that all you'll taste this day is the cold blade of my claymore," Iain taunted, slicing the air with his broadsword. The winter rays of the late afternoon sun glinted off the blade, mirroring the light and disorienting the leader of the pack, while his voice, strong and sure, echoed through the trees as if he were an army instead of a single man.

In answer to his challenge, the wolves backed away, one by one disappearing into the shadowed forest.

"You spooked them," Leeanne said, her voice trembling with relief. She didn't know where she'd gotten the courage to fend off the wolves. Knees weak, she sagged against the rough bark of the tree, dropping the limb from her nerveless fingers.

Resheathing his sword, Iain turned on her, gripping her shoulders with every intention of shaking her teeth until they rattled. Gathering her into his arms and crushing her against his chest instead, he said, "That was my intention."

"You spooked me too," she accused. Her words were muffled against the fleece of his jacket, but he heard and responded.

"Did I now? Well, I'm glad to hear it. You need a good spooking. Or perhaps the correct term would be *spanking*." His tortured expression seemed oddly mismatched with his vehement words.

"I don't need a spooking or a spanking, thank you very much. And where did you learn to scream like that?"

"It's no' a scream. It's the Macdonald battle cry, lass. It's meant to strike fear into the stoutest of hearts."

"Well, it works." Leeanne could still feel her heart pounding like a jackhammer against the wall of her breast. She had no doubt Iain could feel it too, through her cloak and his jacket.

"You think so?" His voice was low, his azure eyes tinted with the concern that his anger had previously camouflaged.

"They left, didn't they?"

"Aye, but only because our strategy prevailed," he said savagely. "Parlan is upwind gutting a red hind. I was merely a moment's distraction. It was the smell of fresh blood and the promise of an easy meal that saved you from disaster."

Suddenly in need of support, Leeanne tightened her arms around Iain's neck.

"You placed yourself between me and the wolf, knowing that only a dead deer could possibly save you?" she asked, horrified by thoughts of what might have happened had the men's plan failed.

"Lord luve me! You can no' imagine I would stand idly by and do nothing, though for a moment I was sorely tempted. You deserved it for the anguish I've experienced since discovering the mare, winded and perspiring, outside the barn. We've been tracking you for hours, wolf tracks upon hoof marks and later upon footprints."

"The wolves scared the pony off."

"Aye, we figured as much."

"We? Are you saying you've brought Parlan with you?" Sesi asked as she scrambled down from the tree.

Iain released Leeanne to catch Sesi as she dropped the last four feet.

"I did, and he is wild with anxiety, I might add. I'm thinking you'll still be hearing of this escapade when you're gnarled and gray, you capricious young *bodach*." He smoothed Sesi's hair away from her face, glancing down at Elizabeth. "How is the wee bairn?"

"Hungry."

"I take it that's a good sign?"

Sesi nodded.

Mouth stern, Iain turned once again to

Leeanne. "Do you have any idea what you've put me through, lass?"

"I assure you there is good cause."

"That remains to be seen."

"I have a second character flaw I forgot to tell you about. One I doubt you'll like as well as the first."

"And what might that be?"

"I'm a woman of action, Iain."

"That you are—miscalculated action. You could no' wait for me to consider all that you said last evening. Nay, you must go off on your own and endanger my sister's life, and that of her child, as well as your own."

Leeanne couldn't argue with that. In her world, she knew the variables, the options, and the consequences. In his, it was another story.

"You don't understand! You cannot think to blame Leeanne," Sesi interjected.

"You plan to champion her."

Sesi's chin came up. "I'm a woman of action too, Iain."

"Enough! Let us cease and desist before we say something we might regret. Parlan will be joining us at any moment. We decided that if we found you three alive, we'd stay at Alasdair's summer cottage for the night. We'll discuss this again at Gleann-leac-na-muidhe when we're all of calmer minds."

"Iain, there is something so vile—" Sesi began.

"That's my final word on it, Sesi."

"Be reasonable, Iain."

"I am being reasonable, sister mine."

Now that the danger was passed, Sesi's temper flared.

"You can be as hard and unmalleable as iron sometimes, and I don't mind telling you so, even if you are my very own dear brother, Iain MacBride."

Iain shook his head. "I vow I do no' know how Parlan contends with you. A man is never allowed the final word, is he, Sesi?"

"Not when I have something of grave importance to impart."

Leeanne watched the exchange between brother and sister, suspecting that stubbornness ran rampant in the MacBride family. She found breaking through Iain's to be the ultimate challenge.

Leeanne didn't realize how cold she'd become until she was inside the summer house, bathed, and sipping tea alone by the fire in the master chamber. She sat wrapped only in her plaid and a fur robe she'd found on the foot of the four-poster bed. Curled in a padded armchair, she felt her stomach tensing in anticipation of what was yet to come. To calm her nerves, she allowed her gaze to roam around the room.

The last time she'd stayed at the summer house, she'd been too sick, too confused, and too aggravated with Iain to properly enjoy the decor. Now she realized that the headboard of the massive bed was carved with a family crest, the canopy was draped in curtains and valances of crimson silk and satin, while the mattress itself was made up in coverlets of midnight velvet. She'd heard that bedding had once been bequeathed down through the generations. Now she knew why.

An oak chest of drawers stood in one corner of the room, a clothes chest much like Iain's strongbox in the other. And against the wall was a writing table that Leeanne surmised might double for a dining table since twin chairs stood at either end.

Parlan and Sesi, along with Elizabeth, were settled in a smaller yet similar room across the hall. Leeanne noted that the furor she'd heard earlier had died down and silence reigned. At least until Iain opened the master chamber door, regarding her dispassionately from the threshold.

Leeanne doubted that his rugged good looks would ever cease to amaze her.

"Now you may explain yourself," he said, striding into the room.

"What about Sesi and Parlan? Aren't they going to join us?"

As if on second thought, Iain retraced his steps to firmly close and lock the master chamber door.

"I advised them to discuss the matter privately while we do the same."

It wasn't what he'd said, but what he didn't say that bothered her.

"So you and Parlan can compare notes later on?"

"So the truth can be told without resulting in a fighting match. You must have heard how Sesi is this evening. I'm thinking it's best that Parlan be left to calm her down."

"She's acting that way because she's worried out of her mind. Parlan must be gentle with her."

"Parlan wouldn't touch a hair on her head, no matter how outdone he is with her! I would never have allowed her to marry that sort of man."

"Good Lord! I didn't mean that. I know Parlan's kind of rough around the edges, but he's no wife beater. I mean she's upset over what we heard today. It's the eleventh hour, Iain."

Iain grabbed one of the desk chairs. Placing it with the back toward her, he straddled the seat, his knees peeping at her from beneath his kilt. She'd never noticed what nice knees he had. They weren't a bit bony, but smooth and well formed like the rest of him, Leeanne thought.

"All right, lass. Have at it. Tell me everything you know, and then tell me all you think you know."

Leeanne's gaze drifted to the fire and she stared pensively into the flames.

"Now that you're finally ready to listen, I'm not sure I know where to begin."

"I suggest you begin with the information you and Sesi overheard."

Lacing her fingers in her lap, Leeanne nodded.

"All right." She breathed deeply, exhaling through her nose. "At dawn the day after tomorrow, Robert Campbell plans to invoke the letter of fire and sword in Glencoe."

Iain rose so forcefully that his chair tipped sideways, clattering to the floor.

"Sweet reason, lass! Do you have any idea what you're saying?"

"Sesi overhead the conversation between Robert Campbell and Charles as well."

"The man with no neck?"

"Yes, Campbell's aide-de-camp. I went over to the main house to pick up the potatoes-and-turnips for lunch. Needless to say, I left without the vegetables, but in the process, I got a lot more than I bargained for."

"Robert Campbell wouldn't dare to attack us in our own territory! Besides that, he'd be daft to oppose us. We're three to his one, lass."

"Only if you count the women and children, Iain. Besides, someone from Fort William is supposed to bring reinforcements. You've heard Campbell mention him before—a Lieutenant-Colonel Hamilton," Leeanne informed him, studying her hands rather than look at him.

Iain righted the chair. "You do have an imagination."

She glanced up. "Do you think I'd make this up?"

Iain did not deign to reply.

"You do, don't you? You think I'm angry because you wouldn't let me confront Campbell. You think I'm trying to force your hand!"

"Or perhaps this is a simple case of boredom," he offered. "Glencoe is a mild place compared to the rigors of London. Almost mundane to my way of thinking," Iain said smoothly.

"*Mundane!* You call delivering a baby mundane! You call *camanachd* mundane! How about a ballet on the spur of the moment, performed in someone's living room? Or a wolf attack? No—a stroll around the lake at a city park is commonplace. Grocery shopping is ordinary. Watching television or mowing grass is mundane. I'd hardly compare a stint in Glencoe to any of those."

"You've lost me, lass."

It was the moment of truth. Destiny awaited. Not the destiny of a dance studio, but the destiny of a Highland glen and its proud clanspeople.

Surging to her feet, Leeanne said, "That's because I'm a fraud, Iain."

"What are you saying now?"

"I'm not from London. I'm not a *sassenach*." Leeanne took another deep breath. "I'm a

324

teacher, but not from a school for ladylike deportment in London."

"I'm thinking that's the first entirely honest statement you've made since I met you."

"Well, here's another one. I'm a—" Her voice faltered. "—time-traveler."

"Is this another of your stories, like the ones you told at the *ceilidh?*"

"No. I actually have transcended time. Breached the time barrier. Taken a giant leap through history."

Iain chuckled to himself. It was a dry sound. Hardly humorous. "We must both be daft. You for making such an outrageous assertion, and me for listening."

"I know it's a lot to take in all at once. How do you think I felt? One minute I was dancing the Blades of War in a modern studio at 1692 Highland Avenue . . ." Her voice trailed off, her brow furrowing in concentration.

Is that how it had happened? There were so many Celtic immigrants in the Carolinas and Georgia that one needed only glance around to see Scottish heritage. Why, every October the town of Waxhaw, North Carolina, held Highland games. As did Grandfather's Mountain and the city of Savannah, Georgia, during the summer months.

Her own family had been of Irish descent, her grandparents disembarking at Ellis Island at the turn of the century.

"Didn't it seem odd to you that I just

appeared out of nowhere?"

"A large number of people did that day. There was a crowd of guests. A crush. For the love of . . . it was a wedding, lass!"

"Take a moment to think over what I've said. I believe I'm here because this is a pivotal time for the Highland clans, when the clanspeople and their leaders must face the future head-on."

Iain was silent, though he looked as if he'd like to shake her.

"I can see the skepticism in your eyes."

"You're—"

"I'm not a wacko. I can prove it!"

Leeanne snatched up her T-shirt and shook it at him.

"Look at this! I've been terrified someone would see it and question me."

"I've seen it. In my strongbox. What of it?"

"It's a screen print T-shirt, Iain. It's made of a cotton and polyester blend woven in a mill, sewn on a machine, and dyed with aniline dye. That's a synthetic coloring. The words are written in puff paint. That's rubber ink. It says save the whales! That's because they're an endangered species in my world. I bought the T-shirt because our delicate ecosystem is being destroyed and I believe the world powers need to work together to save it."

Reaching to her ears, she slipped the back off one of her pearl earrings.

"The back of my pierced earring has plastic

around it so it won't feel so heavy. Have you ever seen plastic?"

"Nay."

"That's because it wasn't invented until the twentieth century. We use a lot of it where I come from—plastic forks, shampoo bottles, grocery bags. It's not good for the environment because it isn't biodegradable, but we seem to depend on it regardless of the far-reaching consequences."

Iain looked blank.

"There's something else. The reason I couldn't read your book of poetry was because it was written in black letter—we've far surpassed that ancient technique of printing. We have lasers now and we spell things differently."

"I know nothing of lasers, but there are many people who can no' read. That proves nothing."

He still doubted her! Leeanne's mind raced, desperately searching for something that might convince him.

"All right. Here goes. Just take a look at this! There's no way you can write this off as normal! I can't see clearly without them; I wear them because glasses interfere with my dancing."

Leeanne popped out a royal blue, extended-wear contact lens into her palm and presented it to Iain as if her hand were a silver platter.

Iain looked incredulous. Recoiling, he stumbled backwards much as the wolves had done when a higher power smacked them in the face.

Leeanne reached out to him with her empty hand. "I'm sorry. I didn't mean to scare you."

He responded in Gaelic.

"I can't understand you, Iain. Speak English."

"I said you're a witch!"

Leeanne blinked. She hadn't expected that!

"I wish I were," she confessed with a flourish. "I'd twitch my nose and this would all be over. Then all the people I've come to know and love would be safe." Cupping the contact lens in her hand, Leeanne counted on her knuckles as she recited. "Sesi. Elizabeth. Parlan. Iseabal. Alasdair. His wife. Mangus. Barr. Even John Macdonald. And most of all you, Iain Ranoull MacBride. We can't let Campbell do this to them . . . to us."

Advancing toward her, Iain did shake her this time. Gently.

"Iain—"

"Take the other eyepiece out, Leeanne. I'm thinking I'd like to have a look at your eyes without them."

"They're nothing without the contacts—pale gray and as bland as dry toast," Leeanne said softly.

"Let me be the judge of that."

This was something she hadn't anticipated either. Leeanne felt suddenly shy and uncertain, something unique for her.

"I can't leave them out for long. They'll dry out."

"Remove them for only a moment. You can

328

put them right back in again."

Leeanne complied, removing the remaining contact. He looked directly into her denuded pupils, searching for what she wasn't sure.

"They're the color of clouds before a Highland storm. I've always been partial to gray thunder clouds."

"That's one of the things I like best about you—your rough gallantry," Leeanne murmured.

"Tell me true. Have you lied to me? Are you playing me for the fool? Is this some trick like the jugglers at court use to entertain the King?"

Leeanne could hear her own heart beating. It sounded like someone hammering on a clay pipe with a rubber mallet. She knew he must hear it too.

"I have nothing to gain by lying to you, and everything by telling the truth."

"You may put the blue disks back in again now, Lass."

Leeanne placed the lenses on her pupils, raising her face to his. His eyes unerringly met hers.

"Is that no' painful?"

Leeanne couldn't help it. She smiled. "Only if I get dust trapped beneath 'em."

"Then you must have a care no' to do so."

Barely aware of how it happened, Leeanne found herself in Iain's arms. Who had moved first? She wasn't sure. Perhaps they had moved in unison.

"Ach, lass. I've tried to quell my feelings for you. But I can no'." The confession seemed torn from him. "You've bound up my broken heart with your exquisite nonsense. I've come to love everything about you. Your laughter. The flatness of your accent. Your poise. The way you feel in my arms. Your touch. Even your failure to recognize the impossible." His voice was husky with desire. "Even if you were a witch, it would make no difference."

"Though you might doubt it, you've wooed and won my heart as well," she whispered fervently.

After an afternoon bereft of it, Iain's most charming of smiles reappeared.

"This has no' been easy for me. I had planned our handfasting to be in name only."

"This hasn't been easy for me either. One minute, I was in my studio and the year was 1992."

"1992!"

"Yes, that's what I've been trying to tell you— 1992. The next, I had a Highland warrior, a *true* Highland warrior dressed in full regalia, breathing down my neck, accusing me of disrupting his sister's wedding. I was afraid I'd had a heart attack and died."

Though he remained silent, Iain reached out to gently graze the arch of Leeanne's cheekbone with the back of his hand.

"When I realized that I was alive, I was afraid I'd gone crazy. It took me a while to figure out what had actually happened. Everything was so new, and you were so hostile. At least at first."

"Hostility is the last thing I'm feeling now," Iain said, wrapping his arms tightly around Leeanne. He cradled her against his chest, the bulge of his loins pressed against her lower body.

Leeanne turned her cheek into his throat, feeling his Adam's apple bob as he swallowed. Muscles quivering, she stood in the circle of his arms, acknowledging there was nowhere in the world, his or hers, she'd rather be.

"I know. I can tell."

He leaned away from her a moment, his gaze roving over her face.

"And what do you propose we do about it?"

She sensed his expectancy. "I'm entirely open to suggestions."

"I've never met a woman like you."

"And I doubt you ever will again."

"Aye and aye to that."

With a sigh, Iain's head descended, his lips enkindling Leeanne's. She whimpered, opening her mouth to his fevered demands. There existed between them some mystical bond. They were right together; soul mates. And like the waters of the torrent rushing past the summer cottage, she allowed desire to wash from her the cares of the day.

She did not protest when he swept the sumptuous clothes from the tester bed and spread the velvet quilts and silk curtains on the carpet before the fire. She helped him, joining him on the elegant pallet.

This time, he was the aggressor, straddling her hips as he tugged his shirt tails from his kilt, pulling the shirt wrong side out over his head and flinging it across the room. She hooked her fingers in the kilt, rising on her elbows to study the checkered wool.

"You've changed setts on me, Iain," she said, unwrapping the woolen kilt and adding it to their layers of bedding. She ran her hands along his bare torso, spanning his muscular shoulders, his narrow waist, his trim flanks.

"Aye."

"I think I know why."

"Do you now?" he asked, stretching full length beside her beneath the covers.

"Will we ever be able to talk about it openly?"

"Later," he said, nuzzling her ear with his tongue.

"Later?"

"Aye, much later," he confirmed as he pushed the fur robe along with her plaid aside, cupping her breasts in his hands. Delicious tingles raced through her as he thumbed her nipples into standing peaks of sensation. His lips teased, tasted, tested as his hands roamed over her thighs, touching her intimately.

"I love you, Iain," she said, returning the sensual favor, tasting the natural saltiness of his skin mixed with the lingering freshness of soap.

For a split second, Iain stilled. "Luving a man is a perilous proposition, lass," he said, passion making his voice husky.

"I'm up to it." She pushed his trews below his waist, then to his knees, kicking them off the pallet with her foot to find him fully aroused. "And I think you are too," she said, writhing provocatively against him.

Leeanne nipped playfully at the fullness of Iain's lower lip.

"What was that for, lass?"

"Just to make sure I have your undivided attention."

Hands on either side of her face, he returned the kiss fiercely, maneuvering her body beneath his, tempting her with his hardness, branding her for eternity.

Leeanne moaned, reaching to touch him with feather-light strokes, to guide him.

"No' so fast, lass," he rasped, his eyes dark with wanting.

"I ache for you," she sighed raggedly, raising her lips to his. Her hands dug into his firm flesh.

Their warm breaths mingled, became one as she moved against him naturally. Thrust for thrust, they performed in harmony, perfectly attuned to each other's needs. And when he would have pulled his heated length from within her, she held him fiercely to her and they achieved surcease together.

Replete, they rested face to face on their sides, his leg settled possessively around hers, Leeanne nestled in Iain's arms.

She raised her head to look into his eyes. "Do I make you happy, Iain?"

He planted a wet kiss on her brow. "You please me well, lass."

"But do I make you happy?"

"You're a persistent wench," he said, plopping her on her naked buttocks.

"Ouch!"

Pulling her on top of him and massaging away the sting with strong, sure strokes, he said, "Aye, you make me very happy. I can no' longer see myself without you. No' in a year and a day. No' ever."

"As happy as your first wife?"

His hands stilled. "I'm thinking you've a right to know about her, lass."

She no longer detected grief in his voice. Just the sadness for something lost. And a hint of hope for something newly gained.

"I thought we'd never reach this point," Leeanne said.

"Aye and aye. We've far surpassed it this night."

"So tell me. . . ." she said, rolling off him only to snuggle against his side.

"She was a MacGregor. She was young, like Sesi. And she loved me. We were married less than a month when she discovered she was with child. I was overjoyed. You see, I wanted a son to carry on the MacBride name." He paused as if reliving the episode in his mind.

"That's only natural," Leeanne interjected, wishing she could somehow ease his pain. Knowing in her heart she already had.

Iain raked his fingers through his hair. "And eventually her time came. But she was so small. The labor lasted for days. I can still hear her screams . . . at least, I could before I met you." He covered his eyes with his arm. "My son was born horribly malformed . . . stillborn. I actually thanked God."

Concerned that he might not continue, Leeanne prompted, "And your wife?"

"Within the week, she'd followed the path of the poor wee bairn."

Leeanne swallowed the lump in her throat, blinking back tears. She wanted to console him and she didn't quite know how. She was relieved when Iain uncovered his eyes, turning to her of his own accord.

"I buried them both myself, vowing I'd never again be responsible for bringing a woman to such a sorry end. I lived the first six months after that with a bottle in my hand."

Now she knew why the handfasting had suited him so well, Leeanne thought. It also explained the infant's christening gown packed in the strongbox. It served as Iain's talisman against temptation—correction, *had* served.

"Is that when you sent Sesi off to boarding school?"

"Aye, but as I told you before, she gave them such a fit I had to bring her home again."

"I imagine that was because she wanted to be with you during your time of grief."

"I suppose. Anyway, Sesi finally got sick of my drinking and had Gabhan MacGregor lock me in my room. They tell me I was like a madman for a while, calling for Parlan and Alasdair to free me from my prison. I do no' remember. Eventually, Sesi finally sent for Parlan. He straightened me out quick enough."

"That's how Sesi first met Parlan."

"Aye."

"And you blamed yourself for her pregnancy."

A small grin hovered at the corners of his mouth. "I blamed myself for inviting the reiver back for a second visit. I had nothing to do with the pregnancy. That was of their own making. Now, with you, lass, that would be a different story."

"You bet it would."

Leeanne slipped one arm beneath Iain, the other around him. Hugging him against her as she wove her fingers through his, gazing into his compelling azure eyes.

"It's going to be all right, you'll see," she said. "We'll make it all right," she said, stirring restlessly against him.

From that point on, Leeanne allowed her body do all the talking, all the consoling, and all the explaining they would ever need between them. And this time, neither of them slept before dawn.

The next morning, after seeing Parlan, Sesi, and Elizabeth safely beyond Meall Mor, Iain and Leeanne turned their ponies toward Glencoe.

"We'll seek Alasdair out as soon as we've bedded the ponies down in the barn," Iain said. "But I warn you, he will no' forgive us easily for our transgressions against the sacred Highland tradition of hospitality."

An icy breeze had traveled with them down from the northern entrance and stark white snowflakes were beginning to powder the ground. Leeanne glanced overhead. Dark clouds hung low in the sky, heavy with the promise of added precipitation.

It seemed to Leeanne as if the weather worked against them, turning ugly only to further complicate Captain Robert Campbell's immediate departure from Glencoe.

Chapter Sixteen

Alasdair and Iseabal were waiting for Iain and Leeanne when they returned to Glencoe.

Iseabal jumped up from the stool where she'd been perched by the fire at Alasdair's feet. "Where have ye been?" she chirped as soon as Leeanne steeped inside the cottage.

Alasdair rose from the armchair, smoothing a forefinger over his curling moustaches.

"That would be my question too, lad."

"I did no' know I was no' free to come and go at will," Iain replied evasively.

"Ye ken ye are. 'Tis only that we were concerned for ye. We expected some word from ye and Parlan after the hunt. The next thing I discover ye missing."

"My apologies. Parlan and Sesi decided to take the bairn to the manor house at Loch Lomond to bide a wee. We stayed at Gleann-leac-na-muidhe overnight. This morning, we saw them as far as Meall Mor."

"A hasty trip, that," Alasdair observed.

"Aye," Iain agreed.

"But I suppose 'tis their decision."

"Aye and aye."

Alasdair cleared his throat. "I trust ye did no' mind if we let ourselves insides in hopes of yer return. 'Tis turning a trifle too cold to wait outside so I thought I'd build a fire."

"You know I would no' deny you the warmth of my hearth," Iain said.

"'Twas me that informed his lairdship o' yer absence. I've been looking for ye everywhere, mistress! How is it that ye forgot today's performance?" Iseabal asked. It was then Leeanne realized that beneath her cloak Iseabal wore her *Nutcracker* costume.

Leeanne drew a quick breath, glancing at Iain as her protégée danced across the room.

"Oh, no . . . the matinee performance! It completely slipped my mind. I'm so sorry," she said. It seemed that for the first time in her adult life she'd discovered something more important than her career.

Iseabal reached out and took Leeanne's arm. "They've been waiting for ye, ye ken . . . a full house. The laird's wife has been playing harp music to soothe the audience's impatience, but we've no more time to dally if we're to avoid a riot."

Iain's gaze traveled from Leeanne to Alasdair and back again.

"Iseabal's correct. Go ahead, lass. Alasdair and I will be along directly," Iain said solemnly.

His look spoke volumes, and Leeanne found herself wanting to protest, but Iseabal had a death grip on her arm, dragging her toward the cottage door.

Leeanne heard Iain say something in Gaelic to Alasdair, though she couldn't make heads or tails of it.

The old chief's face flamed vivid red against his white beard.

"I banned ye from the main house only in the heat of the moment, Iain. Since then, I've had time to reconsider. After all, she is yer wife and ye have every right . . ." Alasdair was saying as Iseabal propelled Leeanne over the threshold, firmly closing the cottage door on the men's conversation.

The matinee performance of the *Nutcracker* passed in a magnificent blur, the audience enthralled by Leeanne while she anxiously scanned the crowd for Iain.

By the time he finally appeared, Barr Macdonald had cranked up his sheep's-hide bagpipe to test the reedy quality of three upper drones and the lower melody chanter in preparation for the conclusion of the show. As during the evening performance, Iain stood at the back of the room, a head taller than any other man. Leeanne did not need to see Alasdair's face to know the outcome of Iain's conversation with him. Iain's haggard expression was testimony to that. It told her that it wouldn't have mattered if she had remained at the cottage. A stickler for tradition, and more stubborn than she and Sesi combined, Alasdair Macdonald obviously wasn't going to listen to accusations against his guests.

"Swords, the lass needs swords to dance the Blades of War," Barr called out to the audience between breaths as the first stirring strains of "Gillie Chalium" wafted through the great hall.

From the corner of her eye, Leeanne saw Charles Hamilton rise from his chair just off stage. She was positive he would have once again offered his sword for the dance, if not for Robert Campbell's glare of disapproval. Charles slowly resumed his seat, clutching his flute so tightly his knuckles whitened against the dark grains of the oak.

Instead, Robert Campbell astonished Leeanne by withdrawing his military sword. Bending with a courtly flourish, he placed it on the stage floor near Leeanne's feet. When he straightened, Leeanne could not help but notice the challenge in his drink-reddened eyes. They also professed, in no uncertain terms, his dislike for her.

"I'm surprised to see you at both performances, Captain Campbell," Leeanne commented, eyeing his sword and wondering what grisly use it would be put to by the misty morning light.

"I've passed a most agreeable thirteen days here in Glencoe, my lady. Your performances have only added to my pleasure."

"This is my final performance. Perhaps it's time you and your men were moving on. They say thirteen is an unlucky number." Her stance was unflinching. Defiant.

"Mayhap in some cases," he replied with a villainous smile. "But not in this instance. Thirteen is an entirely lucky number, one I shall remember well for all the days of my life."

Leeanne might have sent Robert Campbell's sword spinning across the stage with the toe of her dance slipper if not for Iain. Mouth set in a grim line, he wasted no time in making his way through the crowd to the corded-off stage. Gracefully unsheathing his weapon, he crossed Robert Campbell's plain sword perpendicularly with his own double-handed, sapphire-encrusted claymore. The symbolism of Iain's act escaped all those around him, even Robert Campbell. But not Leeanne.

Iain's eyes met Leeanne's for a tension-filled moment as Robert Campbell backed away to disappear into the audience.

"It was futile. He wouldn't listen to you, would he?" Leeanne whispered, wanting Iain to take her in his arms right there and then and knowing that he could not.

"He vows he'll ask the clansmen to hide their weapons in the event they're needed. And send some of the younger, unwed women like Iseabal to the summer house for their protection. But he'll agree to nothing beyond that."

Leeanne glanced at the ceiling, at the tapestries fluttering in the breeze created by the peat fires burning at either end of the hall. "It's not enough!" she said finally, clenching and unclenching her fists while she fought the tears of frustration welling in her eyes.

Iain's face reflected the inadequacy she herself felt.

"There's a place known as Coire Gabhail. It's a hidden valley where the Macdonalds are fond of hiding their stolen cattle. There's a shieling there."

"A shieling?"

"A herdsman's hut. It's no' as nice as the cottage, but it's a safe place—I'll be taking you there after the performance," he informed her beneath his breath.

"Will you stay with me?" she asked in a low voice, fearful of his answer.

"Do no' ask that of me, lass. There's only disappointment waiting for you if you do."

She realized what Iain was telling her. That Alasdair was a stubborn old chief, addicted to and dependent on a tradition that might very well lead to his doom, but that it did not change Iain's loyalty to him. He would stand by Alasdair regardless.

"You could never disappoint me," Leeanne said.

"Nor you me," Iain responded. "Now dance the Blades of War for them, lass, and be done with it. I'm thinking we should be on our way before full gloaming."

"I agree."

There was only one viable solution, Leeanne thought as she stepped between the sword blades—the dance that had brought her to Glencoe in the first place. It was the only foolproof way to insure Iain's safety, to prevent his death at the hands of Captain Robert Campbell's government troops, she reasoned.

Leeanne wondered if she could do it without the studio sound system and the wall of mirrors. If, now that she was faced with the opportunity, she could actually be transported in reverse, forward to North Carolina, 1992.

She decided her theory *had* to work.

When Iain turned to leave the stage, Leeanne detained him by placing her hand on his arm.

Arching a fair brow at her, Iain spun, asking in surprise, "What is it, lass?"

"Stay close beside me, Iain," she whispered, staring out across the great hall at the sea of faces—some friends, some strangers, some enemies.

"Should I no' move away from the stage so the audience can better view you?"

"No! I mean, please don't. I . . . I need you right where you are, Iain," Leeanne said. Her voice was strained, the hand that held his arm trembling.

"Surely you're no' nervous, lass?"

"Yes. That's it. I'm nervous. Scared out of my wits. I think I feel an anxiety attack coming on. Please, don't leave me here on stage alone, Iain."

With a slightly bemused expression in his azure eyes, Iain said, "Never fear, I'll remain by your side until the end of the Blades of War."

"Good. That's what I want. Okay then, here goes . . ."

Taking a deep breath, Leeanne allowed Barr's pipe tune to lead her forward. Nimbly she avoided displacing the weapons as she swayed counterclockwise inside and outside the squares formed by the blades.

"Discipline, persistence, practice, persistence," she recited as she concentrated on the tempo of the music, on her own strict sense of timing.

The music crashed against her athletic figure, lifting her, dominating her. She allowed herself to be carried away by the melody. And this time, her performance was flawless.

Leeanne felt her face flush red as her heart lurched, beating in double-quick time to the music's climax. Exceeding the beat. Pumping in her ears; in her throat; in her chest.

In the final moments, as she felt herself being sucked forward in time, Leeanne reached for Iain.

She could see the sudden dawning of awareness on his face. "It was the claymore that brought you here to Glencoe," he gasped.

"Iain?" Leeanne was suddenly so afraid of what he might do that her heart almost stopped.

"I can no' go with you," he said with a wry smile.

"Iain! Please!"

As if she were standing outside herself, Leeanne watched the woman in the Highland-green-and-rust-colored plaid whirl faster and faster around Iain's broadsword.

"You're in unnecessary danger if you remain behind in Glencoe! Take my hand! Come with me!"

Instead, Iain grasped her extended hand for a moment, turning it face up to plant a warm, moist kiss in the hollow of her palm. Then, with firm resolve, he closed her fingers over the kiss and nudged her hand aside.

"I can no', Leeanne. Honor and my blood brotherhood with the Macdonalds will no' allow me to do so. I'll no' leave the glen until I've done all in my power to put a stop to Robert Campbell."

"I'll stay with you then. . . ."

Gritting her teeth, Leeanne tried to cease spinning. To her horror, she could not. It was as if she no longer had control of her own muscles. She pressed her hands to her ears. It felt as if "Gillie Chalium" throbbed inside her head rather than outside her body.

"*Please*, Iain! No . . . oh, God!" Leeanne's words were a tearful scream, sucked from her throat by time as it propelled her back into the future.

Iain whisked the dried heather badge from his bonnet, gently tucking it behind her ear at the final second before fate ripped then apart.

"Remember me, my brave bonnie lass," he said, his voice growing thinner, his beloved countenance blurring as he reached to retrieve his sword from beneath her feet.

With tears glistening in her eyes, Leeanne said, "How could I ever forget you? You hold the key to my heart."

Leeanne wasn't even sure Iain heard her.

Leeanne felt as if she'd been dropped from the roof of a twelve-story building. Every bone in her body hurt. Every muscle ached. Every cell. Particularly those of her left arm and back.

Cheeks flushed and breathing labored, she glanced wide-eyed around the darkened interior of her contemporary dance studio, discerning objects by the eerie glow of the parking-lot light filtering in through the picture window. The scarred upright, its ivory keys gleaming like gaping teeth, grinned at her. The sheet music she'd been working on still cluttered the top of the piano, while a stale bagged lunch lay spread on the piano seat. She knew it was stale; she could smell it.

The wastepaper basket was still filled with the aluminum soda cans she'd collected. And slivered pieces of the wall mirror still spattered the shiny maple dance floor.

Could she have dreamed it all?

Leeanne felt her forehead with the back of her hand. She didn't seem feverish.

She stared at herself in the undamaged mirrors. Pale and bedraggled, Leeanne decided she looked like a ghost. A ghost wearing worn dance slippers, a crumpled jumper, and a sprig of dried heather in her wildly tangled hair. Staring at the dirt beneath the fingernails of her right hand, Leeanne reached up to caress the heather badge that Iain had snatched from his bonnet and tucked behind her ear at the last second before time had so cruelly ripped them apart.

No, Leeanne thought, Iain MacBride was no dream. She'd transcended time and space. Twice. She knew it as surely as she lived and breathed.

The phone rang and Leeanne jumped, staring at the touch-tone as the answering machine clicked in and picked up the call.

A vaguely familiar voice, a woman's voice, blared out into the room.

"Stop ignoring the phone, Leeanne! One of the dancers told me you'd stayed late to work the bugs out of the Scottish score, but it's past midnight. If you don't return my call soon, I'm coming over there. You can't *live* at the studio—the way you're pushing yourself over this production isn't healthy! Please, take the weekend off and get a little R&R. If you won't do it for yourself, do it for the good of the company."

Leeanne recognized the concerned voice as that of her personal assistant, but the words meant nothing, the hour of the day even less.

Disoriented, Leeanne wandered down the line of director's chairs, arranged like soldiers against the wall.

Soldiers!

The fragmented bits and pieces of her journey into the past clicked into place.

Leeanne dropped to her knees, searching frantically for the sapphire-encrusted broadsword. It was nowhere to be found. Horrified, she realized it must have remained in the past with Iain.

"Nooooo," Leeanne wailed, gazing toward the ceiling, beseeching fate for some sort of reprieve.

Nothing happened.

"You can't do this to me . . . to him," she moaned.

Still nothing.

Slowly, legs trembling, Leeanne found her feet.

The worn floors flexing beneath her footsteps, Leeanne stumbled to the picture window, starring out across the asphalt parking lot and into the mistiness of an overcast winter night. Her station wagon was exactly as she'd left it—except that the snow on the hood and piled against the tires was now four inches thick. But that too meant nothing.

Only the name *Iain* meant anything now.

Iain.

Reverberating in her brain like a litany.

Iain.

Resounding in her chest like a heartbeat.

Iain.

Singing in her blood like a merry tune.

Leeanne breathed a heavy sigh, no longer able to disassociate herself from the name Iain MacBride. The love she'd felt for the Highlander had carried over into her own century.

Teeth chattering, Leeanne clutched her plaid more closely about her shoulders. She'd never been so miserable, she thought, pressing her face against the cool glass of the picture window. A single tear eased from the corner of her eye, sliding down her warm cheek. Leaning away from the window, she watched her own reflection in the night-darkened glass as she withdrew the heather from her hair and clutched it to her breast.

"Remember me, my brave bonnie lass," he'd said.

A muffled sob escaped Leeanne's lips.

Her time with Iain had been ephemeral, and yet he'd made an unmistakable impact on her life. She had brought souvenirs back with her—

a heather badge, the dirt beneath her fingernails, a pair of soiled dance slippers, an ivory
dealg pin, and a new perspective on the Highlands.

Still, Leeanne wondered how she was ever
to pick up the tattered threads of her exis-
tence when like his broadsword her soul had
remained behind in Scotland with Iain. It
seemed she had done nothing to alter the past.
It, however, had done everything to change her
future.

Chapter Seventeen

Leeanne spent all day Sunday drinking cranberry juice, nursing sore muscles in a tub brimming with hot water, and wallowing in self-pity. By Monday morning, the snow had begun to melt, dripping off the rooftops like giant tears. The weather suited her mood perfectly.

On her way to work, Leeanne stopped to fill her gas tank, ran over a discarded beer bottle left in the service station parking lot, and ended up buying a new tire. The delay threw her into the eight-a.m. rush-hour traffic.

With Patrolman Bob on the radio blaring traffic conditions to her from a helicopter overhead, she battled pollution-blackened slush, steering an invention that resembled a sure-footed Highland pony only in coloring. By the time she parked the station wagon in the studio parking lot, she had decided that the only good thing about a car was that it couldn't run away. And that she preferred the natural aroma of ponies to the toxic smell of exhaust fumes.

Rehearsal proved an ordeal, even though the dance company was finally getting the hang of the Highland number. They played "Gillie Chalium" over and over again, and each time she heard it, Leeanne vacillated between screaming and crying.

At six o'clock, she headed home only to discover that like Mother Hubbard's her cupboards were bare. Changing out of her dance clothes and into jeans and a sweat shirt, she drove to the grocery store. She realized the instant she stepped through the sliding glass doors and wrestled a buggy from the corral that it was hopeless. All she wound up with was spiced tea, a giant box of oatmeal, something from the bakery that reminded her of Hogmanay, and a gnawing hunger that no amount of food could assuage.

After the grocery store, Leeanne drove around listlessly for a while, considering and rejecting a visit to a friend's house, a movie, and the mall.

By seven-thirty, she found herself turning into the parking lot of the neighborhood branch library. It seemed she had spent the entire day jumping from parking lot to parking lot, she mused, turning the ignition key to the off position and levering herself from the station wagon.

Throwing open the glass door of the library, she couldn't help thinking how sterile the low-pile indoor/outdoor carpet and the white walls seemed after the earthiness of Glencoe. Earlier, the decor of her studio had struck her in the same fashion.

The librarian glanced up from the front desk, asking automatically, "How are you today?"

"Fine," Leeanne responded just as automatically, thinking, *what a joke!* She wasn't fine . . . might never be fine again.

Weaving her way through the tiny library, Leeanne stood in line to use the lone service computer, marveling at her own patience. There had been a time not so very long ago when she would have tapped her foot and glanced at her watch, ticking off the minutes as she awaited her turn. But she'd learned something from Iain—it was called tolerance.

Perhaps it was shell shock, or the dazed sensation she'd experienced since returning from Glencoe, but she couldn't seem to find what she was looking for in the computer's catalogue system. She stood for a moment looking blankly at the scene until the man behind her snapped, "If you're finished with that, I'd like to use it myself sometime before the turn of the century."

Leeanne blinked. Funny, she'd never noticed how rude people could be. It made her respond all the more politely.

"Certainly. Be my guest. I hope you find what you're looking for." And oddly enough, she meant it.

Leeanne backtracked to the front desk.

"How can I help you?" the librarian asked from behind a mountain of paperwork.

"Uh . . . I was wondering if this branch has an oversized picture book on Scotland."

"Juvenile?"

"Adult. I'm almost positive I've checked it out from here before. I looked on the shelf, but I can't seem to find it and I don't remember the title."

The woman cleared her throat. "Do you know the author's name?"

Leeanne smiled wanly. "No, I'm sorry."

The librarian's expression said she didn't have time for nonsense.

"That makes it a little more difficult."

"But not impossible. Right?"

The librarian sighed. "I suppose I could try to pull it up on the computer by subject." Placing her hands on the keyboard, she waited expectantly. When Leeanne failed to respond appropriately, she prompted, "Do you think you could narrow it down for me just a little bit. You know, culture, national holidays, Lowlands, Highlands?"

"Oh, of course. Highlands. Glencoe."

"Spell that for me."

"G-l-e-n-c-o-e. Glencoe."

Leeanne glanced over her shoulder, realizing she was holding up yet another line. The people congregating behind her with books in their arms looked as if they would like to punch out her lights. She'd forgotten how rush-push-shove her world could be.

"I don't see an entire book on a place called Glencoe, but I've got several books on the Scottish Highlands. Let me see," she said, scanning the list on the monitor. "One is lost. One is a reference book. And oh yes, here we are."

Adjusting her glasses on the bridge of her nose, the librarian pushed back her desk chair and rose.

"Jamie, would you mind taking over for a minute while I help this lady," she called to a man Leeanne could see through the open office door.

"I guess not," he replied, coming to take the librarian's place at the computer.

"This way," she said, motioning to Leeanne.

Leeanne followed the librarian to a shelf at the back of the library, watching as she scanned the neat row of books without pulling anything.

"Well, it's got to be here somewhere," she said, running her finger down the spines of several travel books. "The computer says it's in." She frowned. "Huh. That's odd. Maybe it's still on the book cart."

Wondering how the most simple process could turn into such a hassle, Leeanne trailed her through two more rows of bookcases, past the copy machine and a display of paperback romances to a cart piled high with returns waiting to be shelved. Sorting through the stack, she finally extracted an oversized book bound in tartan cloth.

"That's it! You don't know how much this means to me. I really appreciate it," Leeanne exclaimed, practically snatching the book from her hand.

"Well, I'm glad I could be of assistance," the librarian said in surprise.

Clutching the book to her breast almost as if it were the heather badge Iain had given her, Leeanne followed the librarian back to the front desk.

The man relinquished her chair and the librarian slid back behind her desk.

Digging through her billfold, Leeanne extracted her library card. She handed it along with the book to the librarian.

The librarian promptly handed them back.

"I'm afraid you'll have to go to the end of the line."

Not even bureaucratic bunk could make her angry today, Leeanne told herself. She had her book and that was all she cared about, she thought, marching to the end of the line, chin high.

Ten minutes later, the librarian ran Leeanne's

plastic card through the computer's validator stripe. A crease appeared between her eyebrows.

"I see you have a two-dollar fine on your name. Would you like to clear that now, or pay it the next time you drop by?"

"I'll do it now."

Leeanne fumbled with the zipper section of her billfold, paying the fine in quarters.

That accomplished, the librarian waved the wand across the inside back cover of the book, closed it, and presented it to Leeanne.

"That's due in three weeks. Because it's a relatively new book, it's not renewable. If it remains on the shelf for a twenty-four-hour period, however, you can at that point check it out again without difficulty."

Leeanne nodded. "Thanks," she said, escaping with her treasure.

Three days later she finally got up enough nerve to read the section on Glencoe. It was the worst Thursday night of her life.

There were few pictures of the glen, but the ones the book contained plunged Leeanne into a whirlpool of nostalgia. The snow-capped summits, rocky crags, and rushing burns tugged at her heartstrings. But nothing touched her more than the photograph of Loch Achtriochtan in the throes of summer, alive with swans.

Eventually she forced herself to move on, to read beyond the captions bordering the pictures. With trembling hands, she turned to the pages recounting in explicit terms the massacre she had attempted to prevent.

"At five a.m. on February 13, 1692, Captain Robert Campbell invoked 'The Letter of Fire and Sword' against the clan Macdonald," Leeanne read out loud. "Alasdair Macdonald was killed in his bed chamber in the main house at Carnoch. His wife was thrown out into the snow to die. Alasdair's sons and grandson escaped with the help of a servant."

With tear-blurred eyes, she read further.

"At Achtriochtan, some of the bards met their fate along with a man of eighty and a child who begged on bended knees to be spared. All in all, thirty-eight perished at the hands of the soldiers. And in the days that followed, many of those who escaped died from exposure and starvation, or at the mercy of hungry wolves."

Leeanne tried to block the tragedy from her mind, tried not to put faces to the nameless victims. It was useless.

Late that evening, emotionally exhausted and physically drained, she finally set aside the tartan-covered book. Crawling beneath the virginal percale sheets of her contemporary waterbed, wishing instead for a pallet of silk and velvet and the heat of Iain's powerful body, she cried herself to sleep.

In the months that followed, Leeanne discovered a budding core of resolve within herself—

a source of renewed strength. Through Iain she had gained not only an awareness of herself as a woman of unlimited potential, but the source of the raw power and passion missing in her performance. Knowing him gave her the confidence to give the very best within herself, as he always did. The time spent in Glencoe had not detracted from, but enhanced her career, putting it in the proper perspective.

Incorporating what she had learned from Iain, drawing from her love for a true Highlander, she immortalized the relationship they had shared in the only way possible. On the stage.

Her modernized version of Highland dance was a hit—Broadway bound. But it didn't take her long to realize that success wasn't all it was cracked up to be, not without the man she loved. Memories of Iain and the Highlands haunted her, leaving behind an intense yearning and an emotional void that not even her career filled.

Three weeks into the season, Leeanne amazed everyone, including herself, by relinquishing the reins of the production into the competent hands of her personal assistant. Next, she purchased an airline ticket to Scotland.

Boarding the jetliner, Leeanne decided she must be possessed; obsessed with the notion that by being in the land that he loved, she would somehow be closer to Iain. Anxiously she fastened her seat belt, feeling as if a time bomb ticked within her, as if she might burst before reaching Glencoe and the calming blue-green waters of Loch Antriochtan.

Chapter Eighteen

Glencoe, Scotland
June, 1992

Parking the economy car she had rented in Edinburgh on the main road, Leeanne strolled across the tranquil fields that surrounded the Mountain Rescue Post at Achnambeithach, meandering beneath the cliffs of Aonach Dubh to the shores of Loch Achtriochtan. Ablaze with renewed life, Glencoe, the glen of weeping, enfolded Leeanne like a mother might a long-lost child.

Wildflowers dotted the greening landscape, softening the winter bleakness she remembered so well. She knew that if she walked along the burn-sides, she'd find Mountain Everlasting and Wild Hyacinth. Or if she climbed the slopes of Gearr Aoach, she would see clusters of white fragrant orchids. And still higher, yellow saxifrage, alpine lady's. mantle, and scurvy-grass. But right now, she wasn't concerned with the flora and fauna described by the guide at the Glen Coe Visitors Centre and Folk Museum.

As if drawn by some mystic force, she had traveled thousands of miles, both physically and spiritually, in hopes of catching a single glimpse of Iain's swans. In due time, she would explore the remainder of the glen from the heather-blanketed moors of Rannoch to Eilean Munde in Loch Leven. But for now, with the smell of the sea wafting to her on the breeze, and the sun shining through the morning mist and warming her shoulders, Loch Antriochtan was enough.

More than enough. Almost too much without Iain.

Dry-eyed, Leeanne gazed out across the water as bittersweet memories of Iain came rushing back, nearly overwhelming her. Memories of the cold winter day when he had shared the magnificence of Loch Achtriochtan with her. Memories of his muscular arms embracing her. Of his deep voice, and how he had coached her in skipping stones. Of their lovemaking.

She had imagined she was ready to let Iain go, to put the past behind her. She had planned this trip as a kind of purge to her system, a way to wind things up, like replacing the fresh flowers on a grave with an artificial wreath.

Leeanne realized now that she had only been fooling herself. Her longing for Iain was as strong as ever. Almost unbearable.

With a wistful sigh, Leeanne picked up a flat-sided pebble from the shore, closing her fingers around the smooth, hard surface.

As if it were only yesterday, she could hear Iain saying, "I'm no' laughing at you, lass. Do you see me laughing?"

"I *feel* you laughing," Leeanne whispered faintly. Borne away on the Highland breeze, her words seemed to undulate, spreading across the loch, then the land, and finally out into the far reaches of the peaceful summer day.

Bound for eternity, Leeanne mused whimsically.

Adjusting the pebble between her fingers, she squinted her eyes against the surface of the water and took careful aim. Turning her hand as Iain had taught her, she drew back, shooting the pebble out across the shimmering loch. It bounced three times across the water before sinking beneath the surface.

"Now that one, Iain Ranoull MacBride, was for good luck," Leeanne commented with a wry smile.

"Was it now?" a teasing voice asked. A voice she'd thought never again to hear so vividly except in her dreams.

She'd heard no movement behind her! No footsteps! It couldn't be Iain! Could it?

Feeling as if she'd been pierced through the heart with the blade of a *skean-dhu*, Leeanne froze, afraid to move, afraid to blink. Afraid even to breath.

"Will you no' turn around and look at me, lass?"

Leeanne swallowed hard. Her world had seemed so unsettled since losing Iain. Had returning to Glencoe sent her over the edge?

"I've wanted this so badly that I've actually daydreamed you up," she said, denying him because she couldn't bear to do otherwise.

"I'm no dream. Dreams can no' miss people. And, Lord luve me, lass, I've missed you with all my heart. We've been apart so damnably long, I thought I'd go mad with the want of you. What took you so long?"

As his voice grew increasingly stronger, Leeanne allowed herself to breath—just a little. Still, she dared not turn around for fear of discovering she was imagining things.

"I . . . I'm not sure. I—"

"Do no' trouble yourself so. I'm thinking what counts is that you're here with me now."

"Am I? Am I really?" Leeanne asked raggedly, a strange sense of anticipation assailing her.

"Aye. And as I promised you they would, the swans have returned to the loch as well."

His voice sounded deep and low and wondrous—pure music to her ears.

"I know. I can see them. They're . . . beautiful." A small sob escaped her throat. "Can you see them as well, Iain?"

"I hope to tell you I can, though there aren't as many as there once were. Nor ducks, nor herons, nor sandpipers either."

He sounded so real, as if he stood just behind her. She could almost feel his warm breath fanning the side column of her throat, her ear, her jawline.

"I also see you're wearing your T-shirt. I'm glad. It made you all that much easier to spy."

For some reason, she'd dressed carefully that morning, washing her hair and brushing it until it shone, applying the slightest bit of makeup to give her pale cheeks color. At the last moment, she'd decided on the neon-pink save-the-whales T-shirt.

"Is that what women are wearing these days? Ankle-length trews? I've no' seen them up close until now."

She'd chosen the comfortable denims, along with her Reeboks, because she had planned to spend the day hiking the hills and valleys of Glencoe.

"Most people call them blue jeans," she said, holding back the dam of her emotions by talking of irrelevant things.

"They suit you well, lass, though they make my hands burn to tug your hips against my own and have my way with you," he said huskily.

God in heaven! I can feel his breath on my cheek!

Blood singing in her ears, Leeanne did a pirouette toward the sound of Iain's voice. Tears gathered in her eyes, slowly tracking twin paths down her cheeks.

"Here now. We'll be having none of that, lass," he said softly.

Iain reached up to tenderly brush the salty droplets away with the back of his hand. Leeanne's uncertainty dissolved in a heady rush of pure emotion. Squeezing her eyes shut, she captured his hand, pressing it against her cheek, praying he wouldn't vanish when she opened her eyes.

Leeanne opened her eyes; Iain didn't vanish.

His Highland-green-and-rust-colored kilt was dirty and torn as if he'd been sleeping in a bed of nettles, and he'd grown a beard slightly darker than the blond hair which fell in waves well below the collar of his stained linen shirt.

He had never looked so drop-dead gorgeous. A familiar tingle skittered down her spine.

"You look as if you've lost something, lass."

"I thought I had," she rasped, emotion choking her voice. Her eyes surveyed him from the crown of his head to the tips of his hide boots, drinking him in. "You're thinner," she managed finally.

"You also," he replied in a strained whisper, opening his arms to her.

Her body came achingly to life as Leeanne reeled against Iain, melting into his trembling embrace.

Burying his face in her hair, he inhaled deeply, kissing the hollow of her throat, her eyes, her nose, her lips.

"What with the game so poor and a sword that would no' cut warm butter, I'm fortunate to be alive," he said against her mouth.

With a long, low moan of joy, she arched against him, returning kiss for kiss until he threaded his fingers through the hair at the nape of her neck. "For the luve of . . . hold still, lass," he said hoarsely. As he slanted his mouth across hers, his tongue delved deeply between her lips.

She felt his free hand slide over her lower back to the swell of her hips to gather her more tightly against him, and the time bomb that had been ticking inside her exploded. Heat coursed through her body. His heat. Her heat. Their heat. Inseparable.

"I can't believe it, Iain You've been hiding out in Glencoe, living off the land while I . . ." It hurt so much she couldn't finish the thought out loud. "I've been through hell, and all the time you were here, patiently waiting for me to show up."

He caressed the fullness of her lower lip with the pad of his thumb. "Here. And Lomond."

"Lomond? You traveled all the way to Loch Lomond on foot?"

"I could no' even find the foundation for the cottage that was once here in Glencoe. I felt compelled to see if my holdings near Loch Lomond were in a similar state. I discovered the manor house to be nothing more than an ancient pile of rubble. And Sesi, and Parlan, and the wee bairn all gone, like dust on the wind."

Compassion for the man she loved welled within her. "I know how difficult it must have been. I wish I had been here for you," Leeanne murmured.

He closed his eyes a moment before proceeding.

"I discovered their headstones in the kirk cemetery—side by side as Sesi would have wanted. It seems they lived a long and prosperous life—thanks to you, lass."

"Oh, Iain! What if I hadn't come back? What if I had *never* returned to Glencoe?"

His hand moved to her shoulder where he rested it for a moment. "Eventually I'd have discovered a way to come to you, lass. You taught me to soar beyond the impossible."

"God, to think I could have—"

"Hush, luve. It's all right now. I knew that defying fate would be risky. But feeling you in my arms again was worth any cost I might have paid. Besides, I trusted that, like the swans, you'd return to Glencoe sooner or later." Once again, Iain drew Leeanne into the secure circle of his muscular arms.

"How? How did you do it?" she asked, sagging against his long length.

His eyes shadowed with pain.

"Everything happened just as you predicted." Leeanne could feel his body tense. "The soldiers were demented, rushing through the glen cutting doon everything that breathed."

Via the library book, she had obtained a bird's-eye view of the massacre, knew things that he could not possibly know. But she could not bring herself to tell him that the ravens he'd seen on the roof of the main house at Carnoch had been an omen. Not now. That would come later. Much, much later.

"Surprised as they were, the Macdonalds did no' have a chance to defend themselves," he continued.

Leeanne could feel Iain's despair; experience it in the darkest recesses of her mind as he had in reality. If she could have suffered the tragedy for him, she gladly would have. His beliefs, all that he held sacred, his very way of life, had been blown apart by Robert Campbell's treachery, and she knew beyond a shadow of a doubt that the massacre had very nearly shattered him as well.

Looking into Iain's eyes, Leeanne also realized that sometime between then and now, he had come to terms with it.

"Those of us with the stamina fought Robert Campbell until we were cornered on Aonach Dubh near the entrance to Ossian's Cave."

Iain pointed briefly toward the towering cliffs overshadowing Loch Achtriochtan, and Leeanne thought he shuddered.

"We opposed them doon to the last remaining man—me. By then, my strength was waning. As they closed in for the kill, much like the wolves that attacked you and Sesi, I placed my claymore on the ground. You should have seen their incredulous faces when I began humming 'Gillie Chalium' and performed my abbreviated version of the Blades of War."

Slowly he extracted the claymore from the leather sheath slung across his shoulders. It was pitiful, rusty and pockmarked, and missing its sapphires.

"I believe this belongs to you, lass."

Leeanne could hardly credit it. The same sword that had transported her to him had carried Iain safely and intact through time into 1992. To her.

She gingerly accepted the claymore as he lowered his head, pressing a moist kiss upon her lips.

"I love you," she said simply.

"I luve you as well, lass, and will until the very day I die," he said softly.

"Kahlil Gibran once wrote, 'Love joins our present with the past and the future,'" Leeanne quoted, marveling that fate had awarded her her own heart's grandest desire. "I guess we're living proof."

Smiling his most charming of smiles, Iain said, "Aye, though I would no' pass the word around lightly."

He gathered her more intimately against his vibrant body.

Gazing up into his beloved face, she returned his smile.

"I think you're probably right about that."

"I know I am, lass. Now have done with the talk and kiss me," he commanded. "We've two worlds of love between us. And I'm thinking it's high time they merged into one."

Like a flower reaching toward the sun, Leeanne dropped the sword at their feet, offering her mouth to Iain. With a groan, his head descended, his lips capturing hers. Souls surging to meet head-on, they shared a kiss filled with hope and the promise of a future fluent in tomorrows.

The winter it is past, and the summer comes
   at last,
   And the small birds, they sing on ev'ry tree.
                              "The Winter It Is Past"
                                    —Robert Burns

Author's Note

The massacre at Glencoe appalled Highlanders and Lowlanders alike. Today, a monument commemorating the Macdonalds stands near The National Trust for Scotland Visitors Centre at Glen Coe. My fictionalized version about the events of those thirteen days in February 1692 is based on fact, substantiated by research which includes materials supplied by The National Trust for Scotland.

The people mentioned in the book who actually existed include Alasdair Macdonald, chief of the clan Macdonald, also spelled Alastair McDonald and Alastair MacDonald; John Campbell, Earl of Breadalbane, and Sir John Dalrymple of Stair, who together engineered the massacre; Lieutenant-Colonel

Hamilton and Major Robert Duncanson of Fort William, who issued the Letter of Fire and Sword; Captain Robert Campbell of Glenlyon, who carried out the orders by leading the Earl of Argyll's regiment against clan Macdonald, killing thirty-eight including women and children; Donald Dhu, grandson to the last Lord of the Isles; John Macdonald, the chief's firstborn; Alastair, his grandson by a second son; the chief's wife; Robert Campbell's niece; and King William of Orange.

All other characters are purely fictional.

Vivian Knight-Jenkins
Indian Trail, North Carolina

Don't miss these passionate time-travel romances, in which modern-day heroines fulfill their hearts' desires with men from different eras.

Traveler by Elaine Fox. A late-night stroll through a Civil War battlefield park leads Shelby Manning to a most intriguing stranger. Bloody, confused, and dressed in Union blue, Carter Lindsey insists he has just come from the Battle of Fredericksburg—more than one hundred years in the past. Before she knows it, Shelby finds herself swept into a passion like none she's ever known and willing to defy time itself to keep Carter at her side.

_52074-5 $4.99 US/$6.99 CAN

Passion's Timeless Hour by Vivian Knight-Jenkins. Propelled by a freak accident from the killing fields of Vietnam to a Civil War battlefield, army nurse Rebecca Ann Warren discovers long-buried desires in the arms of Confederate leader Alexander Ransom. But when Alex begins to suspect she may be a Yankee spy, Rebecca must convince him of the impossible to prove her innocence...that she is from another time, another place.

_52079-6 $4.99 US/$6.99 CAN

TIMESWEPT

The Outlaw Heart by Vivian Knight-Jenkins. A professional stuntwoman, Caycee Hammond is used to working in a world of illusions. But she cannot believe her eyes when a routine stunt sends her back to an honest-to-goodness Old West bank robbery. Before Caycee knows it, she is dodging real bullets, outrunning the law, saving bandit Zackary's life, and longing to share the desperado's bedroll. Torn between her need to return home and her desire for Zackary, Caycee has to choose between a loveless future and the outlaw heart.
_52009-5 $4.99 US/$5.99 CAN

Time of the Rose by Bonita Clifton. The dread of all his enemies and the desire of all the ladies, young Colton Chase can outdraw any gunslinger and outlast any woman. But even he doesn't stand a chance against the spunky beauty who's tracked him through time. Soon, Colt is ready to hang up his six-shooters, throw away his spurs, and surrender his heart to the most tempting spitfire anywhere in time.
_51922-4 $4.99 US/$5.99 CAN

Rejar
DARA JOY

Lord Byron thinks he's a scream, the fashionable matrons titter behind their fans at a glimpse of his hard form, and nobody knows where he came from. His startling eyes—one gold, one blue—promise a wicked passion, and his voice almost seems to purr. There is only one thing a woman thinks of when looking at a man like that. *Sex.* And there is only one woman he seems to want. *Lilac.* In her wildest dreams she never guesses that bringing a stray cat into her home will soon have her stroking the most wanted man in 1811 London....

_52178-4 $5.99 US/$6.99 CAN

VICTORIA·BRUCE

"Victoria Bruce is a rare talent!"
—Rebecca Forster, Bestselling Author Of *Dreams*

A faint scent, a distant memory, and an age-old hurt aren't much to go on, but lovely Maggie Westshire has no other recollections of her missing father. Now she finds herself on a painful quest for answers—a journey that begins in Hot Springs, Arkansas, and leads her back through the years, into the strong arms of Shea Younger. He is from a different era, a time of danger and excitement, and he promises Maggie a passion like none she has ever known. And while she is determined, against all odds, to continue her search for her father, Maggie doesn't know how much longer she can resist Shea's considerable charms, or the sweet ecstasy she finds in his timeless embrace.

_52064-8 $4.99 US/$6.99 CAN

Dorchester Publishing Co., Inc.
65 Commerce Road
Stamford, CT 06902

Please add $1.75 for shipping and handling for the first book and $.50 for each book thereafter. NY, NYC, PA and CT residents, please add appropriate sales tax. No cash, stamps, or C.O.D.s. All orders shipped within 6 weeks via postal service book rate. Canadian orders require $2.00 extra postage and must be paid in U.S. dollars through a U.S. banking facility.

Name_____

Address_____

City _____ State_____ Zip_____

I have enclosed $_____ in payment for the checked book(s).
Payment **must** accompany all orders.☐ Please send a free catalog.

FOREVER & A DAY

VICTORIA CHANCELLOR

When Linda O'Rourke returns to her grandmother's South Carolina beach house, it is for a quiet summer of tying up loose ends. And although the lovely dwelling charms her, she can't help but remember the evil presence that threatened her there so many years ago. Plagued by her fear, and tormented by visions of a virile Englishman tempting her with his every caress, she is unprepared for reality in the form of the mysterious and handsome Gifford Knight. His kisses evoke memories of the man in her dreams, but his sensual demands are all too real. Linda longs to surrender to Giff's masterful touch, but is it a safe haven she finds in his arms, or the beginning of her worst nightmare?

_52063-X $5.50 US/$7.50 CAN

Dorchester Publishing Co., Inc.
65 Commerce Road
Stamford, CT 06902

Please add $1.75 for shipping and handling for the first book and $.50 for each book thereafter. NY, NYC, PA and CT residents, please add appropriate sales tax. No cash, stamps, or C.O.D.s. All orders shipped within 6 weeks via postal service book rate. Canadian orders require $2.00 extra postage and must be paid in U.S. dollars through a U.S. banking facility.

Name_____
Address_____
City _____ State_____Zip_____
I have enclosed $_____in payment for the checked book(s).
Payment <u>must</u> accompany all orders.□ Please send a free catalog.

BITTERROOT

VICTORIA CHANCELLOR

Bestselling Author Of *Forever & A Day*

In the Wyoming Territory—a land both breathtaking and brutal—bitterroots grow every summer for a brief time. Therapist Rebecca Hartford has never seen such a plant—until she is swept back to the days of Indian medicine men, feuding ranchers, and her pioneer forebears. Nor has she ever known a man as dark, menacing, and devastatingly handsome as Sloan Travers. Sloan hides a tormented past, and Rebecca vows to use her professional skills to help the former Union soldier, even though she longs to succumb to personal desire. But when a mysterious shaman warns Rebecca that her sojourn in the Old West will last only as long as the bitterroot blooms, she can only pray that her love for Sloan is strong enough to span the ages....

_52087-7 $5.50 US/$7.50 CAN

Dorchester Publishing Co., Inc.
65 Commerce Road
Stamford, CT 06902

Please add $1.75 for shipping and handling for the first book and $.50 for each book thereafter. NY, NYC, PA and CT residents, please add appropriate sales tax. No cash, stamps, or C.O.D.s. All orders shipped within 6 weeks via postal service book rate. Canadian orders require $2.00 extra postage and must be paid in U.S. dollars through a U.S. banking facility.

Name_____

Address_____

City _____ State _____ Zip _____

I have enclosed $_____in payment for the checked book(s).

Payment <u>must</u> accompany all orders.☐ Please send a free catalog.

A GLIMPSE OF FOREVER

LINDA O. JOHNSTON

Her wagon train stranded on the Spanish Trail, pioneer Abby Wynne searches the heavens for rain. Gifted with the visionary powers, Abby senses a man in another time gazing at the same night sky. But even she cannot foresee that she will journey to the future and into the arms of her soul mate.

Widower Mike Danziger has escaped the L.A. lights for the Painted Desert, but nothing prepares him for a beauty as radiant as the doe-eyed woman he finds. His intellect can't accept her incredible story, but her warm kisses ease the longing in his heart.

Caught between two eras bridged only by their love, Mike and Abby fight to stay together, even as the past beckons Abby back to save those trapped on the trail. Is their passion a destiny written in the stars, or only a fleeting glimpse of paradise?

_52070-2 $4.99 US/$6.99 CAN